Eagle Talons

THE IRON HORSE CHRONICLES:
BOOK ONE

EAGLE TALONS

ROBERT LEE MURPHY

FIVE STAR
A part of Gale, Cengage Learning

GALE
CENGAGE Learning

Farmington Hills, Mich • San Francisco • New York • Waterville, Maine
Meriden, Conn • Mason, Ohio • Chicago

GALE
CENGAGE Learning®

Map: Illustrator, Phyllis Mignard, created "The Eagle Talon" map using a crow quill drawing pen and India ink on D'Arches 300 pound watercolor paper.
Five Star™ Publishing, a part of Gale, Cengage Learning.

LIBRARY OF CONGRESS CATALOGING-IN-PUBLICATION DATA

Murphy, Robert Lee.
Eagle Talons / by Robert Lee Murphy. — First edition.
pages cm. — (The Iron Horse Chronicles ; Book One)
ISBN-13: 978-1-4328-2876-9 (hardcover)
ISBN-10: 1-4328-2876-2 (hardcover)
ISBN-13: 978-1-4328-2872-1 (ebook)
ISBN-10: 1-4328-2872-x (ebook)
1. Orphans—Fiction. 2. Self-actualization (Psychology)—Fiction. 3. Union Pacific Railroad Company—Fiction. 4. Western stories. I. Title.
PS3613.U7543E25 2014
813'.6—dc23 2014019677

First Edition. First Printing: October 2014
Find us on Facebook– https://www.facebook.com/FiveStarCengage
Visit our website– http://www.gale.cengage.com/fivestar/
Contact Five Star™ Publishing at FiveStar@cengage.com

Printed in the United States of America
1 2 3 4 5 6 7 18 17 16 15 14

Eagle Talons

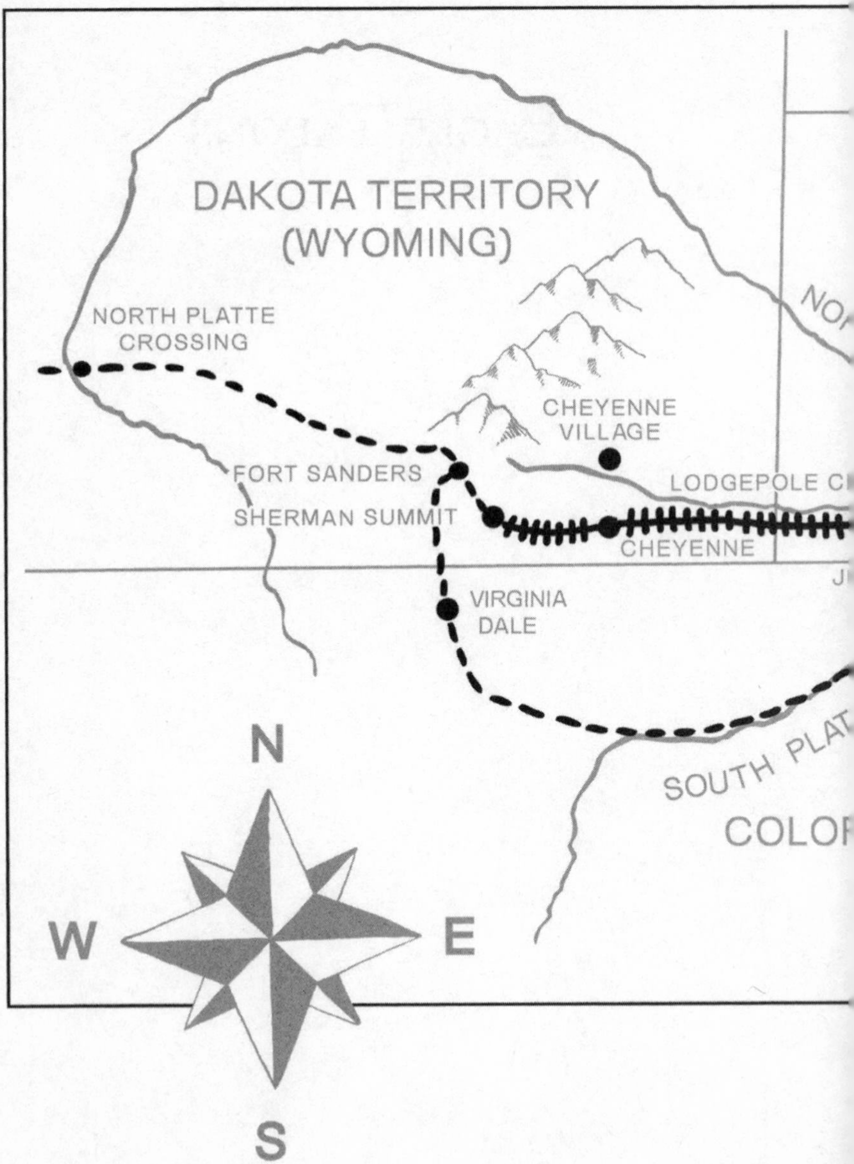
DAKOTA TERRITORY
(WYOMING)
NORTH PLATTE
CROSSING
CHEYENNE
VILLAGE
FORT SANDERS
SHERMAN SUMMIT
CHEYENNE
LODGEPOLE C
VIRGINIA
DALE
SOUTH PLAT
COLOR
NO
N
W
E
S

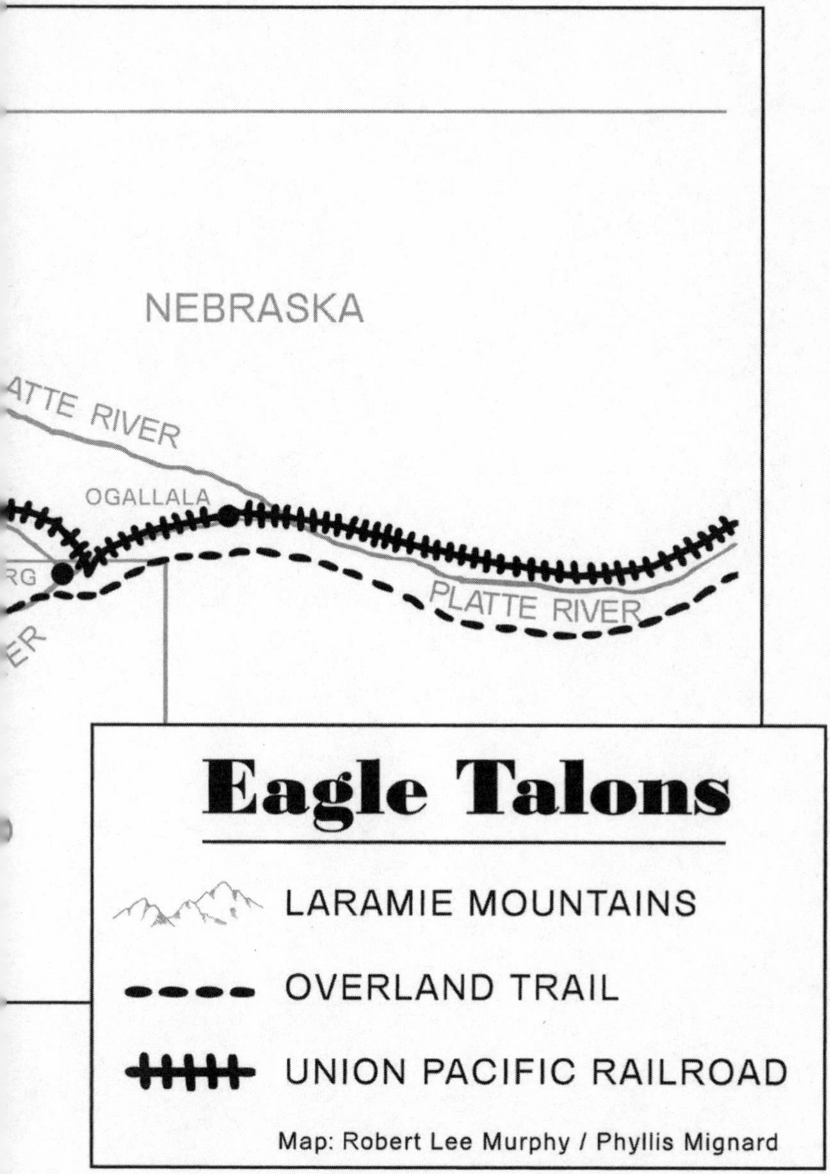
NEBRASKA
ATTE RIVER
OGALLALA
RG
ER
PLATTE RIVER
Eagle Talons
LARAMIE MOUNTAINS
OVERLAND TRAIL
UNION PACIFIC RAILROAD
Map: Robert Lee Murphy / Phyllis Mignard

For Steven and Olivia Tiller

ACKNOWLEDGMENTS

My appreciation to niece Nancy George for being the first reader of this novel and for her helpful suggestions. Doctor Thomas Peters, my primary care physician, provided insight into surviving an arrow wound, adding realism to the book. Jane Penell, Visitor Information Services, Medicine Bow-Routt National Forests in Wyoming, graciously answered my questions about vegetation and the history of beavers along Lodgepole Creek. To enhance the historical accuracy of my writing, I am grateful to the staff of the Henderson, Nevada, Public Library system for obtaining dozens of books (many out-of-print) through the interlibrary loan program. I owe special thanks to my fellow members of the SCBWI Word Worms' critique group and my compatriots in Anthem Authors, all of whom contributed to the betterment of the manuscript as it evolved. Hazel Rumney, Editorial Evaluation and Developmental Coordinator at Five Star Publishing, provided encouragement and expert advice throughout the editorial process. Scott Kirkman provided a much-needed copyedit of the book. My thanks to Phyliss Mignard for taking my rough sketch map and turning it into a printable one. Mary Ann Unger's photo of me used on the book's cover and on my website's homepage is greatly appreciated. Finally, I thank my wife, Barbara, for accompanying me on an extensive research journey covering the route of the first transcontinental railroad's eastern portion from Counsel Bluffs, Iowa, to Promontory Summit, Utah, and for never complaining about the hours I spent huddled before my computer.

Chapter 1

Pushing his eye closer to the crack in the attic floor, Will Braddock tried to get a better view. He'd grown too big to fit easily into this crawl space he used to squirm into as a small child whenever he'd wanted to spy on his parents in the kitchen below. Those two old men down there were talking about him. What was that they were saying about blacksmith apprenticeship and guardianship custody transfer? Will didn't like what he was hearing.

Judge Sampson sat at the table directly beneath Will. "I put the legal papers in the evening mail," the judge said. "I'm sending them to Corcoran in care of my old friend General Grenville Dodge, the Union Pacific's chief engineer."

"Do you really have to get the boy's uncle involved?" Reverend Kincaid sat opposite the judge. "Can't you just issue a court order?"

"I'll assign temporary custody to Klaus Nagel, Reverend, but as the boy's only living relative, Sean Corcoran needs to relinquish any claim as guardian before I make the apprenticeship final."

The judge pulled a cigar from a pocket and lit it from a candle burning on the table. Smoke wafted up through the crack. Will pinched his nose to stave off a sneeze. Moving to avoid the pungent aroma, the rickety boards creaked and a shower of dust floated downward. He froze.

"What's that?" The judge looked up.

"Aw, just a rat, Judge."

"Yeah, guess so."

The judge rose and took half a dozen steps away from the table to stand in the doorway looking at the open coffin in the parlor. "Too bad Annabelle died from consumption."

"Hard to survive here on the Mississippi with congested lungs," the reverend said.

"Have to give her credit for trying to keep the farm going," the judge said. "But, to what purpose? The mortgage is in arrears, and even if he had the money, a fourteen-year-old can't hold title to property in Iowa. The farm goes to auction next week. Under the circumstances, this apprenticeship plan seems to be the best we can do for the boy."

"Like I say, the Lord always provides an answer to our prayers. He'll make a fine blacksmith. He's taller than the other boys his age, and he's developed a strong physique working on the farm. But . . . what if Corcoran won't relinquish custody?"

"He will. Corcoran's a bachelor. Works as a surveyor for Dodge on the transcontinental railroad. The Union Pacific's tracklaying is approaching the foothills of the Rocky Mountains. That's Indian country . . . no place for a boy."

"How long will it take for Corcoran to return your documents?"

"Two . . . three months."

"I hope not that long. Klaus won't be happy with a temporary arrangement."

Judge Sampson stepped back into Will's view. "After Annabelle's funeral tomorrow, I'll have the sheriff turn the boy over to Nagel."

"Good."

"I'm going home now, Reverend. Good night."

"I'll walk you out, Judge."

The men's steps receded through the house.

Will eased out of the narrow space, back into the loft bedroom. He stretched out on the narrow cot. A blacksmith apprentice may be the answer to the reverend's prayers—but not his.

After his father was killed at the Battle of Atlanta, Will had helped his mother work the farm. Raising skimpy crops, milking their old cow, and gathering eggs from six chickens did little more than provide subsistence living. Will supplemented their meager diet with squirrels and rabbits he shot with his father's old musket. But his mother had pushed herself too hard. When she contracted tuberculosis, she had no strength to fight it.

He stared at the ceiling. His mother used to scold him for lying on his cot wearing his dirty boots. A tear trickled down his cheek—she would never scold him again.

He squeezed his eyes. No time to cry—must concentrate. Can't stay here and be forced into a blacksmith apprenticeship. Not that he didn't like horses—but he wanted to ride them across windswept prairies and through forested mountains—not nail horseshoes onto hooves in the dark confines of a barn.

Will listened to the rumble of snoring from below. Reverend Kincaid had planned to hold vigil for his mother throughout the night. Obviously, he'd fallen asleep.

Morning's first light glowed at the attic window. If Will didn't act now, it would be too late. He sat up. The cot's leather strapping supporting the mattress squeaked. He paused. The reverend snored on.

Boots would make too much noise. Taking them off, he wiggled his toes through holes in his socks. His mother hadn't gotten around to mending them. Oh well, they'd have to do. He tied the laces together and hung the boots around his neck. Descending the loft's ladder, he stopped at the bottom. The snoring continued.

He tiptoed to the parlor doorway. Half a dozen candles illuminated his mother's body, stretched out in the pine-board casket. She would've thought it wasteful to burn so many candles.

The reverend's wife had clothed his mother in her only good dress, the one she wore to church. It was the black mourning dress she'd worn to his father's funeral—now she would wear it to her own.

Her hands lay folded across her slender body. She'd lost weight the past three years. The neighbor ladies called her skinny, but to Will she was the most beautiful mother in Burlington. He was proud to go to church holding her arm tucked under his.

A stammering gargle interrupted Reverend Kincaid's snoring. The preacher sat before the fireplace, his head hanging over the back of a rocking chair. After a snort and a throat clearing, the snoring resumed its regular cadence.

The family musket hung above the fireplace. To retrieve it, Will would have to climb over the preacher. It wasn't worth the risk. He'd make do with his father's pistol.

He approached the coffin. His mother looked so pale in her final sleep. He didn't realize he was crying until a tear dropped to her face and slid down her cheek. Will brushed the wetness from her cold skin.

"Sorry, Mama," he whispered, "I can't go to your funeral. They want to make me an apprentice under old man Nagel's custody. I can't let them do that, Mama."

He laid a hand over hers. "You always said if I got an education, I'd amount to something. I know I didn't do well in school, but I don't think you meant for me to be a blacksmith."

A quick glance confirmed Reverend Kincaid still slumbered.

"Mama, I'm going out west to find Uncle Sean. I have to talk him out of signing those papers. I'll ask Uncle Sean to help me get a job on the railroad. That'll make you proud of me." He squeezed his mother's hand, then tiptoed into the kitchen.

From the cupboard, where his mother kept it, he took down his father's old Army Colt .44-caliber revolver and placed it and two black leather belt pouches on the table. The larger pouch contained lead bullets, each encased in a paper wrapping filled with black powder. The smaller pouch held the percussion caps that provided the initial spark to fire the pistol.

On the top shelf, he located the ceramic canister in which his mother hid the cash she got from selling eggs and milk. He withdrew a handful of coins and one paper banknote. Slipping the bill into the bottom of the smaller pouch, he concealed it beneath the handful of percussion caps, and dropped the coins into his pants pocket.

At the back door, on a row of wall pegs, hung his father's old Army haversack and canteen. He packed the revolver, the pouches, and the canteen into the sack and slung it over his shoulder. He reached to take his cap from its peg, but stopped. Beside his cap hung his father's faded black officer's hat. The gold braid had long since been stripped off the brim. His mother had worn the old slouch hat when she ran to the barn on rainy days. He squared his father's hat on his head. It fit.

"Goodbye, Mama. I love you. Wish me luck." He stepped onto the back stoop while looking one last time toward the parlor.

"Ow!" He'd stubbed his toe against a milk pail he'd forgotten to return to the barn. The pail toppled off the stoop, clanging to the ground.

"What's going on?" The noise had awakened the reverend. "Who's out there?"

"Dang it!" Will didn't stop to put on his boots, but jumped off the stoop and raced in his stocking feet to the barn. "Sorry for cussing, Mama. Couldn't help myself."

He sidled into the stall beside the old Belgian gelding. "Morning, Chester." Slipping a bridle over the plow horse's head, he led him outside. The Braddocks didn't own a saddle. He'd ride bareback, just as he did when taking Chester to pasture. Will grabbed the horse's mane and swung onto his back.

"Stop!" The reverend shouted from the back stoop.

Will kicked the old horse hard—something he'd never done.

"Come back here! Where do you think you're going?"

"Run, Chester, run!"

CHAPTER 2

Twenty-seven days after running away from Burlington, Will walked up one of the main thoroughfares of Omaha, Nebraska. He'd done a lot of walking the past two weeks, after Chester had worn out and died. Shoppers hustled along the boardwalk on both sides of the dirt street. Buggies and carriages jostled for right-of-way as they rattled past on the dusty road.

"Watch where you're going, son!"

Will jumped back onto the wooden sidewalk. He'd been so preoccupied studying the building across the street that he'd stepped off the walkway and hadn't noticed the horseback rider bearing down on him.

Grabbing an opening in the traffic, he dashed across the road, stopping at the bottom of a long stairway that climbed in a dozen steps to the second-floor entrance to the United States National Bank. The brick structure rose two and a half stories above ground—the lower level being sunk a half story below the street. Along the side of the building, a narrow stairway reached from street level at the front corner directly to a doorway on the top floor. A sign above that third-floor entrance indicated it was headquarters for the Union Pacific Railroad.

The railroad office was what he'd come looking for. The ferry operator had told him that's where he could find General Dodge.

Will slapped the old slouch hat against his leg. Dust flew from pants and hat. He ran a hand through his grimy hair and jammed the hat back on. The bank would close in a few minutes, and not open again until Monday. He had to go there first.

He retrieved the percussion pouch from his haversack and took out the twenty-dollar banknote. The ferry ride earlier that day across the Missouri River from Council Bluffs had taken his last coins. He'd hoarded the paper bill since he'd run away from Burlington. Now it was the only money he had left.

Climbing the dozen steps, he reached for the bank's front door. It flew outward and a man talking back over his shoulder to someone in the bank barged into him.

Will grabbed the railing to keep from tumbling down the stairs.

"Sorry, young fellow. Wasn't paying attention."

"That's all right, sir." Will released his grip on the railing and straightened up.

The middle-aged man smiled through a graying mustache and beard. "We'll both watch where we're going next time. Eh, son?" He patted Will on both shoulders and hurried down the steps.

Will entered the bank and crossed the empty lobby to where a scrawny teller stood behind a barred window. He waited, but when the teller continued to ignore him, he cleared his throat. "Excuse me."

The teller laid a stubby pencil beside a paper on which he'd been writing a column of numbers. Looking out through thick-lensed, wire-framed glasses, owlish eyes bored a hole in Will. "What do you want, boy?"

Will laid the banknote on the counter, keeping the fingers of one hand on an edge. Should he trust the teller with his money? "I'd like to change this."

The teller snatched the bill from beneath Will's fingers and held it up to allow sunlight to shine through the paper. Sweat stains discolored the armpits of his rumpled shirt, the sleeves of which were bound with elastic bands around skinny biceps. "Where'd you steal this?"

"I didn't steal it!" Will jerked his hand off the counter and clenched his fists.

The teller glanced toward a heavyset man sitting at a rolltop desk. "Mr. Rogers?" A name sign atop the desk read: *Chief Cashier Guy Rogers.*

"What it is, Harry?"

"This boy wants to change a twenty-dollar note issued by the Burlington State Bank."

"I'm not a boy."

The teller glared back at Will. "How old are you?"

"I'll be . . . fifteen . . . on my next birthday." Will decided not to mention that his birthday was ten months away.

"That sure don't make you a man."

Rogers heaved himself out of his chair, shuffled to the teller's window, and accepted the proffered money. Bushy black eyebrows drew together as he scrutinized the banknote. "We don't see many bills from Burlington, Iowa. Where *did* you get this?"

"It's from my mother's egg money. We had a farm there. But she died. So I left."

"Omaha's a long way from Burlington. That's near three hundred miles away. What're you doing here?"

"I'm looking for my uncle, Sean Corcoran. He works for General Grenville Dodge, chief engineer of the Union Pacific Railroad."

"Don't know your uncle, but that was General Dodge you ran into at the front door."

"That was General Dodge? He isn't wearing a uniform."

"He's not in the Army anymore. Folks call him 'general' out of respect. Has an office on the floor above the bank." Rogers pointed up with the banknote. "He stopped in here to inquire about a horse I'm stabling for him. He'll be heading for the ferry now to go to his home over in Council Bluffs."

"Please hurry, sir. I have to talk with General Dodge."

Rogers handed the bill to the teller. "Give him the change, Harry."

The teller counted out a stack of coins and pushed them across the counter. Will scooped them into the cap pouch, dropped the pouch into his haversack, and dashed out the door.

Jumping down the steps two at a time, he raced toward the ferry crossing. He dodged around wagon traffic and horseback riders, who shouted at him to get out of the way.

He wasn't going to make it. The ferry had already pulled away from the landing. He skidded to a stop at the end of the dock, gasping for breath.

General Dodge leaned against the vessel's railing, talking with the ferryman. Will cupped his hands around his mouth. "General Dodge!"

The general looked in his direction, waved, then returned to his conversation.

"Dang it!" Will banged a fist against the wooden bollard where the ferry tied up. "Sorry, Mama," he muttered.

Walking off the dock, he trudged back up the road that led from the river through the business section of Omaha. He'd have to wait until tomorrow to talk to General Dodge. He choked and coughed on dust churned up by a passing buggy.

Tipping his father's old canteen, its canvas cover still faintly stenciled *7th Iowa,* to his lips, a drop trickled into his mouth. He shook it. Nothing came out. His stomach growled. He squinted at the sun low on the horizon. Nearly supper time. Not only was he thirsty, he was hungry.

He had the twenty dollars in coins, but half of them would be needed for his railroad ticket. Posters plastered on walls around town advertised that the one-way ticket to the end of the line cost ten dollars. Not sure what lay ahead, he didn't want to part with any of his money for food or drink—just yet.

Someplace west of here he hoped to find his uncle—had to find his uncle. If his uncle signed those guardianship transfer papers, he'd be committed to seven years of servitude as a blacksmith apprentice. The thought of becoming a blacksmith filled him with dread. He dreamed of the excitement of helping to build the first transcontinental railroad. He craved the freedom to determine his own destiny.

But what would he do if he couldn't find his uncle in time—before his uncle signed those papers?

Chapter 3

Passing through the last of the business section, Will came upon a row of dwellings. There should be a well here. At least he could fill his canteen and quench his thirst. He'd gone hungry a lot during his four-week trek across Iowa. Being hungry wasn't a comfortable feeling—but he could do it.

In the backyard of a two-story house surrounded by a white picket fence, he spotted a stout woman hanging laundry. A bonnet concealed her face. "Ma'am?" he called.

She didn't respond. He leaned over the fence and raised his voice. "Ma'am!"

The woman looked his way. Strands of white hair poked from beneath the wings of her bonnet. Will hoisted his canteen. "Ma'am, might I trouble you to fill my canteen at your well?"

The woman peered at him for several moments before answering. "Yah. Come. The well be here in back." Her lilting accent reminded him of a Swedish woman he'd known in Burlington.

In the backyard, Will cranked a bucket of water up from the bottom of the well and pushed his canteen into it. When the gurgling down the spout stopped, he tipped it up and gulped the chilly liquid. He filled the canteen again and tapped the cork stopper into the neck.

Behind the house he spotted a woodpile. An ax leaned against it. "Ma'am, I'll chop that firewood for a bite to eat."

The woman nodded. "Yah, that be good trade." She gathered

up her laundry basket and disappeared into the house.

He laid the first log across an old stump that served as a chopping block and attacked the log with a vigorous swing. Three swings later the log split in two. Chopping firewood had been one of his chores at home. He could probably do the job in his sleep.

As he worked to diminish the log pile, he imagined what it'd be like to swing a hammer against an anvil. Why'd Judge Sampson think it was his job to decide Will's future, anyway? He swung the ax harder, almost splitting that log with one blow.

He had to find his uncle—had to talk him out of agreeing with the judge. "I don't want to be a blacksmith apprentice!" One more fierce blow with the ax and the log flew apart.

"Who be you talking to out there?" the woman asked him from the kitchen window.

"Nobody, ma'am." He gritted his teeth and laid another log on the block.

Will chopped for over an hour until he'd reduced the logs to a size suitable for a cookstove. When he finished, he knocked on the back door. "I'm done, ma'am."

The woman stepped out onto the porch. "Yah. And good job it looks, too. Come in."

Will followed the woman into the kitchen. She motioned to a chair at a table. "What be your name, son?"

"Will. Will Braddock." He sat where she'd pointed.

"I be Mrs. Svenson . . . Helga Svenson . . . housekeeper for Mr. Rogers."

"The banker?"

"Yah. You know Mr. Rogers?"

"Not really, ma'am. I just met him at the bank today."

She set a plate of stew in front of him. Will inhaled the aroma of beef, potatoes, carrots, and onions. He raised the first bite to his mouth and reminded himself to chew before swallowing.

His mother had frequently criticized him for eating too fast.

"Mm." My goodness, he hadn't eaten this well in days.

Mrs. Svenson sliced an end from a loaf of bread and placed it beside his plate. She pushed a crock of butter to him. Will buttered the bread and sopped up the broth.

"Delicious, ma'am. Thank you."

"You be welcome." She wiped her hands on her apron. "Why be a young boy like you in Omaha?"

"I'm not so young. I'm . . . fourteen." He decided not to tell her the same story he'd told the bank teller.

"Fourteen. Yah, not so young . . . maybe." She grinned.

Will told her about his mother's recent death and that he'd come to Omaha to find General Dodge, who he hoped could help him locate his uncle.

"How did you get here?" she asked.

"At first I rode Chester, our old plow horse. But he wore out and died. After that I hitched a ride on a farmer's wagon . . . whenever I could. Mostly I walked."

Mrs. Svenson replaced Will's stew plate with a smaller one containing a slice of apple pie.

"Nebraska is yust not safe like Iowa," she said. "Savages be attacking the railroad all the time. You can defend yourself?"

"I have a revolver."

A few minutes later, Will scraped the fork across the plate and licked it clean. He ran his tongue around his lips savoring the final tastes of the pie. "My mama was a good cook. Just like you."

"Thank you, Will. That be nice compliment."

Will pushed back from the table and stood.

"Where be you going tonight?" she asked.

He shrugged. "I don't know. Find a tree to sleep under, like I've been doing."

"You sleep in the stable tonight. Yust be careful of that big gelding. General Dodge be coming in the morning to fetch him."

"I will, ma'am." Mr. Rogers had mentioned he was stabling the general's horse. Now the general was coming here in the morning. He couldn't ask for anything better.

Will opened the back door, but Mrs. Svenson caught his sleeve. "Wait."

She hurried across the kitchen and returned with two red apples. "Horses like apples, yah? One for horse, one for you."

"Thank you, ma'am."

Will jumped off the back porch, gathered up his haversack, canteen, and hat from where he'd left them beside the woodpile, and headed toward the stable. While he'd eaten supper, the sun had set. He pulled one of the squeaky stable doors open far enough to slip through, stepped inside, and eased the door closed behind him. He paused to let his vision adjust to the dim light.

A horse snorted and shuffled nearby. There were no windows in the stable, but twilight filtered through cracks between the wall boards. In a stall, he made out the shape of a horse.

"Hello, boy." He spoke in the same soothing voice he'd used to talk to Chester. "Easy, fellow."

When Will entered the stall, the horse tried to step back, but was restrained by a halter rope tied to the front rail. "Easy, now." He stroked the horse's withers. The hair rippled beneath his hand in shivered response. He held out one of the apples, keeping his fingers and thumb pressed together, so the horse couldn't nip them. The horse devoured the apple in two chomps.

"Pretty good, huh?" The horse reached for the second apple, but Will pulled it behind him. "No you don't. That's mine."

Will ran his fingers through the mane, encountering numerous tangles. "Well, boy. In the morning I'll groom you up so you'll look nice to greet General Dodge. What do you say to that?"

The horse whinnied and tossed his head.

"You and I seem to get along all right, fellow. Guess you won't mind if I bunk in the loft tonight."

An old buggy sat against the opposite wall. Mr. Rogers must've kept a horse for the buggy at one time, but there was no evidence of a second horse now.

He climbed to the loft, ate his apple, and washed it down with sips from his canteen. He took the revolver out of his haversack and weighed the heavy gun in his hand. How many Rebels had his father killed with it before he'd lost his own life? What was it like to shoot another man?

Maybe he should load the pistol—but it was dark, he was tired, his belly was full, and the threat of attack was far to the west. He'd load it in the morning. He returned the gun to the haversack and raked some stale straw into a pile with his foot. Yawning, he stretched out on the makeshift bed, pulled his hat over his face, and fell asleep.

Chapter 4

Will fidgeted. Surely it wasn't morning already. He pushed his hat back off his face and sat up. A faint voice coaxing the horse to be quiet came from the floor of the stable. Shadows cast by the light of a lantern flitted across the ceiling.

Uh-oh, Mr. Rogers had come to check on the horse. Had Mrs. Svenson told the banker she'd given Will permission to sleep in the loft?

"Ah, now, boy. Easy." The Irish brogue was distinctive. It wasn't Mr. Rogers.

Will inched toward the edge of the loft. Below him, a slender fellow stood in the stall holding a lantern above the brim of his bowler hat.

"Ah, now, boy. Ye be still."

The lantern's glow bounced off the horse's black coat. The horse turned his head back to look at the man, revealing a large white star blazed on its forehead between wide-open eyes. The horse pricked his ears forward, snorted, and stamped a hoof. He reared his head up and away from the light, pulling tightly against the halter rope.

"Easy, boy. Sure, and we won't be taking long doing this now." The fellow grasped the halter rope—but the horse pulled back, tightening the line even more. The Irishman set the lantern atop the end post of the stall and again grasped the rope with both hands.

Oh no! A horse thief! How could Will convince General

Dodge to help him find his uncle if he sat here and did nothing to stop someone from stealing the general's horse?

Will pulled his revolver out of his haversack and leaned out over the edge of the loft. "Stop!" He hoped his quivering voice didn't convey his fear. "Leave that horse alone."

The Irishman released his grip on the rope and looked up. The lantern light revealed the thief to be a youth. A long scar ran across his left cheek, from the base of his ear to the edge of his mouth. A saber might make a cut like that, Will thought.

The would-be horse thief grinned, the scar wrinkled. "And who be saying so, now?" His open mouth disclosed stained and broken teeth.

Will extended the pistol and double cocked the hammer. Two loud clicks echoed through the confines of the stable. "Me . . . and this Colt." Could the thief tell the revolver wasn't loaded?

The grin disappeared from the Irishman's face. "Hold on there. Ye seem to be having me at a mite of a disadvantage."

The Irishman reached for his lantern, but the horse lunged sideways and bumped him against the side of the stall. The jolt knocked the lantern off the post.

The glass globe shattered. Liquid fire spewed from the lantern's oil. The straw scattered about the stall's floor burst into flame.

The Irishman bolted out of the stable.

Fire raced across the floor and climbed the far wall. The old buggy erupted in flames. The horse reared and slashed at the stall's boards with his hooves.

Will rolled off the loft and landed belly first on the floor. Oomph! He sat up, spitting strands of straw. He slid the pistol under his belt.

"Easy, fellow. Easy." Squaring his hat on his head, he got to his feet. "I'll get you out of here."

The horse's eyes bulged—nostrils flared. The black head

reared back from Will's reaching hand, screaming his whinny. Will needed to calm the horse if he hoped to get him out of the stall.

The fire jumped from the far wall to the loft. The dry straw where Will had slept ignited. The reds and yellows of the flames reflected in the horse's eyes.

Will grabbed a saddle blanket from the stall's railing and flipped it over the horse's head. The horse settled once he could no longer see the flames. "That's it, boy."

The fire burned hot against Will's face. Smoke filled the stable. He choked. His eyes burned. He coughed hard. "Come on fellow. Easy now."

He couldn't untie the halter rope. The horse's rearing and pulling had cinched it tight. Will leaned into the horse with all his weight, forcing the animal to step forward. He unsnapped the rope from the halter beneath the horse's jaw, gripped the halter strap with one hand, and steadied the blanket over the horse's eyes with the other. He backed the horse out of the stall and led him through the stable doors.

Will gasped for air. He faced into the breeze and blinked his eyes to clear the smoke.

Fire leaped with a roar through the roof of the building. The timbers sagged, groaning against one another. With a whoosh the entire roof collapsed into the stable.

Whoom! Whoom!

Will's pistol ammunition and percussion caps detonated in rapid succession, accentuating the roar of the fire and the crashing of timbers.

"No." Will moaned. His pistol was useless without ammunition, but that was the least of his worries. The haversack had contained his money—the coins he'd obtained at the bank. How was he going to buy a ticket?

"Oh my God, the stable's on fire!" Mr. Rogers leaned out of an upper window in the house. "And that boy's stealing the general's horse!"

Chapter 5

Will sniffed the sleeve of his shirt. Whew! Would he ever get rid of that smoke smell? Maybe he should've jumped into the Missouri River last night and washed everything he wore. But after running away from banker Rogers's house, he couldn't think of anything to do other than lay low. Mr. Rogers might have the sheriff out looking for him right now.

Omaha's big railroad yard spread out before him. He wasn't sure why he'd chosen this road to follow. What good would it do to wind up at the depot? He couldn't buy a ticket—that's for sure.

He kicked a rock out of the middle of the road with his scruffy boot. "Dang it!" He didn't bother to apologize to his mother's memory this time. He meant it. What a mess he'd made of things. He'd tried to do a good deed, and look where it'd gotten him. Now how would he get General Dodge to help him find his uncle? Mr. Rogers was sure to tell the general Will had tried to steal his horse.

Why hadn't he thought to slip a few coins in his pants pocket yesterday? His father's old haversack was gone—and his canteen. He didn't have any ammunition or percussion caps to load the pistol. He looked down at his waist. That may not be a good idea to have the revolver so visible. He pulled the tail of his shirt out of his pants and let if fall down over the outside of his trousers.

"Out of the way, son!"

A buckboard rumbled down the road toward Will, forcing him to step into the ditch.

General Dodge sat ramrod straight on the buckboard's seat, staring straight ahead, flicking the reins over the horse's back. An officer wearing a blue Army uniform, with two stars on his shoulder boards, sat beside the railroad's chief engineer. Both men wore full beards and bushy mustaches—but the similarities ended there. Dodge's cheeks glowed from a robust suntan. The other man's pale cheeks sagged beneath sad eyes.

As the buggy drew abreast, the uniformed man covered his mouth with a handkerchief and coughed. Blood speckled the handkerchief when he lowered it. Will remembered his mother suffering from that same harsh cough.

Tied to the tailgate of the buckboard, trotted the black horse Will had rescued from the fire. Its strong shoulder and quarter muscles quivered with each stride. The animal held its head high, nostrils flared wide, short ears pricked forward. Large, bright eyes observed its surroundings with evident intelligence. In the bright morning sunlight, Will identified the horse as a Morgan.

Maybe here was his chance to get General Dodge's attention. Will opened his mouth to call out, but closed it. Maybe he shouldn't attract attention to himself. Dodge might have him arrested. How could he prove he hadn't intended to steal the horse? He crouched down.

After General Dodge passed, Will trotted down the road, keeping a safe distance behind the buckboard. Dodge drove up to a passenger coach coupled to the rear of a train parked on a siding a short distance from the depot and reined in.

Will slipped behind a pile of railroad ties, a few paces away from the siding, squatted down and peeked through gaps in the stack of wood.

The two men stepped down from the buckboard. Dodge

waved to a man standing on the rear platform of the passenger coach. "Morning, Mr. Johnson," Dodge said. "Meet General Rawlins, General Ulysses S. Grant's chief of staff."

"How do, Generals." Johnson's unbuttoned coat revealed a gold watch chain strung between the pockets of his vest. His pillbox hat bore the initials *UP* above its short bill.

"General Rawlins," Dodge said, "this is Hobart Johnson, conductor on our train today."

Rawlins covered his mouth with his handkerchief and coughed. "Forgive me, Mr. Johnson. This blasted consumption has just about gotten the better of me. General Grant thought it would be helpful if I came west to partake of the dry air. General Dodge has agreed to be my host."

"Welcome to Nebraska," Johnson said. "The weather'll get a lot dryer than this the farther west we go. I guarantee it."

Dodge moved to the rear of the buckboard and untied the black horse. "Mr. Johnson, this magnificent Morgan is Bucephalus. Coal black, except for the blaze star right in the center of his forehead. Just like Alexander the Great's horse."

He ran his hand down the horse's forehead. "We just call him Buck. General Rawlins will be riding Buck once we leave the railroad. See to getting him into the stable car, Mr. Johnson."

"Looks tall for a Morgan, sir." Johnson stepped down from the car's platform and took the reins from Dodge.

"That he is . . . fifteen hands," Dodge said. "Buck's a bit feisty. If he gets away from you, I'll let you in on a secret. Just whistle Morse code for the letter B. He'll come."

Johnson whistled one long note, followed by three short ones. Buck reared his head, jerking the conductor's hand upward. The three men laughed.

"Works every time," Dodge said.

Dodge reached under the buckboard seat and brought out a briefcase. "Have someone transfer our luggage into the coach,

Mr. Johnson. And see that this rig is returned to the livery stable."

"Certainly. Shall I take your briefcase, General?"

"No. I never let these maps and surveys out of my sight."

Will watched Dodge mount the steps into the coach, swinging his briefcase. Judge Sampson's custody transfer documents destined for his uncle might be in General Dodge's briefcase, along with his maps and surveys.

Dodge paused on the coach's rear platform and looked down at the conductor. "As soon as you get Buck into the stable car, summon our guests on board and we'll get underway."

"Yes, sir."

Conductor Johnson led Buck to a boxcar coupled directly behind the engine and its tender, then up a ramp into what Will assumed to be the stable car. A few minutes later the conductor exited the car, shoved the ramp to the ground, and pushed on the heavy door. It closed only part way. "Humph!" he said. "Bloody maintenance people didn't fix that door."

Johnson walked toward the rear of the train, flipped open the cover of his pocket watch, then clicked it closed. "Boarrrd!" he bellowed. A dozen men, dressed in suits, clambered off the nearby station's platform and headed for the coach. The conductor motioned for them to mount the rear steps into the passenger car.

The locomotive's whistle sounded two quick blasts and the engine lurched forward with a loud "choof" of escaping steam. The engine's driving wheels screeched on the iron rails—slipping, spinning, churning to gain traction. The connecting couplers banged one after the other as the locomotive pulled the string of cars into motion. With each "choof," a blast of black smoke belched upward from the diamond-shaped smokestack.

Will jumped out from behind the stack of ties, ran up the

tracks alongside the slowly moving train, grabbed the half-open door of the stable car, and heaved himself aboard.

Chapter 6

Inside the boxcar, the Morgan stood between two other horses, each tied to a rope that stretched across the width of the rear half of the car. Opposite a center aisle, three other horses were tied to another rope extending across the front half. The three horses in front faced the three in rear across the walkway that separated them. As the train gained speed, the horses swayed like sailors heading out to sea.

The "choofing" of the accelerating locomotive settled into a steady, rapid rhythm, accompanied by the "clickity-clack" of the wheels bumping over track joiners. The train rocked back and forth, wending its way along snaking rails that were neither straight nor level.

Will stepped in front of the big, black horse and ran his hand across the star on his forehead. "Byoo-*seff*-ah-lus." He stumbled over the pronunciation. "Funny name for a horse. I agree, Buck's a lot better."

He returned to the half-open door, and sat with his legs dangling outside. "Wow, Buck! I'll bet we're doing forty miles an hour. Can you run this fast?"

The Morgan whinnied in reply to Will's question.

When they passed through a sweeping, concave curve, Will could see the length of the train, from the engine to the coach. Four flat cars, stacked with wooden cross ties and iron rails, trailed the stable car. The single passenger car brought up the rear.

The UP's tracks paralleled the north bank of the Platte River. Will had heard old-timers describe the Platte as "too thick to drink and too thin to plow." The river's shallow, slow flowing water, had a well-known reputation for creating treacherous quicksand, waiting to trap the unsuspecting.

A bald eagle soared above the river, its white head and large golden beak swinging to and fro, its yellow eyes searching for prey. Long legs, stretched full length beneath the tail, ending in yellow toes tipped with black talons.

Cedar and cottonwood trees, and an occasional willow, lined the river's muddy banks. In places, cleared fields extended along the tracks where farmers struggled to carve out homesteads. Blocks of sod piled against a dugout bank served as crude houses. Will laughed at a cow grazing on the grass growing on the roof of one.

Near the noon hour, the stable car glided past a station building with *Columbus* painted on its side. The engine wheezed and sighed as the engineer braked the train to a stop, positioning the tender opposite a water tank.

Will slipped in beside Buck and knelt down. "Sh, Buck. Don't give me away."

"Half hour for the noon meal, gentlemen." Conductor Johnson's voice advised the chattering passengers Will could hear hurrying from the coach to the station.

Will watched the stable car door slide open from beneath the horse's legs. Conductor Johnson looked right at him. "What's this? Come out of there this minute."

Will rose and rubbed a hand along the Morgan's withers. "You tried, Buck. Wasn't your fault." He stepped out into the center aisle.

"What's going on here, Mr. Johnson?" General Dodge appeared beside the conductor. General Rawlins joined them.

"Stowaway, General," Johnson said.

Dodge leaned into the doorway beside the conductor. "Why, you're the young fellow I ran into on the steps of the bank. And the one who tried to steal my horse!"

"No, I didn't, sir."

Will clasped his hands in front of him. He was glad he'd left his shirttail out to cover his pistol. Otherwise, General Dodge might perceive him a threat.

"Mr. Rogers saw you running out of the burning stable with Buck last night."

"I know, sir. But I wasn't stealing him. I was just trying to save him from the fire."

"You'd better explain yourself," Dodge said.

Will described how he'd confronted the Irish horse thief who'd been the cause of the fire.

"Interesting story," Dodge said. "You describe Paddy O'Hannigan, a troublemaker we fired a while back for stealing railroad property. Wonder why he was trying to steal Buck?"

Dodge looked at the conductor. "What do you think, Mr. Johnson?"

"Sounds reasonable. I saw a fellow matching this O'Hannigan's description boarding this morning's regular train bound for Julesburg. Hard to miss that scar running down the side of his face . . . and he was wearing a bowler hat."

Dodge turned back to Will. "Would be hard to fabricate all those details, I guess. What's your name, son?"

"Will. Will Braddock."

"Why are you on my train, Will?"

"I'm looking for you, General."

"Me?"

"Yes, sir. I was hoping you'd know where I could find my uncle. He works for you."

"Works for me? Who's your uncle?"

"Sean Corcoran."

"Sean Corcoran, the surveyor? Of course I know him. He's worked for me a long time. Served with me during the war. Why are you looking for him?"

Will told him about his mother's death and explained that his uncle was his only living relative.

"Interesting," Dodge said. "A few days ago I received a package of documents from Judge Clyde Sampson of Burlington to deliver to your uncle. Do you know the judge?"

Will nodded. The judge's guardianship transfer papers had reached General Dodge.

"You have any idea what the package contains?"

"Telling my uncle about my mother's death? I'd be glad to deliver them to my uncle for you."

"Thanks for the offer, but the judge is an old friend of mine and asked me to deliver the package personally. Now . . . just how do you plan to find your uncle, anyway?"

Will shrugged. "I was hoping you'd help me, sir. I don't know who else to turn to."

"Your uncle heads up my special survey inspection team. He's out in the Rocky Mountains someplace. We've got tracks laid as far as the corner of Colorado. He'll be well beyond there. The survey crews stake the route out a hundred miles or more ahead of the construction crews. Might be hard to find him right away. How'd you plan to get there?"

"The money I had saved to buy a train ticket burned up in the stable fire. I couldn't think of anything else other than jumping on your train, when I saw the chance."

Dodge looked at Johnson again, then shrugged a shoulder. "Mr. Johnson, put him to work helping you water and feed the horses. He can ride with us as far as Hell on Wheels."

"All right, sir."

Generals Dodge and Rawlins walked toward Columbus's station.

Conductor Johnson motioned toward a water barrel and a bucket sitting in the center aisle of the stable car. "You heard the general. Take that bucket, water the horses, then refill the barrel from the station's water tank. You'll find hay and grain in a shed behind the station."

Will hurried to do the chores. When he'd finished, he sat in the open doorway of the car.

Mr. Johnson walked up from the rear of the train. "Done?"

"Yes, sir."

"You're lucky General Dodge didn't throw you off right here. Guess giving you a free pass to Hell on Wheels is your reward for saving that horse."

"What's Hell on Wheels, Mr. Johnson?"

"A ramshackle, portable town full of gamblers, drunkards, gunfighters, loose women, and other no-accounts . . . all out to take the railroad workers' hard-earned pay. Hell on Wheels picks up and moves west every now and then, keeping up with our construction effort. The buildings, if you can call them that, are false-fronted tents for the most part. Right now, Hell on Wheels is in Julesburg, Colorado . . . and that's where we're headed."

Conductor Johnson held his hand up to the bill of his hat and looked down the tracks that stretched ahead of the locomotive. "West of here we stand a good chance of running into Indian trouble."

"Indians?"

"Savage Indians . . . Sioux and Cheyenne, even Arapahoe. They don't like us building a railroad across their hunting grounds. This town of Columbus was originally a Pawnee village. Unlike other Indians, the Pawnees are friendly to whites. You've heard about the Pawnee Scouts?"

"No, sir."

"You will. The Army organized a bunch of them into a battalion of scouts. The Sioux and the Cheyenne fear them more than the regular soldiers. The scouts help protect the railroad. But we have to look out for ourselves, too. General Dodge's private coach is an arsenal. We've got enough guns and ammunition to fend off any attackers . . . and we may have to."

Johnson looked at his watch. "Thirty minutes is up. That's all we allow for a meal stop." He snapped the watch closed. "Boarrrrd!"

The passengers scrambled out of the café and hurried for the coach.

"You got anything to eat?" Johnson asked.

Will shook his head.

The conductor reached into his coat pocket, then held out his hand. "Here." He turned and strode toward the rear of the train.

Will held a chunk of jerky and a piece of hardtack. The unleavened cracker had been the soldier's mainstay during the Civil War. His father had told him it'd last forever if it didn't get wet. He tapped the hardtack on the doorsill. He'd have to soak it in the horses' water barrel to keep from breaking a tooth on it.

Will had read about Indian attacks in dime novels, but he hadn't imagined he might face an attack himself. He should've asked Mr. Johnson for ammunition for his revolver.

Chapter 7

Paddy stepped down from the train at Ogallala, the last fueling stop before Julesburg. He waited until the train departed, then entered the depot.

The agent looked up from behind the ticket counter. "You O'Hannigan?"

"Aye." Paddy withdrew a twelve-inch Bowie knife from a scabbard sewn inside the top of his boot. The agent's eyes widened. Paddy chuckled. It always pleased him to see the fear in people's eyes when he drew the knife. He sliced a sliver from a twist of tobacco and scraped the chaw off the blade with his teeth.

"I got Langley's telegram saying you'd be on this train," the agent said. "There's a horse in the barn behind the station."

"Thanks." Paddy pointed his knife at the agent and went out the back door.

Clarence Langley, the Union Pacific's telegrapher in Omaha, was secretly in the pay of Mortimer Kavanagh, the self-styled mayor of Hell on Wheels. Langley kept Kavanagh apprised of goings on at Union Pacific's headquarters through the use of a secret code he'd learned in the telegraph corps during the war.

After Paddy had failed to steal the Morgan from the banker's stable, he'd gone to Langley's office where they'd telegraphed Kavanagh. He'd hated to inform his godfather that he'd failed, but he had to find out what Kavanagh expected him to do. Coded instructions came back over the wire directing Paddy to rendezvous with a band of Cheyenne Indians to make another attempt at stealing the horse.

An hour's horseback ride west of Ogallala brought Paddy to the designated rendezvous point with six Cheyenne warriors.

Black paint obscured the Cheyenne leader's face from beneath his eyes to below his chin. He tapped his thumb against his bare chest. "Me Black Wolf." The flanks of his white pony bore painted imprints of wolf paws.

Paddy shifted in his saddle to reveal the Colt revolver in his holster. He wanted the half dozen Indians to know he was armed, though he seldom drew the pistol. He carried the Colt Navy .36-caliber model, because its kick was less than the larger .44-caliber Army model.

Paddy leaned over and spat a stream of tobacco juice onto the ground in front of Black Wolf's pony. "Ye speak English?"

Black Wolf shook his head and motioned for one of his band to join him.

A younger man eased his pony forward. He rode with the erect, confident bearing of an Indian. A strip of red cloth tied to his head held braided black hair in place. He sat bare-chested, bare-legged, wearing a breechclout and moccasins, like his companions—but his skin was pale.

"Ye speak English?" Paddy asked.

"Yes." Stripes of vermillion and yellow paint highlighted the Indian's cheekbones. On each pectoral muscle a two-inch scar stood out between similar paint streaks. He's been through the Sun Dance ceremony recently, Paddy thought. That'd make him about the same age as Paddy—around fifteen or so. That's when an Indian youth submitted himself to the torture of the Sun Dance. Those livid wounds weren't fully healed. That must've hurt.

"Got a name?" Paddy asked.

"Lone Eagle."

Paddy counted eight eagle talons strung on a rawhide thong that encircled the Indian's neck. A talisman related to his name, no doubt.

"I be Paddy O'Hannigan. What do ye know of this job?"

"Chief Tall Bear sent us to steal horses. Kavanagh promised whiskey."

"Aye, that's the deal. There be six horses coming on the next train. I only want one . . . a black Morgan. Ye braves can keep the other five. Who's the best horseman?"

"Me," Lone Eagle replied.

"Well now, ye'll ride the Morgan to Julesburg. Hide it in the big clump of bushes on the riverbank below the town, do ye see? I'll fetch it from there."

Lone Eagle nodded.

"Ye're not full-blooded, are ye?" Paddy watched Lone Eagle's eyes narrow. "Ye're a half-breed."

"My mother was Cheyenne." Lone Eagle hissed through gritted teeth. "I'm Cheyenne."

"All right, ye're Cheyenne. What do I care?" Paddy spat another stream of tobacco juice.

Paddy and Lone Eagle glared at each other. Black Wolf broke the silence and spoke to Lone Eagle.

"Black Wolf wants to know your plan, Irishman," Lone Eagle said. "If you have one."

Chapter 8

Mid-afternoon General Dodge's train slowed to a crawl. Will leaned out the door of the stable car to see what was going on. Hundreds—no, thousands—of shaggy buffalo covered the plains on both sides of the rails. The engineer blew the whistle in a long, uninterrupted wail and clanged the bell repeatedly, trying to scare the animals away. The locomotive inched forward, shoving the beasts off the tracks with its cowcatcher.

The passengers in the coach blasted away at the herd with rifles and pistols. They couldn't miss, the buffalo were packed so closely together. The carcasses remained where they fell—not a slab of meat, nor a single hide taken. Will had never purposely shot an animal and left it. What a waste.

It took an hour to clear the herd and regain normal speed. The train proceeded west, pausing late in the afternoon to refuel at the new town of North Platte, Nebraska. Here, where the North and South Platte Rivers joined to form the Platte River, the tracks angled southwest and followed the north bank of the South Platte on the final leg of its journey to Julesburg.

Will occupied himself wiping off his revolver with the tail of his shirt. His uncle Sean had brought his father's pistol to his mother when he'd escorted his father's body back to Burlington following the Battle of Atlanta. Will's father had taught him how to shoot the family's single-shot musket, but he'd never fired the pistol. He could hit what he aimed at with the musket. He wasn't so sure about the revolver. He returned the handgun to his waistband.

Lightning streaked through billowing clouds visible to the west. The rumbling, creaking, groaning of the train drowned out any thunder. The wind blowing through the doorway turned chilly. Will tugged on the heavy car door, but the door refused to close.

He reached out, grasped the outside door handle, and placed a foot against the doorjamb. He pushed back with his other foot just as the engine's wheels screeched on the rails from hard braking.

He flew out the open door.

"Aiyee, aiyee, aiyee!" Indian war cries competed with the engine's screaming whistle.

He hit the ground with a thump and tumbled down the slope of the roadbed. Each roll jammed the pistol painfully into his stomach. He ended on his back in the bottom of the ditch alongside the tracks.

The passenger car rolled past above him. He raised himself onto his elbows. At the front end of the train, sparks shot from between the locomotive's locked driving wheels and the rails. Each railcar jammed into the one in front of it with a succession of bangs. By the time the train stopped, Will lay twenty yards behind it.

He rolled over, raised to a crouch, and retrieved his hat. His belly ached where the revolver had pounded into it.

A short distance ahead of him, passengers fired from the coach at a half dozen Indians who raced by on ponies. One Indian pealed away from the others and launched himself into the stable car.

Will took a step toward the train. A shot whizzed overhead. He ducked. He hadn't been shot at before.

Shots zinged between the coach and the Indians. He realized they weren't aiming at him. No one knew he was in the ditch.

He crouched low and trotted parallel to the tracks, between the train and the attackers, staying in the ditch. Ahead of him, five horses jumped one after another from the stable car. Then Buck, with the Indian astride, leaped from the car. The warrior leaned over Buck's neck and rapped the horse's flank with a long stick.

What was going on?

Rifle shots blasted from the passenger car. Indians returned the fire with arrows and bullets. From time to time glass shattered when a shot broke a window pane in the coach.

Will continued up the length of the train, passing each of the flat cars, until he reached the open doorway of the stable car. Ahead of the locomotive's cowcatcher he saw a rail jutting off to the side. The Indians had pried up the tracks to force the train to stop. The engineer and fireman fired weapons from the locomotive's cab. Passengers and the conductor shot from the rear. But the midsection, where he stood, remained quiet.

The Indians had ridden entirely around the train once and now raced past the front of the locomotive again. They ceased firing at the coach and veered away from the train, herding the stolen horses ahead of them, shouting and whirling blankets above their heads. Black paint obscured the lower portion of the lead warrior's face. His white pony's flanks bore black imprints in the shape of paws.

Will noticed something peculiar about one of the riders. He didn't wave a blanket. Instead of a feathered headband, he wore a bowler hat. The rider turned and looked in Will's direction. A scar ran down his left cheek. Paddy O'Hannigan!

A shot from the passenger car found a mark. An Indian screamed and fell to the ground, dragging his pony down with him. One of the other warriors swung back and aided the wounded man in swinging up onto the rear of his pony.

The Indians, the Irishman, and the captured horses raced

east. The Indian riding Buck suddenly swerved away from the group and rode south, toward the South Platte River. Why was he separating from the larger group? Why was he taking Buck in a different direction?

Will had to stop that Indian from stealing Buck!

Chapter 9

The wounded Indian's pony got back to its feet. Will edged up beside the animal. The pony eyed him with a cocked head. Before it could back away, Will grabbed its horsehair bridle. He tried to mount the pony from the left, but the animal shied away. Then he remembered reading in one of his dime novels that Indians mounted from the right. He ducked beneath the pony's neck and threw himself onto its back from the opposite side.

Will kicked his heels into the pony's flanks and took off in pursuit of Buck. But how could an Indian pony catch a Morgan?

Will leaned forward, hoping to reduce the wind resistance. He kicked the pony again and again. Still, the gap between the pony and Buck increased.

Buck raced in easy, long strides down the slope toward the river's edge, a mile away. Suddenly, Buck slowed. The ground closer to the river was broken by gullies. The Indian picked his path more carefully around thick underbrush, evidently concerned with providing Buck secure footing.

Will's pony was well suited for running over broken ground and around obstacles. The Indians would have trained it to pursue buffalo, dodging and shifting to stay abreast of a stampeding herd.

Ahead of him, Will saw Buck stiffen his forelegs and slide out of sight down the embankment near the river's edge. The pony reached the embankment and leaped forward, landing on the sandy riverbank on spread legs. He'd almost caught up.

Will chased the Indian along the river's edge. The Indian slapped Buck's flank with the long stick. Flecks of foam flew from Buck's mouth.

What was that he'd heard General Dodge say about getting Buck to stop? Whistle. That's it! Maybe he could get Buck's attention if he whistled.

"Tseeeee, Tse, Tse, Tse." Too weak. Will had never been a good whistler. He wasn't going to get Buck's attention if the horse couldn't hear his whistle.

He blew harder through his teeth. *"Tseeeee, Tse, Tse, Tse."*

Buck's ears laid back. Maybe he'd heard that one.

Each pounding stride of the pony's hooves jolted Will. He needed to stop the jarring, even if he gave up ground. He pulled the pony to a halt.

He sat up straight, sucked his lips back against his teeth, and blew. *"Tseeeee! Tse! Tse! Tse!"*

The Morgan threw up his head, pricked his ears forward, and jammed his forelegs into the ground. Buck stopped so abruptly the Indian pitched over the horse's head in a tumbling, twisting somersault. The Indian's arms flailed outward. The stick flew from his hand. He landed feet down facing back toward Will—and sank to his waist.

Quicksand!

Will's whistle not only resulted in the Indian being pitched off, it saved Buck from taking a fatal step into the grasping, wet sand.

Will walked the pony forward, reached out and patted Buck on his flank. "Good boy." He slipped off the pony and stepped to the edge of the quicksand. Far enough. He didn't want to become mired himself. He drew his pistol from his waistband.

The Indian stroked at the quicksand with his arms, trying to pull himself forward.

Will double cocked the pistol. "Don't move, or I'll shoot."

The Indian stopped stroking and stared at Will. "You won't shoot."

"You speak English."

"Of course. I went to school . . . just like you."

A band of red cloth gathered the Indian's black hair behind his head. A single feather hung down behind his left ear. Two horizontal streaks of paint outlined his cheekbones, the upper one vermillion, the lower yellow. Identical paint streaks outlined scars on each pectoral muscle. The scars were new—puckered and raw. The Indian's skin was browner than Will's suntanned skin, but not red. He was certainly not the "red man" of the dime novels. Encircling his neck he wore a leather thong on which were strung several talons.

"What makes you think I won't shoot?" Will asked.

"Gun's not loaded. I can see into the empty chambers."

Will released the hammer and jammed the revolver back into his waistband. That's the second time he'd pointed an empty gun at someone.

"No need to shoot. Just watch me sink." The Indian raised his arms and sank to his chest.

"Why'd you steal the horses?"

"A scrawny Irishman promised whiskey for the black horse." He nodded toward Buck.

"Paddy O'Hannigan?"

"That's him."

Will had never killed a man, and watching this Indian drown in the quicksand would be murder. He didn't want that hanging over his head. He leaned over the edge of the quicksand and reached toward the Indian. It was too far.

"Use the coup stick."

"The what?"

"The coup stick. I dropped it." He pointed behind Will to the long stick.

Will picked up the coup stick and extended it toward the Indian's outstretched hand. The limber end drooped, like a buggy whip, and fell short. Will whipped it gently and the end brushed the Indian's outstretched fingers. Still too far.

The Indian lifted the necklace of talons over his head. "Try again."

Will flipped the coup stick at the same time the Indian flicked the necklace. The necklace wrapped around the end of the coup stick. The talons tangled and hooked together. The Indian tugged and cinched the extension tight.

Will gouged a hole in the grass with his heels, braced himself, and pulled. If he slipped, he'd be dragged in with the Indian.

The Indian wriggled his torso to and fro, working against the drag of the quicksand, while Will took short steps back from the edge. Will's hands grew sweaty, the handle of the coup stick slippery. He tightened his grip and pulled harder. The quicksand relinquished its grasp. The Indian surged from the prison with a sucking noise and staggered to his feet. The coup stick slid through Will's fingers and he fell backward onto his butt.

The slender, muscular figure, stood over him. Will's eyes focused on a mud-covered knife at the Indian's waist.

The Indian followed Will's gaze. "I will not kill someone who just saved my life."

Will blew his breath out with a whoosh.

"Cheyenne are fierce people . . . but not ungrateful."

"You're Cheyenne?"

"Yes." He sat down beside Will.

The two stared at the quicksand. The surface had returned to its deceptive smoothness, leaving no evidence of the danger ready to trap the next victim.

"I suppose you'll get to keep the other horses," Will said.

"I'm glad I was able to stop you from stealing Buck, though. I guess that means your people won't get their whiskey. That's probably a good thing from the white man's viewpoint."

"White man's viewpoint!" The Indian snorted. "What about the Indian's viewpoint? This is our land. The railroad brings white settlers who dig up the prairie with plows, destroying the grassland. They shoot the buffalo, wasting the meat and hides my people need. When the Cheyenne fight back, the white man cries for help from the 'Great White Father.' Then the President sends soldiers to kill my people and force us off our land."

"Haven't you heard of Manifest Destiny?" Will asked.

"Humph! They preached that doctrine at the boarding school in Saint Louis. Politicians proclaiming it's the white man's right to expand across the continent does not make it right."

"But the Indians signed treaties. The white man has gained the right to the land."

"Most Indians do not speak English. They do not understand what they sign."

"But when a chief signs a treaty it has to be honored."

"One chief does not speak for all Indians. Each tribe has many bands, and each band has more than one chief. If one band does not like a treaty signed by another, they don't abide by it. Indians do not have a central government like whites."

Will studied the Indian beside him. "You learned English in boarding school?"

"My father taught me first. He's a mountain man."

"A fur trapper?"

The Indian nodded. "Bullfrog Charlie Munro is a famous trapper. My mother, Star Dancer, was the daughter of Tall Bear, a great Cheyenne chief. She wanted me to learn white man's ways. She thought the Cheyenne and the white man should live in peace together . . . like she lived with my father."

"You said she *was* the daughter of a great chief?"

"She caught a sickness from a passing wagon train and died. I ran away from school when I learned about it. I did not want to be forced to become a farmer. I want to be free. I am Cheyenne."

Will understood the desire for freedom. He told the Indian about his search for his uncle.

The Indian rose and stepped into the river. He washed the mud from his body. The paint on his chest streaked. "I am Lone Eagle."

Will stood and extended his hand. "Will Braddock."

Lone Eagle shook Will's hand. "Speak any Indian languages, Will?"

Will shook his head.

"Learn sign language. Next time you may not find an English-speaking Indian." Lone Eagle grinned.

"How old are you, Lone Eagle?" Will asked.

"Fifteen."

"I guessed we were about the same age. I'll be fifteen on my next birthday."

Lone Eagle nodded.

Will pointed to Lone Eagle's chest. "Our reverend preached once that an Indian coming of age performs the heathen Sun Dance and mutilates himself. Is that how you got the scars?"

"Heathen? Not to Cheyenne. I did the Sun Dance last month. My grandfather cut my chest muscles and pushed bone skewers through the cuts. He tied leather thongs to each end of the skewer and hung me on a post. Four days I danced around that post. No food. No water. I pulled back all the time. When the bones tore through my chest muscles, I became a man."

Will stared at the scars. The pain of the Sun Dance was hard to imagine.

"I changed my name then." Lone Eagle rubbed a hand across his scars. "My mother called me Little Eagle. Now I am Lone

Eagle. Now I am truly Cheyenne."

Lone Eagle picked up his coup stick and unwrapped the eagle talon necklace from it.

"What kind of weapon is that?" Will asked.

"Not a weapon." Lone Eagle tapped Will on the shoulder with the limber end of the coup stick. "If a member of my tribe witnesses me doing that, it counts as a coup. Indians do not have to kill an enemy . . . just touch him. Humiliate him, to claim victory. But I did not touch you to humiliate you, but to show you how it is done."

Lone Eagle untied the talisman's thong. A knot separated each of eight talons strung along the length of the rawhide. He slid a talon off each end of the thong. "You saved my life from the sinking sand. I owe you."

Lone Eagle removed the pony's woven horsehair bridle and cut a short length from it. He returned the shortened, but still serviceable, bridle to the pony's mouth, looped it around the lower jaw, and tucked the ends back through the loop. The Indian bridle was a simpler solution to controlling a horse than a metal curb bit—Will would have to remember how to fashion one.

Lone Eagle threaded the two talons onto the length of horsehair, knotted it, and dropped the talisman around Will's neck.

"May they bring you luck," Lone Eagle said. "I used one to pick the lock at the school the night I took back my freedom. And now their strength helped pull me free from the quicksand."

Will touched the talons. "Thank you."

Lone Eagle retied his thong around his neck. "You take the black horse you call Buck. I will take the pony." The mixed-blood swung onto the pony, slapped its flank with his coup stick, and raced away.

A flash of lightning illuminated black clouds that obscured

the setting sun. Thunder clapped. The storm he'd watched developing from the stable car was upon him. Drops of rain pattered Will's cheeks and hands. The drops grew larger, pelting him hard.

From the bank of the South Platte, he couldn't see the Union Pacific's tracks. Two short blasts of the engine's whistle told him that General Dodge's train was underway again. Will and Buck stood alone in the storm.

Chapter 10

"It's no use, Papa!" Jennifer McNabb shouted. "The wheel's jammed."

She pointed to a large, flat rock that barely broke the surface of the shallow creek flowing around the heavy covered wagon.

"Last night's flash flood raised the water level too high," her father said. "That rock would've been in plain sight yesterday. Let's try again, Jenny."

He raised his bullwhip with his good right arm and snapped it over the heads of the oxen. They surged against their yokes. The wagon lurched forward.

Crack!

"It broke, Papa!"

Her father sloshed back through the creek and joined her at the rear of the Conestoga wagon, looking at the wheel. A broken spoke jutted to the side. "We'll have to unload the wagon before we can replace it."

He tucked his bullwhip under the stump of his left arm, reached up and grasped an overhanging branch with his good hand, and pulled himself out of the creek.

"Alistair, I'm sorry to have caused this trouble." Jenny's mother spoke to her father from her seat in the jockey box on the front of the wagon.

"It's not your fault, Mary." Her mother had come down with a bilious fever only two days after the family had crossed the Missouri.

Jenny waded through creek water that rose halfway to her knees. She stopped at the front of the wagon and looked up at her mother. "Mama, we'll get out of this. Don't worry."

Her mother laid a hand atop her head. "We're lucky to have your strength, Jenny. But dear, put on your bonnet."

"Oh Mama, it's hard to work with that thing on."

"Jenny, dear. You must look after your complexion. This prairie sun is too damaging to a Southern lady's delicate skin."

The bonnet dangled behind Jenny's neck on a string. She gathered her long, black hair behind her neck and pulled the bonnet back onto her head. Her complexion had been ruined weeks ago. She didn't look like much of a lady dragging the skirt of her calico dress through muddy water. But, if it soothed her mother, she'd wear the bonnet.

Jenny swished back to the rear of the wagon. "Elspeth! Duncan! Get over here and lend a hand."

"Who said you're the boss?" Elspeth glared at her from the creek bank. "I'm older than you."

"Then act like you're sixteen and lend a hand. You stayed back there to gather up buffalo chips because you didn't want to get your dainty feet wet."

"Wasn't my idea to go to California. I was perfectly happy to stay in Virginia."

All the McNabbs spoke with a Southern accent—Elspeth's cultivation of hers increasingly annoyed Jenny. "You mean starve in Virginia. You forget the damned Yankees burned our house to the ground."

"Ladies, that's enough," her father said. "Jenny, I know damned Yankees is a single word, but it upsets your mother to hear you curse." He winked.

"Yes, Papa."

"Not much daylight left. We're an easy target here. I heard a lot of gunfire yesterday from across the river . . . up where the railroad tracks probably run. We've got to get to Julesburg before the wagon train pushes on." He stepped back into the creek. "Duncan, climb into the wagon and drag things to the rear. Your sisters and I'll carry them to dry ground."

Jenny's mother rose to her feet.

"Sit down, Mary," her father said. "We'll do it. Save your strength, please."

Duncan splashed through the creek, scrambled up the tailgate, and disappeared into the bed of the wagon. Jenny admired her skinny, eight-year-old brother's spunk. He was always willing to help, but he wasn't very big. She was sure he'd eventually develop into a strong man like their father, but now he was just a growing boy.

Jenny chuckled when Elspeth stepped into the creek, clutched her fists against her breast, and grimaced. Even though her blonde sister was three years older, Jenny was as tall as Elspeth. They stood toe to toe in the stream and glared at each other. Elspeth stuck out her tongue.

Duncan dragged a heavy trunk to the tailgate where Jenny and her sister grabbed the end handles. They staggered backward with it, muddy water swirling around their skirts.

"Look at my dress." Elspeth moaned. "I'll never get it clean!"

"Watch where you're going, Elspeth!" Jenny tightened her grip. "This is mother's china."

"I know what it is. You think you're so smart."

"That's enough!" Their father pointed an admonishing finger first at Jenny then Elspeth. "Stop this bickering. If we had horses, instead of oxen, I could ride for help . . . but we don't. We'll make do the best we can. Let's get this done quickly, and quietly. It's going to be dark in a few hours. We'll have to spend another night out here alone on the prairie as it is."

Jenny's father grasped a spinning wheel that Duncan had hauled to the tailgate and lifted it one-handed. Swinging a cavalry saber throughout the war had increased the power in an already strong right arm. He refused to talk about the battle in which he'd lost his left one.

"Papa?" Duncan called from the interior of the wagon. "Do you want to unload the stove?"

"No. That cast iron thing's too heavy. We'd never get it loaded again."

They worked steadily, transferring the remaining contents from the wagon to the dry ground. Their feet slipped in the mud of the creek bottom under the weight of the bundles. Both girls' full-length skirts were heavy with water and coated with mud. Their father's old cavalry boots helped keep his feet dry, but the girls' shoes gave them no protection.

Jenny wrapped her arms around a wooden butter churn. The last item. She turned with the unwieldy burden and tripped over Elspeth's outstretched foot. She caught a fleeting glimpse of the smirk on Elspeth's lips before she fell into the creek. The current rolled the churn hard against her and tumbled her facedown in the water.

She sat up sputtering and yanked the sopping bonnet off her head. She gritted her teeth and wiped her eyes clear of muddy water. The force of the stream kept bumping the churn into her backside.

Where'd that horse come from? Her eyes scanned up the legs of a black horse standing beside her in the creek. A young man looked down at her from astride the animal.

Jenny glared. "What're you staring at?"

The young man jerked back, but continued to stare.

"Are you just going to sit there . . . or are you going to lend a hand?" She scowled at the rider and pushed her wet hair off her face.

"Oh," the horseman said. He slid off the horse into the creek, picked up the churn, and set it on the bank.

"That's not what I meant by lending a hand."

"Oh." He extended a hand and pulled her out of the creek.

"Is *oh* all you can say?"

"Oh, sorry. I've never seen a pretty girl so wet and muddy before."

"Pretty, my foot!" Jenny's wet shoe squished when she stomped it.

"What'd you mean by lending a hand?" he asked.

"Can't you see our wagon has a broken wheel?"

"Oh."

"There you go again with *oh.*" Jenny looked into brown eyes that didn't waver from looking back at her. "Where'd you come from? Who are you?"

"Will . . . William Braddock. I grew up in Iowa. I'm heading west to find my uncle. Yesterday, Indians attacked our train and tried to steal Buck." He patted the horse's neck. "They stole all the other horses, but not Buck. I got him back. But the train went on without me. I didn't want to take a chance running into the Indians over there last night, so I crossed the river and hid out along the bank on this side. Now I need to get on to Julesburg."

"We're headed there ourselves . . . as soon as we get this wagon rolling again."

"Well . . . I guess I can take time to lend you folks a hand."

"That's mighty kind of you. We'd appreciate that. My name's Jennifer McNabb . . . call me Jenny." She waved a hand toward her family members. "Meet my father, and my mother . . . my little brother, Duncan . . . and my *older* sister, Elspeth."

Will jerked off his slouch hat and nodded to the McNabbs. "How do you do." He pushed back a mop of unruly brown hair before returning the hat to his head.

"What's a boy like you doing out here alone?" Jenny asked.

"I'm not a boy. I'm fourteen. Won't be long till I'll be fifteen."

"Oh." Jenny giggled.

"Now who's saying *oh*?"

"Sorry." Jenny flicked a drop of water off the end of her nose with the back of a muddy hand. "Mama's been sick ever since we left Missouri. We fell behind the other wagons. We need to get to Julesburg to join back up with them. But, as you can see, we're not making much progress. We can use some help."

"We don't need help from a damned Yankee," her father said.

"Papa," Jenny said. "Please. We need help. Just because he comes from Iowa makes no difference. The war's over. Think of Mama. This boy may be able to help."

"I'm not a *boy*!"

Jenny cocked her head to the side and looked at Will. "Maybe this *young man* can help."

She grinned and watched Will blush. He wasn't going to be hard to manage—not the way he stared at her. "Any ideas?" She raised an eyebrow.

"You have a spare wheel." Will pointed to a wheel suspended by chains from the underside of the wagon. "We'll have to lift the wagon to get the broken one off."

"Humph." Jenny snorted. "That's rather obvious."

"We need leverage," her father said. "The wagon's too heavy for us to lift without a jack. I loaned ours to a fellow who forgot to return it. If we were with the wagon train there'd be enough strong-bodied men around to hoist the wagon by hand."

"We can do what my pa did when the wheel came off our hay wagon one time." Will pointed at the rock against which the wheel was wedged. "We'll use the rock to gain leverage. We just need a pole strong enough to take the weight. We'll wedge one end of the pole under the wagon, balance the middle of it across the rock, run a rope from the other end of the pole down under that exposed root and back up over that branch of the tree. Buck can pull the rope."

Jenny's father nodded slowly. "Might work." He pointed along the creek bank. "That sapling looks both strong and limber. It should take the weight."

Duncan picked up an ax that was almost as big as he was and headed for the small tree. Jenny saw the young man glance at her father's one good arm.

"I'll chop it," Will said. He removed his shirt and draped it over a bush.

Maybe she should be embarrassed, but she was too fascinated by the muscular build that showed through his tightly fitting undershirt to turn away. A cord of some kind—horsehair maybe—encircled his neck. From it hung two talons. A talisman? Funny. She wouldn't have imagined a boy wearing such a thing.

Will felled the sapling with a dozen strokes of the ax, lopped off the branches, and dragged the crudely shaped pole to the wagon. "Is that a harness on the bank?" he asked.

"Yes," Jenny said. "We don't have a horse right now, but we will when we get to our new home. Then we'll need it for plowing."

"We'll put the harness on Buck."

"I'll bet that Morgan's never been harnessed," her father said. "Looks like a cavalry mount."

"He is," Will said. "He's General Rawlins's riding horse."

"John Rawlins? Grant's chief of staff?"

"Yes, sir."

Jenny's father shook his head. "Well, I never expected to get help from a damned Yankee officer, much less his horse."

"Papa, stop it," Jenny said.

Her father nodded. "All right. Let's get on with it."

Buck snorted and shuffled when Will draped the harness over his back. "Easy, fella. This won't hurt. It's just different. I really need your cooperation, Bucephalus."

"Bucephalus?" Jenny asked.

"Yeah. We call him Buck for short."

"Bucephalus was Alexander the Great's warhorse," Jenny said.

"How'd you know that?"

"Anybody who's read Plutarch knows who Bucephalus was."

"Blue starch?"

"Plu-tark. The Greek philosopher who wrote about the lives of famous men from ancient times. Papa had a copy of *Plutarch's Lives* in his library . . . before the Yankees burned the place. You ever read it?"

"No, ma'am, never read it."

"Don't *ma'am* me. You can call my mother ma'am, but my name's Jenny."

Will grinned at her. "Yes, ma'am . . . Jenny."

She liked the twinkle in his eye. She returned his grin.

Will eased the horse collar over Buck's head and settled it around his neck. Buck snorted and reared his head. "Easy, Buck. You can do this."

Jenny could tell the horse trusted Will, even though he didn't like the harness.

Will straightened the leather straps along the horse's flanks and reached beneath his belly to grab the cinch. "Now that's not so bad, is it?" Buck tossed his head and nickered.

That's impressive, Jenny thought. He does know how to manage a horse.

Will buckled the harness to the collar and backed Buck up to the cottonwood, while she helped her father and Duncan position the pole and attached the rope. Will tied the other end of the rope to the harness beneath the horse's tail.

"Buck," Will said. "Young Duncan here is going to lead you away from the tree when I give him the signal."

Jenny choked back a giggle at Will calling Duncan "young."

"Just talk softly to him," Will said, "and you two will get along fine."

Duncan grasped Buck's halter. Will gave Buck a pat and stepped into the creek beside her and her father. "Let's give this a try, sir."

Chapter 11

The leverage scheme required an hour to replace the broken wheel. Jenny didn't know what they would've done if Will hadn't ridden into their lives.

Will helped the family reload the wagon. "You sure have a lot of books," he said. He set a box of them on the tailgate, and Duncan dragged it back into the body of the wagon.

"A fraction of what Papa's library used to be," Jenny said. "You have a favorite book?"

"*Ivanhoe.*"

"Humph. Sir Walter Scott. That's one of the reasons the Confederacy lost the war. Many Southern boys died believing in that chivalry nonsense."

She looked sideways at Will who opened his mouth, but closed it without speaking.

They completed the reloading and the oxen pulled the wagon up the far bank. Jenny grasped Elspeth by the elbow and pointed her upstream. She clutched a dry dress in her hand.

"Ladies upstream to freshen up . . . men down." She pointed the direction she wanted the males to take. "Mama, you rest here until we get back. And Will, you wash that shirt out. It stinks of smoke."

A few minutes later they all assembled back at the wagon.

"Jenny," her father said. "Let's get some dinner cooked. I'm sure everybody's hungry."

"Yes, Papa." Jenny squeezed her hair one more time with the

towel, then reached back to fan her tresses out over her shoulders to dry. The dry calico dress felt comforting and warm in the chill evening air. "Duncan, bring some kindling and chips over here and get a fire started."

"Sure thing, Jenny."

One of the chores Jenny and her siblings performed along the trail was gathering buffalo chips, as well as branches and twigs of wood when they could find any, and stowing them in a tarpaulin slung beneath the wagon. Wood of any kind was scarce on the prairie. The hundreds of wagons that had preceded them over the past dozen years had depleted the limited supply. Dried buffalo dung was the most readily available fuel. Dry chips made a hot fire that, surprisingly, was free of offensive odor.

"Elspeth, get over here and lend a hand," Jenny said.

Her older sister sighed her displeasure at having to help, but she sashayed over to join Jenny.

Duncan built the fire while his sisters prepared the meal. Jenny had to tell Elspeth what to do—her sister avoided the cooking chore when she could.

"Whew!" her father exclaimed. "Where'd we get that fresh chip? Get it out of the fire, Duncan, or the stink will ruin our appetites."

Duncan scraped the offending patty out of the fire. The stench of manure was potent when the thin crust of a fresh one broke.

"Elspeth," Jenny said, "you weren't paying attention when you gathered up that chip."

"Wasn't me."

"Had to be you. Duncan used the latest batch you gathered up."

Elspeth snorted and stalked away.

After they'd devoured the simple meal of bacon, beans, biscuits, and coffee, they sat around the fire and listened to Will tell why he'd come west. Jenny sympathized with his not wanting to become a blacksmith and understood why he was anxious to find his uncle.

"Will?" her father asked. "Do you think you could find the wagon master of our train when you get to Julesburg? That is, if they're still there. Tell him we're not far behind. His name's Dryden Faulkner."

"Yes, sir. I can do that."

They'd all placed their wet footwear close to the fire to dry while they ate. Jenny saw that Will's toes stuck out through holes in his socks.

"Sorry about the holes," he said. Will pulled his boots on.

Jenny laughed. "Look at mine." She wiggled her toes through holes in her own stockings, then slipped her feet into her shoes. "Walking across the Kansas prairie wears out shoes and socks."

"Walk? Don't you ride in the wagon?"

"Oh, no. We walk . . . except Mama. It's easier to walk than ride in that jarring wagon. Besides, it'd be too much weight for the oxen to pull if we all rode. Mama has to ride. She hasn't been strong enough to walk." Jenny looked to where her mother rocked in a wicker chair they'd placed by the fire. Everybody else sat on the ground.

"Where are you heading after Julesburg?" Will asked.

"California, maybe Oregon. Papa will decide when we get to where the trails divide at Fort Bridger." Jenny took his empty plate and added it to a stack of dirty dishes beside the fire. "And what are you going to do, Will?"

"Return this horse to General Dodge in Julesburg. After that, find my uncle . . . I hope." He tied the laces of his boots and stood. "I best be going . . . or I can stay and accompany you folks to Julesburg."

"Thanks, but that's not necessary. We just have to push on for two or three more days and we'll be there." Jenny held out a hand and Will helped her to her feet.

"Thank you for the good meal, Jenny."

"You're welcome. Wasn't that good. We're running low on supplies. Need to restock in Julesburg."

Jenny walked with Will to where Buck grazed under a tree. Will gathered up the halter line and heaved himself onto the horse's back. "I'll find your wagon master. Promise."

The light breeze blew Jenny's black tresses across her face and up against Buck's mane. They were the same color. "Will, we do appreciate your help. You were true to your name."

"True to my name?"

"Will means 'resolute'."

"I didn't know that."

"It does. My grandfather told me. His name was William. You were certainly resolute in helping us get that wheel replaced." She looked into Will's brown eyes and grinned when he blushed. How long would she be able to do that to him?

"Goodbye, Jenny. Good luck."

"Good luck to you too, Will."

Will slapped Buck's neck with the halter rope and the horse broke into a trot, taking them away from the creek and out across the grassland.

Elspeth had slipped up behind her. "You're sweet on that boy," her sister said.

"Am not."

"Are too."

"Hush up, Elspeth. Just you hush up."

Jenny watched until the horse and rider disappeared. Would she ever see him again? He really was just a boy—but a nice boy.

Chapter 12

Will rode late into the night. The waxing moon drifting across a cloudless sky lit his way along the rutted wagon trail. He'd pushed Buck hard enough though. They both needed rest. He halted in the shelter of a copse of trees beside a dry creek bed, another tributary of the South Platte. He used the halter rope to hobble Buck, then stretched out on the ground, his only cover the stars overhead.

But they weren't stars that twinkled back at him—they were pale, blue eyes. Or were they gray? When she'd first confronted him in sunlight, he thought they were gray. By the light of the campfire, he decided they were blue. She'd stared straight at him while they'd talked after supper. She didn't drop her eyes—not even once.

Helping his mother on the farm hadn't left him much time for girls. Alice Armstrong may have been the prettiest girl in his class in Burlington. She'd made it clear she wasn't interested in a farm boy like him.

Then there was Rebecca Bottomley. She'd embarrassed him in front of his friends at the church social last Christmas. He'd refused her when she'd asked him to dance. He didn't know how to dance.

He couldn't say Jenny was beautiful. Her sister Elspeth was beautiful. But Jenny? She was—what? Independent—stubborn—physically tough. Not big and strong—just tough.

Jenny, with the help of a complaining Elspeth, had wrestled

the broken wheel off the hub. The two girls had climbed under the wagon and dragged out the replacement wheel, then slid it onto the axle, while Will and her father lifted on the side of the wagon to aid Buck's efforts. Elspeth may be the older sister—but Jenny was clearly the leader. Yes, Jenny McNabb was different. And the way she talked—that soft drawl.

He hadn't been able to keep his eyes off Jenny when she'd returned from washing up. She'd stood beside the campfire and unwound a towel she'd wrapped around her head, letting her hair spill over her shoulders, shimmering in the firelight.

Will drifted off to sleep picturing Jenny McNabb.

Long black hair, as black as Buck's mane, brushed across his cheek. It tickled. He awoke with a start. "Dang it, Buck! What'd you do that for?" The horse stood over him, swinging his mane back and forth across Will's face.

He pushed Buck's head away. "All right. It's time to go."

He only had the clothes he wore and the empty revolver. He had no saddle. He undid the hobble, snapped the rope back onto the halter, and heaved himself onto the horse's back.

He rode toward Julesburg with the morning sun growing warmer against his back. He fished the cold biscuit Jenny had given him the night before out of his pocket and bit into it. It sure beat that hardtack Mr. Johnson had given him in Columbus.

The deep wagon ruts led him toward the Upper California Crossing on the South Platte River. Buck pricked his ears at a shrill train whistle. Will scanned the horizon to the north. The rolling landscape blocked the view of the tracks, but a faint trace of smoke moved steadily westward on the opposite side of the river.

The undulations of the prairie ended and Will looked down a long slope to the meandering, muddy river. The banks on either side were denuded—just stumps remained. The thousands of immigrants crossing here had chopped down every tree for firewood.

Off to his right, a large Union flag flapped over what must be Fort Sedgwick. Why was the fort on this side of the river? The town was over on the opposite bank.

A half mile away, across the river, the Union Pacific's twin ribbons of rail glistened in the sunlight. Three locomotives puffed clouds of black smoke from where they were coupled as pusher engines, one behind the other, at the rear of a long construction train idling at track's end. Dozens of workers scurried around dragging ties and rails into position.

To the east of the train, a jumble of tents and wooden shacks ranged along the single dusty street of Julesburg. To the west, scattered along the north bank of the river, a half dozen circles of covered wagons delineated that many different wagon trains.

Will kicked the horse and Buck splashed across the shallow ford. He inquired at the first wagon train he came to and received directions to Dryden Faulkner's outfit. He rode into the center of a circle of wagons—the makeshift enclosure serving as a corral for oxen and horses. He found Faulkner and briefed the wagon master on the McNabbs' dilemma.

"Mr. Faulkner," Will said. "I thought wagon trains followed the Oregon Trail, up the North Platte River. Why are you all assembled here along the South Platte, heading southwest?"

"Too much Indian trouble along the old Oregon Trail right now," Faulkner said. "Last December a loud-mouthed Captain Fetterman bragged he could whip the entire Sioux nation with his eighty-man company. Crazy Horse and a band of Sioux and Cheyenne lured him into an ambush and massacred every last soldier, Fetterman included. The Indians have gained confidence they can stop any wagon train crossing their hunting grounds. The Army claims they don't have enough soldiers to guarantee safe travel up that way, so General Sheridan has ordered all wagon trains to follow the Overland Stage Trail out of Julesburg. We won't rejoin the Oregon Trail until five hundred miles west of here, at Fort Bridger."

"How's the Army going to protect all these wagon trains when the fort's over there?" Will pointed across the South Platte.

Faulkner laughed. "Julesburg used to be over there, right next to the fort. When the railroad showed up a while back on this side of the river, the townsfolk picked up, lock, stock, and barrel, and moved over here."

Satisfied that Faulkner's train wouldn't receive the Army's permission to leave before the McNabbs reached Julesburg, Will rode into the town to find General Dodge. He wished he could've saved the other horses, but maybe General Dodge would be appreciative enough with the return of Buck to tell him where to find his uncle. What was he going to do if his uncle got his hands on those guardianship papers before he had a chance to talk to him?

Carts and buggies, riders on horseback, and staggering drunks mingled along the roadway. A stagecoach boarded passengers at a Wells Fargo station. A single telegraph line, sagging between skinny poles, stretched the length of the street. Shouting and laughter drowned out the music from a tinkling piano, making the tune unrecognizable. Hell on Wheels was in full voice this late June morning. Many rowdies hadn't gone to bed last night.

Will pulled up sharply on Buck to avoid knocking down a man who staggered in front of them. "Watch where you're going, sonny." The drunk slurred his words, brandished a half-empty whiskey bottle, and stumbled on across the street.

The owner of the Lucky Dollar Saloon, the largest structure on the street, obviously wanted to give the impression of permanence with its elaborate false front. Conductor Johnson had told him that the whole town could be torn down in less than a day's time and hauled to the next Hell on Wheels location.

"Out of the way!" a freighter shouted at him, flicking the reins at a team of horses pulling a heavy wagon. "Don't stop in the middle of the road, boy."

"Come on, Buck. Let's find the depot."

Shacks and tents of all descriptions lined the narrow street. Hand-painted signs distinguished one from another: a laundry, a general store, a blacksmith. Wagons, horses, and pedestrians jockeyed for the right of way. A pistol shot punctuated a shout from an alley.

At the end of the street, Will pulled up at the Union Pacific depot and dismounted.

"Well, I'll be." General Rawlins looked down at him from the depot's platform. He turned and called over his shoulder. "General Dodge. Come see who just rode in."

CHAPTER 13

Following the raid, Paddy had spent a miserable night with Black Wolf and his Cheyenne warriors. He'd kept his Bowie knife within reach the whole time—afraid one of the savages might jump him. At daybreak, when the Indians took the five stolen horses and rode away, he'd made his way back to Ogallala. From there he'd gotten on the first westbound train earlier today.

As the train slowed, Paddy descended the steps of the coach's platform on the side away from Julesburg's depot. The other passengers jostled for position to exit on the depot side and paid no attention to him. He jumped from the platform steps before the train stopped. His feet hit the ground running and he stumbled. He quickened his stride, regained his balance, and ducked between two boxcars parked on an adjacent track.

"Sure, and Mort's gonna like this." He chuckled and peered out from between the boxcars. He saw no one on this side of the rail yard. He trotted across an open area and turned in behind the row of ramshackle hovels that stretched along the single street of Julesburg. He hurried down an alley, staying in the shadows.

"Aye. Mort's really gonna like this. I got that black horse this time. Sure, and I did." He glanced down to the South Platte, to the clump of bushes where he'd told Lone Eagle to hide the Morgan. After he reported to Kavanagh, he'd go retrieve the horse.

He easily located the back entrance to the Lucky Dollar Saloon. The large tent structure extending behind the false wooden front could accommodate a small circus. Paddy pushed through the rear canvas flap door. Chandeliers crowded with candles struggled to illuminate the smoky interior. It was too early for the railroad construction workers, but the Lucky Dollar always had a few customers.

Paddy kicked a drunk passed out on the earthen floor beside the rear entrance. He got a groan in response. One of Kavanagh's ladies sat beside the piano player, who plinked away on the keys. Later in the evening, she would circulate among the tables encouraging men to drink up and buy a dance with her. At one table, a professional gambler tried to con three men into wagering against him in a game of faro. A handful of customers leaned on the elaborately carved wooden bar that extended the length of one wall of the tent.

"Randy, me good man." Paddy tipped his bowler to the stocky, bearded man polishing the bar.

"Humph," Randy Tremble grunted. "The mayor's been wondering what happened to you." Randy wiped his hands on his apron and tossed a wrinkled envelope to Paddy. "This came in the mail couple days ago."

The envelope revealed no return address, but one wasn't necessary. Paddy recognized the handwriting. He received frequent letters from his sister. They were all the same. His mother didn't know how to write, so it was his sister who kept reminding him they couldn't survive on what they earned as laundresses in Brooklyn. He jammed the unopened letter into a vest pocket. Somehow he'd have to scrape up some money to send to them. He never seemed able to satisfy their demands.

Paddy crossed the hard-packed dirt floor and stepped up onto the irregular wooden floor of the false front, where one corner was walled off to serve as Kavanagh's office. Paddy knocked on the door.

When a gruff voice beckoned from within, Paddy entered the small office and tipped his bowler to Kavanagh.

Sally Whitworth sat in front of Mort's desk. She glared at Paddy.

"Darling," Mort said, "be a good girl and fetch me a bottle of that fine Irish whiskey Randy's got stashed behind the bar."

"Sure thing, Mort." Sally stood and smoothed her skirt. Her red curls brushed the tops of her bare shoulders. She was the prettiest of the half dozen girls who worked for Kavanagh, and she knew it. Paddy's eyes followed her swaying hips as she left the office.

"Where the hell have you been?"

Paddy spun around to face the powerfully built man sitting behind the desk. Why'd Mort use that tone? Paddy had expected praise. "Sure, and I been doing like ye said, Mort. Stealing the Morgan horse."

"Well, you didn't do a good job of it now, did you?" Kavanagh brushed a large mustache away from his lips with a finger. In addition to his physical size, he used a keen business sense to control everybody and everything in the portable sin city. Hell on Wheels moved only when "Mayor" Kavanagh said it was time to move.

Paddy furrowed his brow. His upper lip twitched. He fingered the scar on his cheek. Mort must be referring to the bungled attempt at the banker's stable. The raid on the train had been a success.

"Step over here and look out the window. What do you see in front of the depot?"

Paddy pushed open the window and leaned out. His mouth fell open. Tied to the hitching post at the depot stood the Morgan.

Paddy looked back at Kavanagh. "Well, now, sure and it must

be a different horse."

"No. That's the Morgan. I was in Omaha the day Dodge brought that horse across from Council Bluffs. I got a good look at it. It's the same horse."

"Sure, and I don't understand. That Cheyenne half-breed Lone Eagle was riding that horse away from the train last I seen him, to be sure. I told him to hide it down by the river. What happened?"

"How should I know? I wasn't there."

Paddy closed the window and returned to the front of Kavanagh's desk. He fidgeted with his bowler hat. "Jeez, Mort. Sure, and I done what ye telegraphed."

"What am I going to do with you Patrick O'Hannigan? I wish I'd never agreed to be your godfather. If that Yankee major had killed you at the same time he killed your pa, I wouldn't have had to promise your ma I'd look out for you." Kavanagh shook his head. "I don't know how much longer I can afford to have you working for me."

Sometimes Paddy hated his godfather almost as much as he hated Sean Corcoran. He caressed his scar—a souvenir given to him by the Army major when Corcoran had interfered with his father's attempt to hang a former slave. "Sorry, Mort. It was sure I was that the Indian got clean away with that horse."

"Well, obviously he didn't. I wanted to give that Morgan to Chief Tall Bear. I have to keep bribing the Cheyenne to attack the railroad to slow down the work . . . so I can keep selling whiskey to the workers." Kavanagh leaned back in his swivel chair. "Sit down."

Paddy sat opposite his boss and dropped his hat on the floor. He slipped the Bowie knife from his boot and sliced the end off his twist of tobacco. Wasn't much left of this twist. He'd have to steal another one from some passed-out drunk.

"Twice you've failed to steal that horse. Twice!" Kavanagh

placed the tips of his fingers together and glared over them at Paddy. "How old are you now, anyway?"

"Fifteen."

"Fifteen. Well, maybe that's it. I can't send a boy to do a man's job."

Paddy's lip twitched faster. He felt his face flush. He bit down hard on the tobacco chaw to keep from swallowing it. "I'll get the horse, Mort. Sure, and I will."

"Forget about the horse . . . for now. I've got another job for you. I have it on good authority that General Dodge and his party are trekking up Lodgepole Creek to stake out a new railroad center at the base of the Laramie Mountains."

A soft knock on the door announced Sally's return. "Come in, darling," Kavanagh said.

She entered and set a bottle of whiskey and a glass on the edge of the desk.

Paddy licked his lips when Kavanagh popped the cork and poised the bottle over the glass. "No. You don't get any of this good stuff, Paddy. When you're successful in your assigned task, I might think differently."

Kavanagh splashed amber liquid into the tumbler, downed it in a gulp, and slammed the glass onto the desk. "Mm." He smacked his lips and spun the swivel chair around to a file cabinet.

Paddy gave Sally his best smile. She sneered back at him. "Don't leer at me with those rotten, crooked teeth . . . and don't breathe in my direction either, you slimy Mick. You have the foulest breath of anyone I know."

Paddy spat a stream of tobacco juice through a gap in his teeth toward a spittoon at the corner of Kavanagh's desk, missing on purpose. The brown blob splattered on the floor at Sally's feet. He chuckled when she jumped back, jerking up the hem of her dress.

Kavanagh swung back to his desk. "That'll be all for now, Sally. Leave us for a while. I need to do some strategizing with this slimy Mick, as you call him."

Twenty minutes later Paddy handed Kavanagh's handwritten requisition to Randy Tremble. Randy looked at it and then at Paddy. "A case?"

"Sure, and that's what the man wrote. A case of whiskey for Chief Tall Bear."

"There goes today's profits. Giving away a case of whiskey." Randy heaved a wooden case of bottled whiskey onto the bar. "They ain't getting the good stuff. This here rotgut's good enough for Injuns."

Paddy grasped the case and dragged it off the bar. He staggered under the weight. The case thudded to the floor.

"Don't break the stuff before you get out the door, you scrawny Irishman. Transfer the bottles to saddlebags. You can't ride into Injun country holding a case of whiskey on your lap."

"Well, and be sure I know that." Paddy snorted at Randy, but he wished he had someone to handle one end of the case.

Paddy hefted the box and struggled through the canvas flap door. Once in the alley he set the case down and bent over, holding onto the sides of the box. He spat out his tobacco chaw and gasped for breath.

When he could stand upright again, he patted the pockets in his vest. One pocket held coins to buy a ticket on the stage to Fort Sanders, two hundred thirty miles west of here. They'd decided it would be safer to approach the Cheyenne village from the west, from Fort Sanders, rather than ride up Lodgepole Creek from Julesburg and possibly encounter General Dodge's party. Paddy was well known to the railroad officials since they'd fired him a year ago.

The other pocket contained coins for procuring a saddle horse and a packhorse from the Army's stable at the fort. Mort had told him to find Sergeant Lunsford, a drunk who'd been a regular customer of the Lucky Dollar before his transfer from Fort Sedgwick. Paddy was to bribe the sergeant for the horses and some saddlebags. The Army wouldn't miss the horses for the short time Paddy needed them.

He took a deep breath and hoisted the box. He staggered down the alley toward the Wells Fargo station. "Sure, and I ain't doing your bidding forever, Mort Kavanagh. One of these days I'll settle me score with Sean Corcoran, then I'm gonna strike out on me own."

Chapter 14

General Dodge motioned Will into the depot and pointed at some leftover food on a table. Will fashioned a sandwich from cold ham and cheese. Between bites, he told about seeing Paddy O'Hannigan with the Indians, chasing after Buck, and rescuing Lone Eagle from the quicksand.

"You say this Lone Eagle's father is Bullfrog Charlie Munro?" Dodge asked.

"That's what he said, sir."

"I know Bullfrog Charlie. A genuine relic from the past. He used to show up at our surveying camps wanting to trade an antelope carcass for whiskey." Dodge laughed. "He knows how much I like a good antelope steak. I guarantee we'll run into him on this trip. Bullfrog won't miss a chance to get a bottle of whiskey off me."

A short, full-bearded man stepped into the open doorway of the depot. "You wanted to see me, General Dodge?"

"You ready to travel tomorrow, General Jack?"

"I'm ready."

"Meet General Jack Casement, Will. Jack, this young fellow is Will Braddock. He just rescued the most valuable animal we had on the train."

General Jack Casement stood half a dozen inches shorter than Will's five feet nine. In stature he could be described as diminutive, but his bearing belied that. He exuded confidence as he tapped a riding crop against calf-high boots. "Ah. That's the black Morgan outside, I take it." Casement tipped his head to Will.

"Is *Colonel* Seymour ready to go, Jack?" Dodge snarled Seymour's title.

"Yes. He's been a regular pain in the rear. But he's ready."

"Grenville," Rawlins said, "I've been searching my brain ever since you introduced him, but I can't recall a Colonel Seymour from the war."

"He's not a real colonel, John. Just calls himself that. Have to tolerate him since he's Doc Durant's right-hand man. The vice president and general manager uses him to meddle with our surveys, trying to make the line longer. The more miles of track laid, the more money Durant can collect from the government."

Rawlins shook his head.

Dodge turned back to Casement. "How about Blickensderfer? Is he ready?"

"Yes, Jacob's ready. I feel sorry for him, being escorted by Seymour."

"Can't be helped. Durant specified Seymour was to look after him. I just hope Seymour doesn't antagonize him. We need a favorable recommendation from Blickensderfer on where the Rocky Mountains start. We need the Department of Interior to approve increased government funding for laying track through the mountains . . . no matter how long Durant and Seymour connive to make the line."

"Doc Durant and that fool Seymour will be the ruination of the UP if we're not careful," Casement said.

While the men had talked among themselves, Will had eased closer to a side table where General Dodge's briefcase sat open. Was Judge Sampson's package in there?

"Will?"

Will jerked around, his sandwich partway to his mouth.

"You still set on finding your uncle?" Dodge ask.

"Yes, sir." Will lowered the sandwich.

"Well . . . how'd you like to ride with us tomorrow?"

Will's head jerked up. "I'd like that, sir."

"Can't pay you anything. You can earn your keep looking after our visitors' horses. I'll make that your reward for rescuing Buck."

"Thank you, General." Will grinned. "I won't let you down."

"I'll hold you to that. But I can't have you associating with the dignitaries looking like a bum. General Jack, can you see he gets some gear from the UP's stock?"

"Can do."

"Will," Dodge said, "take Buck, feed and groom him, along with the other horses you'll find at General Jack's warehouse. Get them ready for riding in the morning."

"Yes, sir." Will shoved the last bite of sandwich into his mouth.

Will rode with Casement down Julesburg's only street and out beyond the end of town to the construction train. When they passed the three pusher engines, Casement pointed to them with his riding crop. "Know anything about locomotives, Will?"

"No, sir."

"These are 'four-four-ohs.' That's railroad code for the arrangement of the wheels . . . four leading wheels behind the cowcatcher, four driving wheels beneath the boiler, and no wheels under the cab."

They continued along the line of cars coupled in front of the 4-4-0 locomotives. Half of the cars they passed were outfitted as bunk cars.

"Designed these over-tall bunk cars myself," Casement said. "Three tiers of bunks on a side. Kind of crowded, but it provides sleeping accommodations for the crew. Each worker keeps a rifle suspended in ceiling racks down the central corridor. We're prepared to fend off any Indian attacks . . . and we've been seeing plenty lately."

They rode past a couple of dining hall cars and a kitchen. The tantalizing smell of baking bread wafting from a boxcar bakery stimulated Will's saliva. A worker threw the remains of a cow's carcass out of the open door of a boxcar serving as a butcher shop. Blood coated his apron, his boots, and the floorboards beneath him.

"We trail our own herd of cattle with the train," Casement said. "Slaughter a couple each day for fresh meat. A well-fed man makes a better worker."

Near the end of the train, men banged away in a tool car and a blacksmith car. The last car, a flat car loaded with wooden cross ties and iron rails, was actually the first car in the train as it was pushed down the track backward.

Beyond the end of the train, dozens of tracklayers worked along the prepared roadbed. The clanking of hammers on spikes responded to the shouted instructions of foremen.

"First time to witness tracklaying?" Casement asked.

"Yes, sir."

Will watched workers drag rough-hewn cottonwood ties into position along the grade. A boy, younger than he was, drove a wagon, fitted with railroad wheels, at a gallop down the tracks from the end of the construction train to where the rails ended several yards away. When he stopped, a crew of burly men carrying tongs grabbed the heavy iron rails, one from each side of the wagon, walked rapidly forward on opposite sides of the grade, and dropped the rails into place atop the ties.

"Those fellows are 'gandy dancers.' " Casement laughed. "They waddle like ducks struggling with those heavy loads."

A supervisor checked the spacing with a wooden gauge to align the rails on the ties.

"The rails have to be exactly four feet, eight and one half inches apart," Casement said. "The Romans supposedly established that standard. All wagons have been built to that width ever since, so their wheels fit properly into the old chariot ruts. When England built the first railroad they continued to use that measurement. I don't know that I believe that story . . . but, it's the best one I've heard for using such an odd dimension."

Will watched a supervisor signal he'd verified the width and a crew spiked the rails to the ties. Three quick blows with a sledge hammer drove each spike securely into place. Other men fastened the ends of the newly placed rails to the previously positioned ones with rivets driven through iron connecting plates. The continuous flow of rails from Omaha extended thirty feet farther west.

A boy already had the job of driving the rail wagon. He'd have to convince his uncle to recommend him for a job as a tracklayer. He could certainly drive spikes—maybe even be a gandy dancer. But first, he had to talk his uncle into not signing those guardianship papers.

"The gangs work until 'tools down' is called at sundown," Casement said. "They'll descend on the dining cars for their evening meal first, then they'll be off to Hell on Wheels to let off steam and blow their wages on liquor and gambling. I don't cotton to that lifestyle myself, but I tolerate it to keep them happy."

Casement led the way to a knock-down warehouse erected next to the tracks. He dismounted and shouted into the depths of the building. "Ellis!"

A Negro, much taller than Casement, appeared in the doorway. "This is my servant, Jack Ellis. Will Braddock needs outfitting, Jack. See to it, please."

Will emerged from the warehouse a short time later outfitted in dark-blue wool trousers, a red-and-black-checkered flannel shirt, and calf-high leather Wellington cavalry boots. Strapped around his waist he wore a black leather belt that carried a cartridge box, a percussion cap pouch, and a flap-protected holster holding his revolver. A pair of saddlebags slung over his shoulder contained additional ammunition and a canteen.

Casement nodded approval. "Why didn't you take a new hat?"

Will took off his father's old slouch hat, reshaped the crown, and seated the hat squarely on his head. "I like this one."

CHAPTER 15

Will rode with General Dodge's party out of Julesburg early Friday morning, the twenty-eighth of June, on a planned six-day journey to the Laramie Mountains. The column marched northwest up Lodgepole Creek from its juncture with the South Platte River, following the centuries-old creek-side trail and the stakes set out by the surveyors that marked the route for the track graders.

General Dodge, General Rawlins, and the dignitaries rode at the head of the slow-moving column, with a small cavalry detail close at hand. Two companies of mounted Pawnee Scouts, as well as two companies of regular Army infantry, provided protection for Dodge's party. The infantry hiked from Julesburg, marching the thirty miles each day.

Civilian teamsters drove two dozen wagons hauling tents and provisions. Trailing behind the wagons, a half dozen riders prodded along a cattle herd. The herd would shrink daily as the cooks butchered the animals to feed the travelers and the troops.

Will trailed behind the wagons in company with the cattle. He led six extra saddle horses; one each for Dodge, Rawlins, Blickensderfer, Seymour, and Casement—plus one for himself. Each noon, he guided the remuda to the head of the column so the dignitaries could exchange their mounts for fresh ones.

The first day, Will offered to help General Dodge shift his saddle to his fresh horse, eyeing the briefcase strapped against the saddle's skirt. The general shooed him away. "You help Seymour. He'll slow us down if we wait for him to transfer that mountain of equipment alone. The rest of us will fend for ourselves."

Will reserved the biggest horse in the remuda for "Colonel" Seymour. Not only did the poor animal have to carry the heavy-set Seymour, but also more personal gear than any two of the other officials combined. Seymour insisted on lugging a carbine in a case—although Will wondered if he knew how to fire it—and saddlebags stuffed with food and clothing. Two canteens dangled from his saddle horn. Behind the saddle's cantle he lashed a bedroll and poncho combination rolled up to the size of a cannon barrel.

After Will helped Seymour load his equipment, he had to give the big man a boost into his saddle. Once mounted, Seymour popped open an umbrella, which he held overhead as he rode. The Pawnee Scouts made fun of him behind his back, pretending to carry umbrellas.

When the column pitched camp each evening, the dignitaries turned their mounts over to Will. He fed the dozen horses oats from the supply wagons, rubbed them down, then hobbled each so they could graze without wandering far.

Will didn't finish his wrangling chores until an hour after the column halted. The dignitaries had usually finished their supper by the time he approached the campfire, but Dodge's railroad cook kept a plate of beef steak, sourdough bread, and beans for him. He was allowed to share this elite group's food because he took care of their horses. He was thankful he didn't have to fix his own meals. The soldiers and scouts had to feed themselves, but they were provided adequate rations from the wagons.

After eating, Will found a spot removed from the campfire. The officials relaxed and listened to General Rawlins read poetry. Will wasn't partial to poetry, so he paid little attention.

The first night, a wiry Army officer, wearing silver bars on his shoulder boards, stepped in front of him. The officer bowed, sweeping his campaign hat across his body.

"*Scuza* me." The officer greeted Will in a singsong Italian accent. "Lieutenant Luigi Moretti, at your service. I command the cavalry detail. General Dodge tells me you are Major Corcoran's nephew."

"Major Corcoran?" Will asked.

"Yes, Major Sean Corcoran."

"I never heard him called major. He's always been Uncle Sean to me."

"But of course." Moretti laughed and twirled one end of a waxed mustache that jutted the width of his face. "Your uncle and me, we fight the war together. I was a major too then. After the war, I lost that rank. Everybody lost rank who stayed in. I became first lieutenant once more. Same rank they gave me when I came from Italy to join the Army."

"You know Uncle Sean?" Perhaps the lieutenant could tell him where to find his uncle.

"But of course, we were both with General Dodge during the war. Your uncle was a major of an engineer battalion, rebuilding the railroads the Rebs tore up. I was a major of the cavalry assigned to protect his men. Your uncle and me, we know each other a long time."

"Have you seen him recently?"

"Not for a year . . . maybe more."

Will rose and extended his hand. "I'm Will Braddock. Nice to meet you, Lieutenant."

"Call me Luey. Everybody calls me Luey . . . except my men."

"Luey?"

"Yes. Short for Luigi, not Lieutenant." He laughed. The tips of his mustache jiggled.

★ ★ ★ ★ ★

For the first half of their hundred-forty-mile journey, the column encountered grading teams leveling the roadbed in preparation for the tracklayers who followed. Armed guards sat mounted on the surrounding hilltops to warn the graders of Indians.

The entourage crossed the southwest corner of Nebraska, and on the fourth day entered into that part of the Dakota Territory that would soon change its name to Wyoming. Here they veered away from Lodgepole Creek and headed due west. The final forty miles took them through rolling country, where only survey stakes marked the way.

The column had moved for six days, with Dodge and Rawlins always at its head. Will and his remuda, at the column's rear, ate the interminable dust thrown up by the feet of the men, the hooves of the animals, and the churning wheels of the wagons.

Will had guided his remounts forward in preparation for the changing of horses at noon, when the column halted abruptly on the crest of a low hill. Dodge turned in his saddle and motioned Lieutenant Moretti forward. Dodge saw Will at the same time and signaled for him to approach the head of the column, too. When Will, with his remuda, reached the crest, he saw that the slope stretched down to a grassy plain where two small creeks joined.

Moretti trotted up beside Dodge. Will guided his string of horses up next to Rawlins. Buck whinnied and tossed his head. "Hi, boy," Will said.

"Luey, this is our destination." Dodge pointed at a spot on a map he held unfolded across his saddle horn, then toward the valley before him. "We'll make camp down there, where Clear Creek flows into Crow Creek."

Rawlins eased Buck closer to Dodge to look at the map.

"I stumbled across this spot by accident a few years back, John, when I had to evade a pursuing band of Indians. I knew then that if I survived, I'd found the ideal route for building the railroad over the Rockies. That yonder ridge, between the two creeks, rises at a gentle two-percent grade, well within the capabilities of our locomotives. Where these creeks join is the perfect place for a major railroad center. I've decided to name this spot Cheyenne, after the tribe that claims this as their hunting ground." Dodge chuckled. "And may have been some of the ones who were intent on lifting my scalp a few years back."

Dodge folded his map and returned it to his pocket. "Luey, move the men and wagons down to that meadow and set up camp. Post a strong guard. This is Indian country. The Sioux are on the warpath to the north. The Cheyenne can hit us from the north, west, or south. Farther south are the Arapaho. We're surrounded by hostiles."

"Right away, sir." Moretti pulled both ends of his mustache to straighten them and saluted. He wheeled his horse back toward the column, shouting for his sergeant.

"Will." Dodge leaned forward in his saddle, looked across Rawlins and Buck, and pointed into the valley. "See that grove of trees on the far side of Clear Creek?"

Will lifted his slouch hat and shielded his eyes from the sun with it. "Yes, sir."

"Set up your remuda picket line over there."

"Yes, sir." Will slapped his mount's flank with his hat and headed down the slope with his string of horses.

Dodge called after him. "Tomorrow's the Fourth of July, Will. We're going to have a celebration!"

Chapter 16

General Dodge and his guests sat around the campfire next to Clear Creek and puffed pipes and cigars while Rawlins read poetry to them. The Laramie Mountains loomed above the encampment in the shadows following the setting of the sun. Twilight still illuminated the peaceful valley.

"Halloo the camp!" The call reverberated from the wooded hillside beyond the creek. Everyone around the fire turned toward the shouted greeting. A buckskin-clad figure rode down the slope. An unled packhorse trailed behind. The Pawnee Scouts on guard around the campsite made no attempt to stop the rider.

He rode with stooped shoulders, his face obscured by an oversize, broad-brimmed hat. His white beard would've made Moses proud. He wore a faded, buckskin shirt. Leather-clad legs grasped his horse over an Indian blanket saddle, his moccasins jammed into homemade wooden stirrups. He cradled a rifle in the crook of one arm.

The man's mount splashed across the shallow creek. The packhorse, laden with a pronghorn antelope carcass, followed along like a dog. The mountain man rode up the slope to the campfire, swung a leg over his blanket saddle, and slid to the ground on the right side—Indian style. He walked up the slope with a wiry step, belying the stoop.

"Evening Gen'ral." The mountain man's voice boomed.

"Bullfrog Charlie," Dodge said. "Long time, no see."

"By golly, has been that, I'll grant ya."

Will's mouth dropped open. Bullfrog Charlie Munro. Lone Eagle's father.

"Join us, Bullfrog." Dodge motioned to the log beside him. "Sit a spell and have some supper."

"Don't mind if I do. First, though, I reckon I'd like to trade this here antelope for a couple bottles of rye whiskey."

Dodge laughed. "I thought that might be what you had in mind." Dodge motioned one of the Army cooks to come forward. "Corporal, haul that antelope off that packhorse and dress it out for tomorrow's feast."

Bullfrog helped the corporal unload the antelope. Dodge walked to a supply wagon and returned with a bottle in each hand. "Here . . . two bottles of rye whiskey. I consider that a good trade. You remembered how partial I am to antelope steak. Come, sit. Have a bite and enjoy your rye."

Will listened with fascination to the tales with which Bullfrog entertained the dignitaries. "I joined up with Jim Bridger's Rocky Mountain Fur Company back in twenty-four. Old Gabe . . . that's the name what Jedediah Smith give him 'cause Bridger reminded him of the angel Gabriel . . . anyways, Old Gabe and me had set beaver traps out in a creek up in the Wind River Range and I was bending over the water's edge to check one of them traps when we was jumped by a band of Blackfoot. Now don't ya know, one of them savages shot me in the butt with an arrow and I went tumbling into the creek. Old Gabe said I come up sputtering and croaking like a giant bullfrog landing on a lily pad. Ever since, I been called Bullfrog."

Between stories Bullfrog devoured two plates of food and drank half a bottle of whiskey. Will thought an ordinary man would've passed out from that much liquor. With each drink Bullfrog's voice grew louder and his laugh more raucous.

The mountain man took another swallow of rye. He wiped

the sleeve of his dirty buckskin shirt across the mustache that concealed his mouth. His lips remained hidden when he talked. The mustache jiggled up and down as the words came out.

"I ever tell you fellows 'bout the time Ole Gabe and me rode through the petrified forest? Well sir, this here petrified forest was full of them petrified trees, and sitting on them petrified branches was dozens of petrified birds . . . singing petrified songs." Bullfrog howled. The listeners laughed with him.

After being regaled with tales for two hours, the men seated around the campfire drifted away to seek their bedrolls. Will waited until the last of the lingerers departed. Finally, he was alone with Bullfrog Charlie.

"Sir?"

Bullfrog looked around at the empty logs that had served as seats. "Sir? I reckon them gen'rals done gone to bed, son. Who you calling sir?"

"You, sir. Mr. Munro."

"How'd you know my last name? I don't recollect hearing nobody call me by my last name."

"I know who you are, sir. Lone Eagle told me."

"Lone Eagle, you say. Now just who might this Lone Eagle be?"

Will told him how he'd encountered Lone Eagle at the quicksand.

"Hmm." Bullfrog's gravelly voice caressed the sound deep in his throat. "So he's changed his name from Little Eagle to Lone Eagle. I heard tell he'd gone through the Sun Dance. His ma would be proud of him, even though he didn't take to white-man ways like she'd hoped. Can't say's I blame him. Don't like most white-man ways myself. Too confining, if you get my drift. At least Little Eagle . . . I mean Lone Eagle, will be a better Indian than some. I don't reckon he'll go murdering folks just for the fun of it, like that heathen Black Wolf."

Bullfrog tipped the bottle and sipped from it. "What's your name, son?"

"Will Braddock."

Will withdrew the thong from beneath his shirt and showed Bullfrog the eagle talons. "Lone Eagle gave me these. He told me they would bring me good luck."

Bullfrog reached out and ran his fingers over one of the talons. "He said they'd bring you good luck, did he? Well, I reckon he might think that. He used one to pick the lock at the boarding school the night he run away from there. He give them to you, did he?"

"Yes, sir. Said it was for saving his life."

"He tell you how he got them?"

Will shook his head.

"Well, when he was little, three . . . four years old as I recollect, there was an eagle nest atop a big tree back of our cabin on the North Platte. Junior . . . that's what I called him . . . was fascinated watching the adults raise a chick. One day a band of Shoshone come through and shot one of the adult birds. I reckoned they wanted the feathers for their warbonnets, don't ya see. Well, now, Junior decided to help raise that chick. He took scraps from our table and dropped them under the tree. The big bird gathered up that food and fed it to the young one. Star Dancer, his ma, was so proud of him, she give him the name Little Eagle. We didn't call him Junior no more. I found the carcass of the eagle the Shoshone had dumped and I made the necklace of talons for him."

Bullfrog reached again for the talons and held one up before Will's eyes. "See that marking along the edge? The tiny letters? I carved them real small like."

Will studied the talon, and although worn, the initials *LE* were visible in the firelight.

The old-timer sat quietly sipping his rye, staring into the

flames. Will decided it was time to leave the mountain man to his thoughts. "I guess it's time for me to turn in, Mr. Munro."

"Call me Bullfrog. I reckon we'll run into one another again afore long. Railroad's heading right through the country I trap. This country ain't been much good for trapping lately, truth be told. Beaver been all trapped out of this here Laramie Range for years."

Will rose from the log and slid the eagle talons back inside his shirt.

"You'll be passing my cabin one of these days. Place is on the North Platte, just this side of the Continental Divide. Drop in anytime."

"Thanks. I hope I can stay out here long enough to do that." Was he going to be able to go farther west to find his uncle? Would General Dodge keep him on as a wrangler now that they'd reached their destination? "You staying for the Fourth of July celebration tomorrow?"

"No, reckon I'll be gone afore sunup. Too big a crowd here for my likings. Besides, I got to go hunt up another antelope. Might be able to make another trade with Gen'ral Dodge afore he leaves." He tipped the bottle for another sip. "Good night, Will . . . and good luck."

"Good night, Bullfrog."

Chapter 17

General Rawlins rose from his camp stool and nodded in turn to those seated around the fire. Dodge leaned back in a folding chair with his feet extended toward the flames, even though it was a warm day. Silas Seymour sat on a log between General Jack Casement and Jacob Blickensderfer. Will stood off to one side with Lieutenant Moretti.

Rawlins motioned the soldiers scattered around the perimeter to step in closer. Those Pawnee Scouts who weren't assigned sentry duty around the outskirts of the camp lounged on the far bank of Clear Creek, showing no interest in the proceedings.

"General Dodge, General Casement, Mr. Blickensderfer, my fellow Americans. It is appropriate that we pause on this glorious day of our nation's independence and give thanks for the blessings that God has bestowed upon our country and its momentous endeavors." Rawlins pulled a handkerchief from his pocket and coughed into it, speckling it red.

"My superior, General Ulysses S. Grant, will, I assure you, be the next President of the United States, and he would want me to convey his personal greetings as we celebrate the Fourth of July." Rawlins paused to glare at Seymour. "Notwithstanding the fact that *Colonel* Seymour's cousin Horatio Seymour, presently the governor of New York, has been nominated by the Democratic Party to oppose General Grant, the Republican Party will prevail."

A smattering of applause came from some of the audience.

Rawlins coughed into his handkerchief again. "We are all aware that the transcontinental railroad will join the two oceans of our expanding country. No longer will a traveler have to spend four months sailing around Cape Horn, or stumbling through the mosquito infested swamps of Panama, to reach San Francisco. He will make the trip in a matter of days. The railroad will provide for increased commerce between the East and the West. It will bring civilization to the savages, who are trying to block its construction. This is the greatest engineering achievement undertaken by our nation since its founding ninety-one years ago."

More scattered applause came from the gathering.

Rawlins rambled on for an hour. Will found it difficult to concentrate. Mouth-watering aromas from the roasting beef and antelope drifted up from the creek side where the cooks prepared the special meal. More than one head snuck a look in that direction.

Rawlins paused and sniffed the air. "My, my. Smells like I need to end this speech so we can enjoy what promises to be a truly memorable meal."

All of the officials applauded. The soldiers burst into a round of hurrahs. One trooper strummed a banjo. Another sawed on a fiddle. The soldiers formed a line to partake of the food and joined the two musicians in singing the strains of a familiar tune.

Have you heard tell of sweet Betsy from Pike?
She crossed the wide prairie with her lover, Ike.
With two yoke of Oxen, a big yellow dog,
A tall Shanghai rooster and one spotted hog.

A short time later, Will filled his plate with a second helping of beef and antelope. He was ready to heap on more beans when a shout from the Pawnee sentries caused him to pause with the serving spoon poised above the iron pot. He, along with all the others, looked to the west. Down the far slope, into the meadow, raced four men on horseback. Their horses, blown and lathered, showed evidence of hard running.

At the commands of their sergeants, soldiers raced for their stacked rifles. The Pawnee Scouts along the creek bank ran up the slope, beyond the shelter of the surrounding trees. The officials rose and turned their attention to the approaching riders.

"Why that's Corcoran," Dodge said. He strode down the slope and waded across the shallow creek to meet the arriving horsemen.

Uncle Sean? Here? Will focused hard on the riders. Could it be? He hadn't seen his uncle since the war ended two years ago—but sure enough, he was the lead rider. Two white men and a black man rode close behind him.

Will dropped his plate to the ground, spilling its contents into the grass. He ran to catch up with Dodge, reaching his side just as the four horsemen reined up before them.

"Corcoran," Dodge said. "You look bad. What happened?"

"General Dodge, I'm glad to find you here. We were ambushed by Cheyenne about ten miles back. Lost all our supplies and surveying instruments. We managed to outrun them . . . but it was a close call. Closer than I've had before."

Corcoran dismounted and pointed to an arrow lodged in his saddle. A trickle of blood oozed down his horse's flank where the arrowhead had penetrated the leather saddle skirt.

"The supplies and equipment we can replace," Dodge said. "You and your men we can't. We've lost too many surveyors to the hostiles already. It's fortunate we're camped here in strength. That should dissuade them from further attacks."

Will's uncle cocked his head to one side and leaned forward. "Will? Is that you, Will?"

"Yes, Uncle Sean. It's me."

"What are you doing here?"

"Looking for you."

"Me?" He glanced quizzically at Dodge.

"He stowed away in Omaha," Dodge said. "If he hadn't saved General Rawlins's horse from rustling, twice as a matter of fact, I'd probably have ignored him. He kept insisting he had to find you, so I let him come along. He can fill you in on the details."

"What brings you out here, Will?"

"Ma died."

"Annabelle is dead?" His uncle stepped back and fixed his gaze on Will. "I didn't know."

"Will," Dodge said, "take your uncle to get some of that grub before the soldiers eat it all. He looks like he could use a good meal."

"That I can, General."

Will's uncle turned to his companions. "Homer, Otto, Joe. Take care of the horses, then get something to eat."

"Yes, suh," the Negro he'd called Homer responded. The other two riders touched their hat brims, acknowledging their instructions.

Homer kept looking back up the slope. He must be afraid the Indians were still chasing them.

A raucous hee-haw once again drew everybody's attention to the top of the slope. A gray mule trotted down the hill, braying at the top of its lungs, dragging the remnants of a pack beneath its belly.

"There's Ruby," Homer said. "I knowed she'd follow. She always does. Ain't no redskins gonna get her."

"Ruby's been Homer's mule all the time we've been out here," Will's uncle said. "She thinks she's part of the team."

Will and his uncle sat apart from the celebrating group. While his uncle ate, Will gave his uncle the details on his mother's death and explained why he'd snuck away from the Iowa homestead in the middle of the night.

"I don't want to be a blacksmith apprentice, Uncle Sean. I don't want to be under Klaus Nagel's guardianship. You're the only family I have left. I had to come looking for you." He felt moisture in his eyes. He blinked fast. He didn't want to cry in front of his uncle.

"I'm sorry about Annabelle's death, Will. But I'm not sure you can stay with me. This is no place for a boy."

"I'm not a boy, Uncle Sean."

His uncle stared at him—then nodded slowly. "Maybe . . . maybe not. You've grown since I last saw you. But that doesn't make you a man."

"I want to work on the railroad, Uncle Sean. I want to be a tracklayer, maybe even a gandy dancer."

Dodge walked over from the campfire and joined them. "Get enough to eat, Sean?"

"Yes, sir. That restored my energy. I'll need it. I have to get back to Casement's warehouse to pick up a new surveying instrument. Unless you brought an extra one with you?"

"Only brought one and I plan to use it to lay out Cheyenne, starting tomorrow."

"Cheyenne?"

"That's what I've named this meadow." Dodge indicated the surrounding area with a sweep of his hand. "This will be the UP's last staging yard before trains head up over the Continental Divide. Plan to build a roundhouse here, and maintenance shops."

His uncle looked around the valley and nodded. "Good choice, General."

"I can use your surveying expertise to help me lay out the town and railroad facilities. It's actually fortuitous you arrived. We'll find somebody else to go back to Julesburg."

"I'll go," Will said.

"You?" his uncle said.

"Sure. We just came from Julesburg. I know the trail. All I have to do is follow the survey stakes. I've been to Casement's warehouse. So I know where to go when I get there."

"Will," his uncle said, "that's not a good idea. There are Indians out here who'll do anything to stop our construction efforts. I learned that firsthand today."

"Uncle Sean, just yesterday I overhead General Dodge say that most of the hostile Indians are north, west, and south of us. Heading to the east won't be that dangerous. The grading crew is not much more than a day's ride back from here. Once I get there, I'll have lots of protectors." Will raised his eyebrows in Dodge's direction, seeking his confirmation.

Dodge shrugged. "Oh, the route to the east of here is generally safe. A detachment of soldiers from Fort Sedgwick rides the survey line every few days to make sure the stakes are still there. The Indians knock them down. But, it's not a good idea to go alone. If we had someone to ride with him, Sean, I'd agree."

Will faced his uncle. "Please, Uncle Sean. Let me help."

His uncle stared at him for a moment, then sighed. "I guess I can send Homer. He knows the other supplies we need to replace. Otto, Joe, and I can take our meals with your outfit, General . . . so I won't need Homer to cook."

Will beamed. Maybe he'd found a way to prove to his uncle and General Dodge that he could be of value to the railroad.

"Oh, I almost forgot." Dodge handed Will's uncle a package. "Judge Sampson sent this to you."

Chapter 18

Paddy rode the Army horse at a walk through the Cheyenne camp's outer circle of tepees. He led another horse bearing the whiskey he'd packed in straw in the pockets of two sets of saddlebags. Having departed Fort Sanders the day before, he'd crossed the Laramie Mountains, to reach this large village along Lodgepole Creek. Sergeant Lunsford had provided the horses in exchange for two bottles of the whiskey. Paddy was pleased with himself for managing to keep the coins Mort had given him for bribing the sergeant. He'd send the money to his mother.

Now he only had ten bottles of whiskey to give Chief Tall Bear, but that shouldn't be a problem. The Cheyenne chief wouldn't know Mort had sent Paddy out with a full case. He was fortunate none of the bottles had broken during that miserable stagecoach trip from Julesburg to Fort Sanders, and even more fortunate none had broken on his ride across Cheyenne Pass.

A dozen mangy dogs barked and snapped at his horses' legs, making them skittish. A crowd gathered to watch, but no Indian challenged him. What would he do if they closed in on him? What had his godfather gotten him into this time?

He recognized some of the young braves who'd been in the raiding party on the railroad—at least he thought he did. Hard to tell, most Indians looked alike.

Ah, there's one he definitely recognized. Black Wolf's distinctive, blackened lower face stood out among the others. He nodded to the warrior, but Black Wolf just stared back.

Paddy halted before the council tepee in the clearing in the center of the innermost ring. He spat his tobacco chaw onto the ground and raised a hand in a sign of peace. "Sure, and don't ye know I come seeking Chief Tall Bear."

From out of the council tepee stepped the tallest Indian Paddy could remember seeing. This fellow stood well over six feet. Gray hair, bare of ornamentation, hung over his shoulders in two long braids. His crossed arms clutched a faded, red trade blanket about his broad shoulders.

"Greetings from Mayor Kavanagh. He sends gifts." Paddy motioned to the packhorse. "Ye be Chief Tall Bear?"

Chief Tall Bear stared at Paddy along the length of his aquiline nose. Lone Eagle emerged from the tepee and joined his chief.

"O'Hannigan," Lone Eagle said. "I will translate for Chief Tall Bear. Why do you come here?"

"Ah, now, the half-breed Lone Eagle. And good it is to be seeing ye again. Perhaps ye can be explaining why it is the black Morgan turned up at the Julesburg depot after the raid?"

Lone Eagle ignored Paddy's question. "Chief Tall Bear asks what business the little, ugly Irishman has with the Cheyenne?"

Had Chief Tall Bear called him little and ugly, or was it just Lone Eagle saying that to aggravate him? Tall Bear probably couldn't tell one white man from another. How would he know Paddy was Irish? From his brogue maybe. But it was more likely Lone Eagle generated the insult himself.

"Well, do ye see, if I might join the chief in yonder tepee, I'll be explaining." Paddy shifted in his saddle to dismount.

"Talk from where you sit. Chief will not invite you into council tepee."

"Humph," Paddy snorted. He settled back onto his saddle.

"Mayor Kavanagh sends a gift of whiskey to Chief Tall Bear and asks the Cheyenne the favor of attacking the railroad."

Lone Eagle interpreted for the chief, then turned back to Paddy. "Chief Tall Bear wants to know why the Cheyenne would want to attack the railroad?"

"Sure, and the railroad be crossing the buffalo paths. Or haven't ye noticed? It destroys the Cheyenne's hunting grounds. Mayor Kavanagh knows the Cheyenne don't want the iron horse to frighten the buffalo away."

"Why does Kavanagh care?" Lone Eagle didn't address Paddy's boss as mayor. The Cheyenne probably wouldn't accept Kavanagh's appointing himself mayor, anyway.

"Well, now, the mayor wants to open trade with the great Cheyenne nation. He cannot do that if the railroad destroys the way of life of the Cheyenne. Don't ye see?"

Lone Eagle translated. Tall Bear snorted and spoke through Lone Eagle again. "Chief says he does not believe that is Kavanagh's real reason. But the Cheyenne will attack the railroad if Kavanagh gives us ammunition."

"Ammunition? Mayor Kavanagh sent whiskey as his gift. But ye ask for ammunition?" Giving ammunition to the Indians would anger the Army. Kavanagh might not agree to it.

"Yes," Lone Eagle said. "Soldiers and Pawnee Scouts protect the railroad. We must shoot many bullets to fight them. Then no bullets will be left for hunting."

Paddy sighed. "Sure, and I'll be asking Mayor Kavanagh to send ammunition." If Mort was serious about using an Indian attack to slow down construction of the railroad, he'd probably accept their terms.

Lone Eagle spoke with his chief, who hesitated for a moment before giving his answer. "Tell Kavanagh," Lone Eagle said, "Cheyenne will attack the railroad soon. Chief Tall Bear accepts the whiskey now. Kavanagh can send ammunition later."

Paddy nodded and shifted in his saddle.

"Do not get off your horse," Lone Eagle said.

"But I need to unload the packhorse." Paddy stopped, one leg raised out of his stirrup.

"We will keep the packhorse, too."

Paddy settled back onto his saddle. "Well now, the horse belongs to the Army at Fort Sanders. Sure, and ye can see it has an Army brand."

"We have other horses with that brand." Lone Eagle beckoned to a boy who took the packhorse's halter rope.

Paddy blew out his breath. When he returned to Fort Sanders without the packhorse he'd have to pay that drunken Sergeant Lunsford for a replacement. There went the money he'd planned to send to his mother.

The Indians drifted away from the circle. Paddy sat his horse staring at Lone Eagle. There was something different about that thong around the half-breed's neck. He was sure he'd counted eight eagle talons the day of the train raid—not six.

"Well, now, Lone Eagle," Paddy said. "Is it ye're gonna be telling me why the Morgan horse was not hidden where I be asking ye to put him?"

"Who says he was not there? Who says someone did not find the horse before you?"

Paddy frowned. "Humph. Sure, and ye're lying."

Lone Eagle's eyes narrowed. "You leave now, Irishman."

Bloody half-breed, Paddy swore under his breath. He turned his horse, rode out of the camp, splashed across Lodgepole Creek, and headed toward Cheyenne Pass and Fort Sanders. He waited until he was well clear of the village before pulling his Bowie knife from his boot. He sliced a bit off his twist and stuck the tobacco in his mouth. Bloody Cheyenne hadn't extended him the hospitality of a meal, or lodging for the night. He'd have to eat hardtack and jerky and sleep on the ground again. He wished he'd kept a bottle of that whiskey for himself.

Chapter 19

Will tugged the packsaddle's cinch rope tight around Ruby's belly. Ruby hee-hawed her objection and kicked out with her hind legs. Over the mule's back Will saw General Dodge, General Jack, and his uncle step across Clear Creek and head up the slope to the picket line where he and Homer prepared for their ride to Julesburg. Will turned away from Ruby, gathered up a saddle, and threw it onto the back of his horse. Ruby let loose with a cackling bray.

The approaching men roared with laughter. When Will turned, the reason for their mirth was obvious. Ruby's pack load dangled upside down beneath her belly.

"Got a thing or two to learn about packing mules, eh, Will?" Dodge called out.

Will felt his face flush. This wasn't the way to prove to General Dodge he was capable of working for the Union Pacific.

"There's a trick to tying a pack load." Homer spoke in a low voice that only Will could hear. "I'll show you how."

Homer raised his voice and greeted the approaching men. "Morning gents."

"Morning, Homer," Will's uncle answered. "Ready to ride?"

"We's jest about ready. Soon's we straighten up the pack on this contrary mule."

Homer resettled the packsaddle atop Ruby's back, then hauled off and slugged the mule in the gut with his fist. She bellowed and exhaled from the force of the blow. Homer jerked the cinch tight. "Got's to get a mule's attention first," he whispered.

Homer adjusted the load, then wrapped a rope back and forth across the bundle and tied it with a knot. "We secures the whole thing with a diamond hitch and she's good to go."

"Thank you, Homer," Will said.

The black man smiled at him. "Sure thing."

The three men reached the picket line. "Follow the survey stakes and you can't get lost," Dodge said, "but keep a sharp lookout. Once you reach the grading crews on Lodgepole Creek you'll be safe."

"Yes, sir," Will said.

"A wagon train of Mormon workers from Salt Lake City arrived last night looking for work on the railroad," Dodge continued. "They reported being shadowed by a band of Indians. I expect we'll have trouble before long."

"You have weapons?" his uncle asked.

"Spencer carbines and Colt revolvers," Will answered. "Luey gave us lots of ammunition."

"Good. Let's hope you don't have to use any of it."

General Jack pointed his riding whip at Will. "Find my brother Dan and tell him to give you the best transit from the warehouse."

"Transit?"

"That's the technical name for a surveyor's instrument," Will's uncle said.

"Oh."

His uncle dropped some coins into Will's hand. "Here's money to buy me some cigars. Go to Abrams General Store. Benjamin Abrams is a tightfisted Jew, but he won't cheat you. Buy the best he has. I don't smoke them often, but when I do I like a good one."

"Yes, sir."

"If there's any change left, buy yourself some candy."

"Thanks, Uncle Sean."

Homer and Will mounted. His uncle handed Ruby's halter rope to him. "You know the way since you've just come in from Julesburg. But listen to Homer. He's been in plenty of tough spots and he's been riding these hills with me for the past two years. He can spot danger a long ways off."

"Yes, Uncle Sean."

"We'll discuss your future when you return."

Will had to do this job right. He needed to impress General Dodge, but more importantly he had to show his uncle he could be trusted. If he messed up now—what would happen?

"Off you go, then," Dodge said. He slapped Will's horse on the rump.

Homer and Will rode away from the picket line. Buck, tied to the line nearby, whinnied and tossed his head. "No, Buck," Will said. "You can't come."

"And Will," Dodge called out. "Stop by the depot on your way back and pick up any mail that's accumulated."

Will looked back at Dodge. "Yes, sir."

"And remember. Any Indians you encounter are probably not Pawnee."

Chapter 20

Their horses and the mule didn't have to exert themselves following the gentle two percent gradient marked by the survey stakes leading up and away from the Cheyenne meadows. Will believed they'd have an easy ride and not being encumbered with wagons, should reach Julesburg in three days—half the time it'd taken Dodge's party on the outbound journey. It was early July, two weeks past the summer solstice. Plenty of sunshine would allow for twelve-hour days in the saddle.

They'd ridden in silence for a couple of hours before Homer finally spoke. "How's come you out here all by yourself looking for your uncle?"

Will was glad his companion had broken the silence. He hadn't known how to start a conversation with the older black man.

Will told Homer about the recent death of his mother, as well as the death of his father during the war. "I know Pa went to war because he believed in preserving the Union, and in freeing the slaves of course . . . but, I think if he hadn't been killed, Mama would still be alive."

"I 'spect your right. The war caused a heap of misery for a lot of folks."

Will explained to Homer how he'd made his decision to search for his uncle and try to convince him not to sign the papers making him a blacksmith apprentice. "I don't want to be a slave to some barn."

"Yep," Homer said. "That'd be a kind of slavery, I 'spect. But at least a body can see the end to an apprenticeship, and then a man's got a trade."

"Maybe so . . . but that's not the trade I want."

Will described his experiences after arriving in Omaha, his encounter with Lone Eagle, and helping the McNabbs.

"Hold up, Homer." Will pointed to a rabbit that hopped out from under the cover of a bush. He raised the Spencer carbine, jacked the trigger guard lever down and back up, driving a cartridge into the chamber. He cocked the hammer, aimed, held his breath, and pulled the trigger. The carbine roared. The rabbit flopped dead.

Homer dismounted and retrieved the carcass, holding the rabbit up by its hind legs. "That's some shooting. Clean through the head. You that good all the time?"

Will smiled. "Usually. My Pa taught me how to shoot."

"This'll be supper. Better'n hardtack and jerky." He tied the rabbit to Ruby's pack.

Toward sunset they dropped down off the high ground and intersected Lodgepole Creek. The old trail along the stream had served the Indians for hundreds of years as a thoroughfare between the Rocky Mountains and the great Platte River bottom lands to the east. General Dodge had told the dignitaries during campfire discussions one night that in the Laramie Mountains west of the new town of Cheyenne, near the creek's source, the hillsides were covered with the tall, slender Lodgepole pines the Indians prized for supporting their tepees. But here on the plains, trees were sparse, growing mainly along the water courses.

"I 'spect we's come far enough today," Homer said. "I don't like being on the trail in the dark. General Dodge thought the graders would be this far up the creek by now. Something's held them back."

Will scanned the valley. "Do you think it could be Indians?"

"Maybe." Homer dismounted and pointed up the slope. "We'll camp up away from the creek a bit. Won't make it so easy for anyone to find us in the dark. Let's refill our canteens and let the animals drink."

"Right." Will dismounted. He hadn't thought of the precaution of camping away from the trail.

They found a sheltered copse of stunted trees a few yards from the creek, and staked out the animals with picket pins and enough rope for them each to graze in a small circle.

While Homer skinned the rabbit, Will gathered twigs and kindling to make a fire. Will withdrew a tin of lucifer matches from the supply pack.

"No lucifers," Homer said. "We'll save them. No wind tonight. Easy to make a fire with flint and steel."

"Right." Will didn't have a flint. He'd have to find one.

Will stacked the kindling into a small pyramid and Homer whittled a twig into fine shavings next to it. Then Homer struck a flint chip sharply against the back of his knife blade and dropped a shower of sparks into the shavings. He sheltered the shavings between his hands and blew. They smoldered briefly before bursting into flame. He shoved the burning bundle beneath the kindling with his knife.

Homer tossed one twig aside. "Too green. Smokes too much. Give our position away. We'll keep the fire small. Jest enough to cook this rabbit and boil a little coffee."

Homer pounded a handful of beans into grounds with the butt of his pistol and tossed them into a battered coffeepot, which he set in the embers. They ate the rabbit with their fingers directly from the frying pan, then Homer walked several yards away before tossing the carcass into the brush. "Don't want them leavings to attract no wild critters into our camp," he said.

Homer grasped the coffeepot's handle with his bandanna and

poured the thick mixture into a tin cup. He stirred in two spoons of sugar and leaned back against his saddle. "I likes it sweet. Learned to drink it that way down in Louisiana." He pronounced it *"Luzyana."*

"Louisiana?"

"Yep. That's where I growed up."

Will screwed up the courage to pose a question he'd been pondering all day. "How'd you come to be out here with my uncle?"

"Well now, that's some story." Homer blew into his cup to cool the coffee. "Let me recollect. I'se born in Georgia."

Will studied Homer's face. There'd been only a few Negros in Burlington and Will had no experience against which to judge Homer's age. The salt and pepper in his thin beard and close-cropped hair gave the impression of an older man. Closer scrutiny revealed numerous wrinkles around his eyes.

"How'd you get from Georgia to Louisiana?"

"After I'se born, the plantation owner decided as how he didn't need no woman with a baby. All he wanted was a working man. He kept my pappy and sold my mammy and me to a plantation outside Shreveport. She was a good cook, so she worked as a kitchen slave. I growed up running 'round with the owner's youngsters. That's how I learned to read. Not much, mind you, jest enough so's I can read my Bible." Homer sipped his coffee.

Will wanted to learn more. "Why'd you leave Louisiana?"

"Well now." Homer turned his cup upside down, dumped out the black dregs, and refilled the cup from the pot. "When I'se old enough, they took me away from the big house and set me to working in the fields. I 'spect I'se twelve, maybe thirteen. About your age."

"I'm fourteen."

"I see." Will saw the grin that creased the edges of Homer's lips. "Yes suh, I'se younger than that. After my mammy took sick and died, I kind of lost track of time. I 'spect it was ten years later when I met Mavis. She said her name meant joy. And she was sure a joy to me . . . while I had her."

Homer paused and stared over his cup into the fire.

"Mavis was brought in from another plantation to be a house slave. I'se right smitten. She took to me, too. Weren't no time till Mavis and me was married. Not like white folks, in a church and such. We jest said the vows and jumped the broom."

Homer sighed and sipped from his cup. "But Mavis is gone now. When the war started and things went bad for the South, most plantations couldn't afford to keep all their slaves. Old man Lafontaine, he was the plantation owner, sold her. Damn his soul! Excuse my cussing."

"I say dang myself . . . every once in a while. Mama didn't approve, but sometimes I can't help it. It just comes out."

"I knows what you mean."

"What happened to Mavis?"

"Don't rightly know. Heard tell she was sent to Alabama."

"That's not right."

"Not right?" Homer sat up. "Nothing's right about slavery, Will. Nothing!"

"But you're not a slave now . . . are you?"

"No. Thanks to Mr. Lincoln. He made it official with that Emancipation Proclamation. But I made it happen sooner."

"How'd you do that?"

"I run away. Hightailed it out of Louisiana. It was too dangerous to go to Alabama to look for Mavis. The Rebs delighted in capturing runaway slaves and returning them to their owners. I'd a been captured for sure, and like as not beaten to death. So I followed the underground railroad north. Weren't no real railroad like the UP. They jest called it that."

"Where'd you go?"

"New York City. That's where I met your uncle."

Homer pulled down the collar of his jacket. An ugly white scar encircled his thick black neck. "Ain't pretty, is it?"

Will shook his head.

"Right after the Battle of Gettysburg, I'se working on the docks in New York. President Lincoln wanted to draft more troops to fight the war. But them New York Irish refused . . . said they wouldn't fight to free no Negras. The Irish felt the free Negras were taking jobs away from them, and if they fought to free the rest of us, there wouldn't be no jobs left for them."

Homer pulled his collar back up.

"Now I can understand the Irish, or others for that matter, feeling what you call persecution. But they forget, when they run away from their old country and come here, they was given a fighting chance to be somebody . . . to be free. Now we already had freedom where we come from . . . but when we was brought here, we wasn't given no chance at all."

Homer laid his head back against his saddle.

"It got so bad in New York in sixty-three, the Irish rioted and burned the draft offices. Then they started lynching Negra men. Major Corcoran had come to New York to buy railroad equipment to ship south where the Yanks was rebuilding the lines tore up by the Rebs. I was a stevedore, helping load locomotives onto a ship for your uncle, when a mob of Irish thugs stormed the docks yelling 'hang the nigger.' They strung me up to a lamppost. That's when your uncle lit into them with his sword."

"What'd you do?"

"Nothing, 'cept hang onto that rope . . . and pray. They hung me up so fast they forgot to tie my hands. I'se able to reach up and grab the rope, but my hands was so sweaty they kept slipping. That noose got tighter and tighter. But I kept my eyes on the major. Somehow I jest knowed he was my salvation."

"What'd Uncle Sean do?"

"He slashed at them till they backed off. 'Cept for one bully named O'Hannigan."

Will sat up.

"O'Hannigan was the gang leader . . . louder than the rest, shouting orders. He come up behind your uncle brandishing an ax handle. Somehows, I managed to called out a warning. The major whirled round and slashed at O'Hannigan's arm. Blood spewed everywhere, but that Irishman jest shifted the ax handle to his other hand. When he raised the handle again, the major lunged at him with his sword. Right then a boy ducked in between the two of them, crying 'Pa.' The blade sliced across that boy's face before plunging into the Irishman's chest. That boy knelt beside his pa's body, glaring pure hatred at the major, with blood oozing from that slash across his cheek. I heard him swear to kill the major if it was the last thing he did. Then I lost my grip, and the rope strangled me real good. Next thing I knowed I was coming to on the dock. Your uncle had cut me down with his saber."

"I know who the boy is," Will whispered. "Paddy O'Hannigan."

Chapter 21

Will's eyes popped open. He tried to speak, but Homer's hand clamped his mouth closed.

"Sh," Homer whispered. He removed his hand, touched a finger to his lips, and pointed downslope.

In the early morning light, five Indians rode single-file along the path beside the creek. They kicked each survey stake they passed, grunting satisfaction when they succeeded in toppling one over.

Black paint obscured the lower half of the lead rider's face. Will had seen him someplace before. Of course—the train raid. Cheyenne! He scrutinized the other warriors. Lone Eagle wasn't one of them. For some reason he breathed a sigh of relief.

He lay alongside Homer, peering through the bushes. His heart thumped so loudly he at first thought the Indians might hear its drumming. Don't be foolish, he told himself. Just stay calm.

The two of them remained motionless for what seemed like an eternity before the Indians disappeared up the trail.

Will studied Homer's face. Deep lines creased the older man's forehead, his bushy gray eyebrows scrunched above squinting eyes.

"They're the same Cheyenne who raided General Dodge's train," Will whispered.

The black man nodded, ran a hand through his hair, and

settled his hat on his head. "Come on." His voice low and raspy.

Homer rolled up his blanket and strapped it to the cantle of the saddle he'd used for a pillow. He motioned for Will to do the same, then grabbing his saddle in one hand and his carbine in the other, he shuffled up the slope in a crouch toward the horses.

Will followed, saddled his horse, strapped on his gear, then turned to Ruby. He lifted the pack over the mule's back and lowered it slowly. He tightened the cinch as hard as he could without punching the mule in the stomach, hoping he wouldn't cause her to bray.

Homer slipped back to their dead campfire, retrieved the coffeepot and frying pan, and added them to the pack. He stroked the mule's neck. "Ruby, you behave now."

She snuffled softly.

"So far, so good." Homer climbed into his saddle. "Them Injuns is far enough away now. Let's get going."

Will gathered up the mule's halter rope and stuck his boot into his stirrup. In his hurry to mount he jabbed the toe of his boot into his horse's belly. The startled horse kicked out with its hind hooves, striking Ruby in her chest.

"Hee-haw!" Ruby brayed in protest at being kicked. She bucked up to get away, yanking the halter rope out of Will's hand.

"Aiyee, aiyee, aiyee!" The Indians had heard the raucous commotion.

He reached for Ruby's halter rope, but she backed away and brayed louder.

"Leave the mule!" Homer shouted. Will could clearly see the fear in the whites of his companion's eyes. "She can save herself!"

"Aiyee, aiyee, aiyee!" The cries drew closer.

Will heaved himself into the saddle and pounded his heels

into the horse's flanks. His mount lunged down the slope following Homer, who lashed his steed with his reins.

He looked back. The first Indian rounded a bend in the trail, whooping and motioning to those behind.

"Ride!" Homer shouted. "Gotta get to that grading crew!"

"Yeah! Can't be far!"

A rifle fired behind him. The bullet zipped past his ear. Whew, that was close!

He kicked his horse repeatedly. "Go! Go!"

Another shot rang out. The bullet ricocheted beneath Homer's horse, spattering rock and gravel.

Will twisted around in his saddle and tried to steady the weight of the carbine's barrel over his raised left arm. The jouncing on the horse made aiming impossible, so he just pulled the trigger. The carbine roared. Flame and smoke spat from the barrel.

The Indians kept coming. He hadn't hit anybody. Hadn't even slowed them down.

He levered another cartridge into the breech, but before he could pull the trigger, a third shot erupted from the Indians.

Will's horse screamed.

That bullet had hit its mark. His horse stumbled. Its legs buckled. The horse collapsed under him.

"Homer!" Will sailed over the dying horse's neck and slammed into the ground. The carbine jammed against his chest. He heard a sharp crack.

The fall knocked the wind from him. Dazed, he gasped for air. He fought to clear his mind. He forced himself to take a deep breath. His ribs ached. Had he broken one? He had to get up—now!

"Get behind your horse, Will!" Homer shouted as he wheeled his mount around and raced back. He reined in beside a large cottonwood, swung a leg over his saddle, and slid to the ground behind the tree.

Homer slapped the horse's rump. "Hyah!" The horse raced off down the trail in the direction of Julesburg and the track graders.

Will scrambled up behind his horse's body, dragging the carbine with him. A bullet thumped into the flesh of the dead animal. Another smacked into the leather of his saddle.

He lifted the carbine. Oh no—the crack he'd heard hadn't been his ribs. The carbine's stock dangled below the metal barrel of the weapon. He tossed the broken gun aside and drew his revolver. He steadied the handgun on the saddle, cocked the hammer twice, aimed, and fired.

The shot fell short. The Indians pulled up fifty yards away and dismounted. The warrior with the partially blackened face stepped forward. Will fired again and once more the shot landed short. The warrior, having tested the range of the pistol, stepped back and motioned for his companions to spread out. Will intended to keep the attackers at that distance.

The narrow valley at this point gave the Cheyenne little maneuver room. Will and Homer were in a secure position. Two of the Indians had muskets, muzzle loaders that would be slow to load. The others were armed with bows and arrows.

Will and Homer held a firepower advantage with their remaining seven-shot carbine and two six-shot revolvers. Hopefully, the Indians would think twice about rushing them.

But the arrows—the arrows posed a special danger. A bullet traveled in a straight line—an arrow could be lobbed overhead.

Will fired the last shot from his revolver. It would take several minutes to load. He wasn't practiced at it. "Homer! Keep firing. Gotta reload."

He hunkered down behind the horse and drew the revolver's hammer back to half cock, allowing the cylinder to spin freely. He shoved a paper cartridge containing both black powder and a lead bullet into the front of one of the chambers and tamped it down with the ramrod lever affixed beneath the barrel. He repeated this process five more times. Even then, the gun wasn't ready to fire.

While he struggled to reload, he glanced at Homer, who without exposing himself or taking aim, stuck the carbine around the tree and blasted away. Homer couldn't hit anything that way!

Fishing a pea-sized percussion cap out of the smaller pouch on his belt, he snapped it onto the nipple at the rear of one of the chambers. He sneaked a look over the saddle to check on the Indians while reaching into the pouch with his fingers for another cap.

Dang it! He dropped that one. No time to look for it—just dig out another one. Finally, he completed the loading of all six cylinders.

He clicked the hammer to full cock, raised up, and balanced the gun on the saddle. He aimed at the visible feathers of one of the Indians and pulled the trigger. When the hammer struck the rear of the cylinder it ignited the fulminate of mercury in the percussion cap, driving sparks into the chamber. In a split second those sparks ignited the paper cartridge's black powder, generating the explosion that drove the bullet down the barrel on its lethal spiral toward its target.

But he didn't hit the target. The Indians remained out of range of the revolver.

"Homer, let me have the carbine!"

"Here." Homer tossed the long arm to Will and drew his pistol. "Yore a better shot than me, for sure."

Will unlashed a quick-loading cartridge box from behind his saddle. The leather container held ten tubes, each loaded with seven metallic, rim-fire cartridges. He ejected the empty magazine tube from the butt of Homer's carbine, poured the new cartridges from the quick-loading tube into the magazine tube, then slid it back into the carbine's butt. That quickly he'd reloaded seven shots. Percussion caps weren't necessary.

Faster to load than a pistol, the Spencer was accurate up to two hundred yards. He'd proven to himself that a man couldn't hit a target beyond fifty yards with a revolver.

Will eased the carbine over the saddle, cocked the hammer, sighted down the barrel, and waited. One of the Indians armed with a musket moved in a crouch through the brush, away from his companions, and headed up the slope. He was trying to get above them. He aimed at the Indian's knees. Lieutenant Moretti had cautioned him that the Spencer fired high.

He led the Indian as if he were hunting a running deer. He tightened the tension on the trigger and waited until the Indian stepped into a clearing. He drew in his breath, held it, and squeezed the trigger. The carbine boomed. The Indian reared up, dropped his musket, and rolled back down the slope.

Will stared at the fallen body. The Indian didn't move. Will had killed a man for the first time. Was it murder to kill an Indian who was intent on killing him? He didn't have time to think about that. He levered another round into the chamber.

The firing slowed from both sides. The lack of a breeze held the acrid smoke from the black powder suspended in the air, stinging his lungs.

Will knew the Cheyenne with the second musket, the blackened-faced leader, would be waiting for him to look over the saddle, so he scooted toward the head of his horse and peered around the dead animal's muzzle. An Indian raised his bow and launched an arrow. Will followed the arrow's arc as it descended onto the spot where he'd been lying a moment before.

The Indians would know the greater danger came from Will's carbine, and would concentrate their fire on him. Will shuffled backward along his horse's body and peered over the saddle. The other Indians with bows rose and launched arrows at the same time. Three arrows arced toward him. He pushed himself tighter against the horse's body.

One arrow, then a second, thudded into the ground beside him. A sharp blow thumped against his breast bone. A burning sensation raced across his chest. An excruciating pain exploded in his left arm.

"Agh!" Will shouted.

That third arrow had cut a path across his chest muscles and driven into his upper arm. "Wow!" He'd never felt such pain.

"Whew!" He spat his breath out. He tasted bile. He choked down vomit. He gritted his teeth and clenched his eyes. The pain didn't go away.

"Oh!" He moaned.

"Will? You hit?"

"Yeah . . . arrow."

"Hang on, I'm coming."

"No! Stay there."

Will dragged himself up and balanced the carbine over the saddle with his good arm. He held his injured arm close to his side and took aim at an Indian who exposed himself when he drew back on his bow. Will fired. The Indian collapsed.

He raised his elbow to get a better look at his wound. The movement hurt! The feathered end of the arrow quivered before his eyes, the arrowhead protruded three inches beneath his arm. Blood dripped from the point. The arrow hadn't broken the bone—it'd passed cleanly through the bicep muscle. He didn't see spurting blood—it hadn't pierced an artery. Still, blood soaked his shirt sleeve. His arm felt wet and sticky. He blinked his eyes—needed to focus. He was losing blood.

The roaring sound in his ears grew louder. He shook his head—tried to think. That roaring noise—it was the pounding of hooves. Through bleary eyes he saw a group of mounted men race up the trail toward him. They fired over his head at the Indians.

Will hauled himself up to look over the saddle. The blackened-faced leader and the other warriors gathered up their two dead companions, mounted their ponies, and beat a retreat.

Will's head dropped.

CHAPTER 22

Jenny McNabb's kiss felt wet, yet cool, on his lips. Will opened one eye. Homer held a canteen to his mouth.

Then the pain hit. "Oh!" He groaned. His arm throbbed. He tried to sit up, but his head spun and he promptly dropped back.

"Easy," Homer said.

Will looked at his left arm. The sleeves of his shirt and undershirt had been cut off. A blood-soaked bandage bound his upper arm. The front of his shirts looked like they'd been ripped open with a razor. Through the gap in the material, a streak of dried blood outlined the path the arrow had followed on its way across his chest to his arm.

"You done fine, Will. You kept them pesky redskins at bay till the graders got here. Without your shooting, we'd be goners for sure." Homer helped him to sit up.

"I never thought an arrow packed that much of a wallop." Will touched the bandage.

Homer held the arrow shaft up and pointed to the feathers and the encircling painted rings. "You were right, Will. Cheyenne."

"We're seeing them more often." One of the track graders who'd come to their rescue spoke from a few feet away. "They're joining up with the Sioux to try to stop the railroad. This bunch that attacked you were probably the same ones that made a pass at our camp yesterday, until they realized we had a lot more men than they did."

"Sorry I passed out, Homer."

"Good thing you did. I'se able to cut that arrowhead off and pull the shaft out of your arm without you knowing." Homer handed Will the arrowhead.

Will turned it over in his fingers. Now he had a piece of flint.

Reaching into the front of his shirt, he pulled up the horsehair thong that hung around his neck. He fitted the arrowhead into a nick along the side of one of the talons. The talon had deflected the arrow from slicing into his chest. In the center of his chest a pinprick of dried blood and an ugly bruise revealed where the arrow had jammed the tip of the talon into his skin. Lone Eagle had been right. The talon had brought him good luck.

"I'm Grady Shaughnessy, foreman of this gang." The track grader who'd described the increasing incidents with the Indians introduced himself. "We heard the firing. We could tell it was a Spencer, and when the horse came racing into our camp we knew from the saddle and tack it had to be railroad men in trouble. We came as fast as we could."

"Sure glad you did," Will said.

"Homer tells me you're Sean Corcoran's nephew."

"Yes, sir."

"Your uncle's a first-rate surveyor. He plots a grade that's good to follow."

Will smiled at the compliment to his uncle. It'd be nice if some day he were considered worthy of such praise.

"We best be getting back to camp," Shaughnessy said. "It's about a mile down the trail. That band of savages may round up more braves and come back."

"I don't relish waiting around here no more," Homer said. "We've got to get Will to the railroad doctor in Julesburg."

Homer helped Will stand. Will swayed and leaned against

Homer until his dizziness passed. "I'll be fine. I'm ready to get out of here, too."

"Get the saddle and tack off that dead horse, boys," Shaughnessy said. "Don't want General Jack fussing at me for leaving railroad property behind. You climb up behind me, Will. Homer, you ride behind Caleb there." He pointed to a skinny young man. "The two of you won't make too much of a load for Caleb's horse. What about that mule of yours?"

"Ruby'll catch up," Homer said. "She always does."

Chapter 23

The McNabbs' wagon sat last in line in their column. Once underway they'd eat all the other wagons' dust, but only for a day. Every morning the lead wagons rotated to the rear.

They'd rejoined Dryden Faulkner's wagon train outside Julesburg ten days ago. Finally, the Army had announced it was safe to travel once more. Earlier this morning the wagon master had reformed his charges from their protective circle into a traveling arrangement, four columns abreast. He'd instructed the wagon owners to be ready to head out at first light tomorrow.

The McNabbs finished their typical noon meal of bacon, beans, and biscuits. Jenny's mother rocked slowly in her wicker chair. She'd eaten little from the plate cradled in her lap.

"Mama," Jenny said, "you must eat."

"I have no appetite."

"Mary," her father said. "I wish we could stay here a few days more, but Faulkner says it's time to press on. They've already been here too long."

"It's all right, Alistair." Her mother reached a slender hand out to her husband, who sat on a crate beside her, and laid it on his shoulder. "I can travel."

A tall, young man approached and doffed his hat, revealing fiery red hair. "Afternoon, Colonel," he said. "Afternoon, Mrs. McNabb. Excuse me for interrupting your meal."

"Percival Robillard," her mother said. "It is nice to see you.

And how is the South's finest cavalry lieutenant?"

"Former cavalry lieutenant, ma'am." Robillard had been assigned to the regiment Jenny's father commanded during the war. "I am fine today, thank you."

"That's good."

The young man turned to Elspeth. "Afternoon, Miss Elspeth." A broad smile creased his clean-shaven face. The freckles on his face accentuated his red locks.

"Good afternoon, Percy." Elspeth busied herself picking up dishes, something she normally refused to do. Jenny knew she was pretending not to appear interested in Percy.

"Miss Elspeth," Percy continued. "I came to invite you to the dance this evening. That's why I was so bold as to interrupt your meal. I wanted to ask you . . . before anybody else could."

"A dance?" Elspeth exclaimed. "Why, where on earth out here is there ever going to be a dance?"

"At the head of the wagon train. Mr. Faulkner agreed we can have a dance to celebrate getting underway again."

"This doesn't seem an appropriate time for dancing," Jenny's father said. "Everybody needs to rest before we hit the trail."

"But, Papa," Elspeth protested. "How can a little dancing hurt anything?"

"Alistair," Jenny's mother said. "If the other families are consenting to the dance, why should we object? I don't think our girls will miss that much rest going to a dance."

"Our *girls* aren't going to the dance," Jenny said. "Only *one* McNabb girl has been invited to the dance."

Elspeth stuck her tongue out at Jenny and shoved her stack of dishes into Jenny's hands. With her back toward Percy, he couldn't see Elspeth's gesture.

"Why, I didn't mean to exclude you, Miss Jenny," Percy said. "You come too."

Jenny stuck her tongue out at Elspeth. "So there." She

mouthed the words silently.

"Say it's okay, Papa," Elspeth pleaded.

"All right. I'm overruled by your mother. But not too late, mind you. We have to be ready to travel at an early hour."

"Oh, thank you, Papa." Elspeth ran to her father and hugged him.

"Elspeth, we need to get these dishes cleaned up," Jenny said.

"We? I've got to get ready for the dance. You clean them up."

"I'm going to the dance too. Percy invited me."

"Ladies," their father said. "Both of you clean up the dishes or neither of you goes to the dance."

"Oh, Papa." Elspeth pouted, but took the stack of dishes from Jenny's extended hands.

"I have to fetch that wheel from Julesburg," Jenny's father said. "The wheelwright promised to have it repaired today."

"Papa," Jenny said, "if you'll wait a few minutes, I'll go with you. We'll be finished with these dishes in no time. We need flour and salt, and I want to see what other provisions I can find at Abrams General Store."

"All right. I have to borrow a horse from Faulkner to tote that wheel back from town. Be ready when I get back."

Chapter 24

Will rode a horse Grady Shaughnessy had loaned him. Homer had reclaimed his horse at the graders' camp and Ruby had returned on her own. Will chewed on willow bark, hoping to ward off inflammation. He held his arm close against his side, his fingers tucked into his shirtfront. The arm throbbed with each jolting step of his horse. How much damage had been done to his arm? How was the injury going to affect his chances of landing a job with the railroad?

They topped a small rise and Hell on Wheels came into view in the distance. Even with the delay caused by the Indian attack, only three days had passed since he and Homer had departed Cheyenne. The Casements' tracklaying crew had made the turn up Lodgepole Creek and were leaving Julesburg behind.

When Will and Homer came abreast of the pusher locomotives at the rear of the work train, Ruby spread her forelegs, braced herself, and jerked Homer backward in his saddle with the halter rope which he'd wrapped around his wrist. She brayed her loudest protest and refused further progress. "Dang it, mule! What's the matter with you? It's just a steam engine."

The railroad horses were used to being around locomotives. But Ruby, a mule from the mountains, didn't want anything to do with the snorting, belching iron horses.

Will laughed and wished he hadn't. He groaned and grasped his elbow to steady his arm.

An hour later, the railroad doctor had cleaned and rebandaged Will's wound. He placed the arm in a sling. When Will asked about permanent damage to his muscle, the doctor shrugged and told him it was too soon to know. The doctor said that if Homer hadn't pulled the arrow out right away, the damage would certainly have been worse.

Will and Homer rode on to the knockdown warehouse, where they found Dan Casement. Dan was even shorter than his brother Jack. Will had earlier overheard some of the workers describe Dan as standing "five feet nothing." "I'll bet that arm hurts a mite," Casement said.

Will nodded. "Yes, sir. But I'll be all right soon. I hope to get a job working on the railroad."

"A man with a crippled arm won't be much good to the railroad. Good luck with your recovery."

While Jack Ellis assigned Will a replacement carbine and issued him new shirts, Homer selected a replacement transit and its accompanying equipment.

"Thanks for the transit, sir," Will said. "My uncle will appreciate it."

"Glad to help," Casement said. "You two can bed down in one of the bunk cars tonight. Tomorrow morning a troop of Pawnee Scouts is escorting a wagon train of resupply to General Dodge. You can ride along with them."

"Homer," Will said, "I need to buy Uncle Sean's cigars if we're riding out in the morning. I'm going into town. Be back shortly."

A few minutes later, Will flipped the reins over a hitching post outside Abrams General Store. It was a typical Hell on Wheels establishment—sturdy enough to remain standing until it was time to dismantle it for movement to a new location.

A tinkling bell above the door announced Will's entrance. A gray-bearded man greeted him. "Hello, friend. What'll it be today?" The shopkeeper wiped his hands on his apron.

"I want to buy some cigars."

"Cigars? You're a little young to be smoking."

"I'm fourteen." Will bristled at the challenge. "But, they're not for me. They're for my Uncle Sean. He said he knows you."

"Your uncle Sean?"

"Yes, sir, Sean Corcoran."

"You don't say." The shopkeeper smiled. "Sure I know your uncle. Fine man. Saved my life once."

"He did?"

"Yes, he did. When Hell on Wheels was in North Platte your uncle stepped in and stopped a couple of Mort Kavanagh's thugs from putting a slug into me. They were all liquored up and mad that I didn't have the kind of chewing tobacco they wanted. Fortunately, your uncle came into the store at that time."

This was the second story this week about his uncle rescuing someone. His uncle certainly had a good reputation with everybody Will had come in contact with. He'd have to stay on his toes to not let his uncle down.

The shopkeeper extended a hand across the counter. "Pleased to meet you. Name's Benjamin Abrams, proprietor of this establishment." He raised his eyebrows in an unspoken question that asked for a name.

"Will Braddock."

Abrams pointed to the sling. "Looks like you had a bit of a problem, Will."

"Indian arrow through the arm. Doc says it should be okay, thanks to Homer."

"Homer Garcon? He's still with your uncle. Good. But where is your uncle? Why are you buying cigars instead of him?"

Will explained the reason for his trip to Julesburg.

"I see. It happens I have the same smokes your uncle selected in North Platte. Best I can get." Abrams pulled a cigar box from beneath the counter and placed it before Will. "Dime apiece."

Will laid the handful of coins on the counter and opened the box. The doorbell tinkled behind him.

"Miss Sally Whitworth," Abrams said. "Good afternoon."

"Afternoon, Mr. Abrams."

A slender redhead collapsed a parasol that matched her low-cut, emerald-green dress. Black, high-button shoes peeked from beneath her long skirt. A scrap of horse manure clung to the heel of one shoe. Will grinned when he saw it.

The young lady must have thought he was smiling at her, because she nodded to him. "Afternoon, sir," she said.

"After . . . afternoon, ma'am," Will stammered. She'd called him "sir."

"You'll be stopping by the Lucky Dollar Saloon later to buy a drink and dance with me, I assume." She flashed him a brilliant smile, revealing prominent dimples.

Will shook his head. "I . . . I don't dance."

"Don't dance?"

"No, ma'am. And even if I did, I couldn't." He pointed to the sling.

"Oh, you shouldn't let a little thing like that stop you. And don't call me ma'am. My name is Sally."

"Yes, ma'am . . . I mean, Sally."

"Miss Whitworth," Abrams said. "I don't think Sean Corcoran would approve of his nephew drinking whiskey in the Lucky Dollar Saloon."

"You're Sean Corcoran's nephew?" She cast an appraising eye at Will.

"Yes, ma'am."

"Sally, please."

"Yes . . . Sally. I'm his nephew."

"Do tell." She leaned over the counter and tapped on the glass top. "Mr. Abrams, where is that lovely gold ribbon I saw here yesterday. I've decided I simply must have it."

"Oh, I sold it earlier this afternoon."

"Sold? To whom, pray tell?"

"Oh you wouldn't know her. She's with one of the wagon trains. A pretty, black-haired young woman accompanied by her father, a one-armed former Confederate."

Will's mouth dropped opened. He quickly closed it. Jenny! Has to be Jenny and her father.

"That's too bad, Mr. Abrams. That gold ribbon would have set off my hair perfectly with this new dress Mr. Kavanagh bought me." She turned around slowly, extending her arms to the side. "Don't you agree, Mr. Braddock?"

"Ah . . . yes." Will stammered. A gold ribbon would certainly set off her flame-red hair against the emerald dress.

Sally faced the shopkeeper. "You'll be ordering more ribbons like that, Mr. Abrams?"

"I'll try. I don't always receive exactly what I order. But, I'll try."

"Thank you," Sally said. "Good day to you, Mr. Abrams. And good day to you, Mr. Braddock. Too bad you can't stop by for a dance." She flashed him a smile as she opened the door. When she looked down before stepping out into the street, she saw the horse manure. She scraped her shoe against the doorsill, then popped open her parasol and departed.

"That young lady is trouble," Abrams said. "Best stay away from her. She tried to get her hooks into your uncle in North Platte, but he avoided her. Miss Sally Whitworth is Mortimer Kavanagh's favorite dance hall girl."

Will had read about dance hall girls. But those stories described them as soiled ladies. Sally Whitworth didn't look soiled in the least bit—except for the manure on her shoe. She was one of the fanciest dressed ladies he'd ever seen. She carried herself with dignity. She spoke with grace. And that red hair was spectacular.

"Your uncle wouldn't approve of you going to the Lucky Dollar Saloon. He told me about having a run-in with Kavanagh's Irish thugs on the docks in New York City during the war. He avoids contact with Kavanagh. I expect he'd ask the same of you."

"Homer told me about some of the troubles on the docks, but he didn't mention Kavanagh's name."

"Ask your uncle about him. He'll fill you in on Kavanagh."

"I'll take these for Uncle Sean." Will pushed twenty cigars across the counter. "Mr. Abrams, I think I know the girl who bought the ribbon. You said she purchased it earlier today?"

"That's right. Came into the store with her father to buy flour and sugar while they waited for the wheelwright to finish some repairs."

Will smiled. That's Jenny, all right.

Abrams counted the coins and wrapped the cigars in brown paper. "You have a nickel too much."

"Oh. Uncle Sean said I could buy some candy." He pointed to a jar of jawbreakers. "How many of those will a nickel buy?"

"They're a penny apiece."

"I'll take five."

Will left Abrams General Store. He popped a jawbreaker into his mouth and stuffed the package of cigars and a small poke containing the rest of the candy into his saddlebags. He mounted and turned the horse up the street. Sally Whitworth stood in front of the Lucky Dollar Saloon talking to a stocky man dressed in a suit and vest. Was that Mortimer Kavanagh? Will's curiosity would have to wait—right now he wanted to find Jenny McNabb.

Chapter 25

"Homer, I'm going to ride over to the wagon train to see if the McNabbs are there." Will mumbled as he stepped from his saddle.

"How's that?" Homer paused in fastening sacks of provisions onto the mule pack. "I can't understand you. Your mouth's full of something."

Will spit the remnants of the jawbreaker into his hand. "I'd like to go to the wagon train to find Jenny McNabb."

Homer looked at the marble-sized candy Will cradled in his hand. "Ugh. What's that?"

"Jawbreaker. Want one?"

"No thanks. Go on. Don't be too late. We's leaving at first light, remember."

"I'll be ready." Will climbed back into his saddle. "Oh, keep this." He lifted the sling over his head and tossed it to Homer.

"Doc says you should wear that when yore riding."

"Not this time." He didn't want to be wearing a sling when he met Jenny.

The sun had set by the time he reached the wagon train. A fiddler sawed fitfully away at "The Blue-Tail Fly." A mouth organ tootled along in harmony. Shouting, singing, laughing, and clapping from the far end of the rows of wagons told Will a celebration was underway.

When he'd visited the camp several days ago the wagons were circled. Now they were aligned in the four-column formation used to travel across open prairie.

Will tied his horse to a tree stump along the outskirts of the wagon park and walked up through the center of the four columns. The noise of festivities grew louder with each step he took. When he reached the head of the train, he encountered a large crowd. Through gaps in a ring of spectators, Will caught glimpses of dancing couples whirling around a bonfire. Some of the revelers sang the verse to the song.

When I was young I used to wait
On massa an' han' him his plate
An' pass de bottle when he got dry
An' brush away de blue-tail fly

The volume doubled when all the participants chimed in to sing the familiar chorus.

Jimmie crack corn an' I don't care
Jimmie crack corn an' I don't care
Jimmie crack corn an' I don't care
Ol' Massa's gone away.

Just like in church back in Burlington—not all the folks knew the words to the verse, but they all knew the refrain.

Everybody in the train must be here. He circled around the celebrants and returned to where he'd started. People were packed so tightly he couldn't wedge himself in close enough to get a good look at their faces. How was he going to find Jenny in this crowd?

"That's the way, Elspeth! Show them how Virginians dance!"

He knew that voice. He looked up. Jenny sat on the jockey box of the wagon right next to him. She clapped her hands, the sleeves of her gingham dress fluttering. A gold ribbon held her black hair away from her ears. Will's eyes drifted back down to the high-button shoes that tapped on the footboard. Each tap provided a fleeting glimpse of white pantaloons flashing between her shoe tops and the hem of her dress.

"William Braddock. Didn't your mama ever tell you it was bad manners to stare at a lady's ankles?" Jenny looked straight ahead at the bonfire, tapping her feet and clapping her hands.

Will raised his head. "I . . . I . . . I."

"It's nice to see you too, Will. Even though the cat's got your tongue."

"Sorry, Jenny. Just surprised."

"Help me down, so we can dance." She extended her arms to him.

"I don't know how to dance and even if I did, my arm wouldn't—"

Before he could finish his sentence, Jenny had leaned forward and dropped from the wagon seat.

He instinctively raised his arms to catch her. "Oh!" He winced and jumped back, grabbing his arm.

"What's wrong?"

"Nothing." He pressed on his bicep. "Just a wound."

"A wound?"

"An Indian shot me in the arm with an arrow."

Jenny touched his arm. "Oh, my. Your sleeve's wet. I've caused it to bleed."

"It's nothing, really."

"Come on. We're going back to our wagon to stop that bleeding."

"It can wait until I get back to the railroad doctor. He'll do it."

"You don't think I can?" Jenny planted her hands firmly on her hips.

"It's not a young lady's work."

"I helped Mama bandage many a wounded soldier during

the war. They didn't object that I was a young lady. And I was a lot younger then."

"Sorry." Will dropped his head. "Didn't think about what you might've done in the war."

Jenny stepped around to his other side. "I guess it's all right if I take this arm."

"Sure." He felt his cheeks grow warm and his smile widen when she slipped her arm through his.

They soon reached the McNabbs' wagon, parked last in line in the far right column. Jenny's parents sat near a small fire beside the wagon. Her mother rocked slowly in a wicker chair. Her father perched on an upturned box.

"Nice to see you again, Will," Jenny's father said. "Thank you for notifying Dryden Faulkner about our plight."

"You're welcome, sir."

"Papa. Mama," Jenny said. "I have to dress Will's wound. He's been shot by an Indian's arrow. I've caused it to bleed. Let me have your shirt, Will."

Will removed his shirt and stood before Jenny and her parents in his undershirt. The sleeve of the undershirt was wet with blood.

"That has to come off too," Jenny said.

Will looked at Jenny's parents. He opened his mouth. Then he looked back at Jenny.

"Oh, don't be so modest. They've seen men without their shirts before . . . and I saw lots of soldiers in the hospitals without theirs. But since you're so shy, come over here behind the wagon."

Will unbuttoned his long-sleeved undershirt. She helped him pull it off his injured arm, then she unwound the bloody bandage. She washed the wound, rewrapped his arm with a new bandage, and tugged it snugly to stop the bleeding. Jenny touched the eagle talons on Will's bare chest. "I noticed these when you helped us fix the wheel. What are they?"

He told her about Lone Eagle and how he came to have the talons.

"And did they bring you good luck?"

Will held up one of the talons and pointed to the nick. "Yes. This one deflected the arrow from my chest."

She leaned closer to look at the nicked talon. "I'd say they did bring you good luck."

Will sucked in his breath as he inhaled the cleanliness of her black hair just beneath his nose.

Jenny turned away and pulled a blanket from the wagon. "Here, put this around your shoulders." She smiled at him. "Now, come sit by the fire while I get the blood out of your shirts."

Will sat on the ground across from the McNabbs. Jenny washed the shirts and hung them over the handle of a shovel she drove into the ground next to the fire.

"How'd you get the wound?" Jenny's father asked.

Will told them about the run-in with the Cheyenne and how Homer had pulled out the arrow. He wasn't sure if the McNabbs would understand his praising a Negro.

"Sounds like this Homer is a good fellow to ride with." Mr. McNabb's comment eased Will's apprehension.

"Yes, sir," Will said. "I'll learn a lot from him."

"Mama," Jenny said. "Have you ever heard of a more original excuse for refusing to dance with a lady than being shot with an arrow?"

"I really don't know how to dance, Jenny," Will said.

"Someday we'll have to remedy that shortcoming in your upbringing." She reached out and touched his good shoulder.

The campfire was warm, but the flush he felt on his cheeks didn't come from that heat. "The wagons are lined up like you'll be leaving soon," he said.

"Tomorrow," Jenny said.

"Me too. Tomorrow, Homer and I head back to rejoin General Dodge's party."

"Well then. You need to get some rest before you start that long ride. Your wound will heal, but it needs rest for that to happen."

"You're probably right."

Jenny retrieved his shirts and led him to the rear of the wagon to dress. "Let's fix you a sling."

"I have one at the railroad."

"Then use it, please."

"Yes, ma'am."

"Now what'd I tell you before about calling me ma'am?"

He grinned and she returned it, then led him back to the fire.

"Mr. and Mrs. McNabb," Will said, "I'll say good night and wish you a safe journey."

"Thank you, Will. And you too," Jenny's father said.

Jenny linked arms with Will and they walked away from the McNabbs' wagon.

"Jenny?" Will asked. "Is it too rude to ask how your father lost his arm?"

"No. He was wounded in the battle at Yellow Tavern."

"Where JEB Stuart was killed?"

"Yes. Papa was there when General Stuart was shot. He was devastated he couldn't do anything to save the general, but he was too badly wounded himself. After the surgeon amputated Papa's arm, his men brought him home. Our plantation wasn't far from Yellow Tavern. The Army used it as a hospital. Mama nursed him back to health."

"Jenny—"

When he didn't continue right away, she prompted him. "Yes, Will?"

"It's embarrassing to ask this . . . but I was wondering if you ever owned slaves?"

They had reached Will's horse, and Jenny unlinked her arm from his. She turned him toward her and grasped each of his hands in hers. "I don't mind you asking, Will. My grandfather William owned slaves. But when Grandpa died, shortly before the war, and Papa inherited the plantation, he freed the Negros. Most stayed with us during the war, until it got so bad we couldn't feed them anymore."

"If you didn't own slaves, why'd your father fight in the war?"

"Now that is a silly question." Jenny's eyes flashed gray. "Papa fought for states' rights. He fought for Virginia. Just like Robert E. Lee. Not everybody in the Confederacy fought to keep slaves."

Will was silent a moment, then he pointed to her hair. "May I have your ribbon?"

"What? Do you want to wear it as a lady's favor, like Ivanhoe?" She laughed.

"No. I want to put one of the eagle talons on it. For luck."

She untied the gold ribbon. Her hair dropped loose over her shoulders in long, black waves.

Will transferred one of the talons from his thong onto Jenny's gold ribbon. He motioned with a twirl of his finger for her to turn. He draped the talon around her neck and knotted the ribbon beneath her hair. He breathed in her aroma. The warm flush returned to his cheeks when his fingers brushed her neck.

"Thank you," she whispered. She turned and kissed his cheek, then stepped back. "Will Braddock, you're going to have to start shaving."

Even in the twilight Will saw the twinkle in her blue eyes.

"Now off you go," she said. "I pray you continue to have good luck. Maybe we'll meet again . . . someday."

She whirled and walked away, not looking back. He watched her until she turned down the last column of wagons. He placed a hand against his cheek. It still felt damp from her kiss. “I hope so, Jenny. I hope so.”

Chapter 26

"Agh!" Paddy pushed the plate away. "Bloody awful." The yolk of the egg resisted cutting with a knife, much less a fork. The fatty, salty bacon tasted rancid, and he could've knocked a man out with the biscuit. If he didn't have to eat to stay alive, he'd never come into the Paradise Café—but it was the only place in Julesburg that served an affordable meal. Even the fifty cents the old Chinaman charged for breakfast was too much. Paddy was seldom in Hell on Wheels for a noon meal and he couldn't afford the prices the other establishments charged for supper. So, he ate breakfast here each day rather than not eat at all.

The coffee in the tin cup wasn't hot—never was. Coffee came with the meal, and he was determined to finish it. He tipped the cup to his lips and tried to filter the grounds out of the last sip, but his rotten teeth failed to form a barrier to strain out the dregs. He sputtered and slammed the cup down, spitting black residue back into it. Damn, that was foul.

He sat at a table in front of the café's single window, which provided a view of Julesburg's dusty street. A youth, his arm in a sling, and an African leading a mule rode past.

Paddy leaned closer to the window. "Hmn." Yesterday he'd been lurking in the shadows alongside the Lucky Dollar Saloon listening to Sally Whitworth talk to Mort Kavanagh. She'd pointed out the boy as Sean Corcoran's nephew. What had she called him? It wasn't Corcoran—he had a different last name. Kavanagh had commented to Sally that he was the boy he'd seen ride the black Morgan into town several days ago. Paddy thought he'd seen him before, too. But where?

Of course. The banker's stable!

He's the boy who'd foiled Paddy's attempt to steal General Rawlins's horse in Omaha. He'd also ruined his attempt to steal the horse during the train raid. Well. Sure it is, you put that all together, plus the fact he's Sean Corcoran's nephew—that boy's gonna pay the price. Will Braddock—that's what Sally called him. Will Braddock was the reason he was in hot water with Kavanagh. Paddy didn't like that one bit.

And that Negra riding with Braddock—he looked familiar too. The African removed his neckerchief and wiped his forehead with it. His bare neck revealed an ugly scar.

"Ah!" Paddy's mouth fell open. He gripped the edge of the table with both hands and squeezed hard. Yes! It'd been four years, but the memory of that day seldom left him. In his nightmares that black face was indistinct. That would no longer be the case. The last time he'd seen that face, Corcoran was slashing the hanging rope from around the fellow's neck. Paddy hadn't known his father's intended victim had survived.

Paddy stroked the scar along his left cheek. Ah, now. Sure, and there are three owing to him. Sean Corcoran for killing his father and giving him his ugly scar, the nigger for being the cause of the confrontation in the first place, and now the lad who thwarted his efforts to steal the horse. He would kill all three—the ex-major, the nigger, and the boy. But Will Braddock will be the first.

Paddy pushed back from the table and dropped two quarters for the meal in the middle of the messy plate. He hurried to the rear door of the café, eased the Navy Colt loose in its holster, and stepped into the alley.

Chapter 27

"We've got to get a move on, Homer," Will said. He rode down the center of Julesburg's only street. Homer trailed behind a few paces leading Ruby. "The wagon train's probably left the warehouse already. Mr. Casement said the Pawnees were heading out right after sunup."

Will and Homer had stopped earlier at the Union Pacific's depot to pick up the accumulated mail to take to Cheyenne, but they had to wait for the station agent to show up to unlock the door. Will had hurriedly scooped the letters into his saddlebags, but he had noticed a letter from Judge Sampson addressed to General Dodge. It was probably an inquiry about the delivery of the guardianship transfer papers to his uncle. He was tempted to throw the letter away, but the judge would just write another one.

As he rode, Will tried different positions for holding his carbine. The injury made it uncomfortable to hold it in his left hand. The weight of the weapon put too much strain on his arm, even with the benefit of the sling. If he held the carbine in his right hand, he had to control the reins with the left. When the horse tossed its head up and down, the jerk on his sore arm proved unpleasant. He gave up. Best not to carry the carbine at all. He leaned forward and shoved the weapon beneath his leg, wedging it between the stirrup strap and the saddle flap.

A gunshot cracked to his left. A bullet crashed into the carbine's stock, driving it hard into his horse's side. The horse reared. Will fought to stay in the saddle. A second shot exploded. The bullet zinged past his face. If the horse hadn't reared, that shot would've gotten him for sure.

Through a narrow opening, between two shacks, Will saw a figure wearing a bowler hat turn and race away. He reined his mount hard to the left and urged the horse into the space between the ramshackle buildings. His knees brushed the walls on either side and he slowed to keep from being dragged out of the saddle. He transferred the reins to his left hand and drew his revolver with his right.

He emerged into the alleyway behind the single row of structures. The fractious horse tossed its head, pulling on his arm. He gritted his teeth against the pain and fought to hold the horse steady. He glanced left and right, but saw nothing. A shaking of bushes leading down to the bank of the South Platte caught his attention.

"Hi!" He kicked the horse and forced his way into the thick brush. Branches clawed at his pants legs. The horse struggled to break through the tangle.

"Will!" Homer shouted from behind. "What're you doing? Where're you going?"

"That was Paddy O'Hannigan. I'm going after him."

Will reached the water's edge and surveyed the bank. Heavy brush concealed the shoreline. Paddy could hide in there forever.

Homer joined him. "You sure it was O'Hannigan?"

"Pretty sure. Short and skinny. Bowler hat."

They sat on their horses along the river studying the bank.

"I don't see him," Homer said. "Wait. Down there."

Will looked to where Homer pointed. A bowler hat bobbed up and down above the brush. Will raised his pistol and fired.

The hat sailed away, carried by the force of the bullet into the river.

"You got the bowler," Homer said. "I don't think you got him."

"No, he got away . . . this time."

"We'd better get back. The wagon train's going on without us."

Will returned the revolver to its holster. "Let's find the sheriff and report the bushwhacking."

"Ain't no sheriff in Julesburg," Homer said. "The only law's that self-appointed mayor, Kavanagh. And if O'Hannigan works for him, like we think, what's the use?"

Will shrugged. Someday Paddy O'Hannigan, we'll settle this.

He tugged on his reins and turned the horse away from the river. He looked at the broken stock that protruded in front of his knee, a bullet lodged in the wood. "Looks like I owe the railroad for another carbine. Let's stop by the warehouse and I'll pick up a new one."

After Jack Ellis issued a replacement carbine, Will and Homer trotted after the wagon train. They caught up to it a mile outside Julesburg.

Sergeant Coyote, the leader of the Pawnee escort, had spread his men out in two columns along each side of the dozen wagons, half fifty yards away, the rest a hundred yards farther out. The sergeant didn't intend to be surprised by Sioux or Cheyenne.

The scouts rode in silence. The drivers of the mule teams, ten scruffy whites and two brawny African Americans, did not drive their wagons in silence. The skinners shouted, cursed their teams, and cracked bullwhips over the heads of the mules. Will couldn't remember when he'd heard so many bad words at the same time.

The column followed the trail up Lodgepole Creek away from the South Platte. They stayed off the graded bed for the railroad. The wagon wheels would tear up the prepared surface.

To the southwest, Jenny should be underway too. Will twisted in his saddle and watched a large dust cloud trailing behind four columns of wagons. He felt a flush spread across his cheeks at the thought of Jenny's kiss last night.

"Will," Homer said.

Will jumped. Oh no. Homer had read his thoughts.

"Will, I'se going to drop back and chat with Moses and Ezekiel. I been knowing them two skinners for as long as I been out here."

Will smiled when he realized how foolish it was to think Homer knew his thoughts. "Sure thing. Let me take Ruby. I'll keep her moving along."

Several minutes later, Will screwed up his courage and rode up beside the Pawnee leader. "Sergeant Coyote?"

The Pawnee looked at Will with dark eyes, his piercing gaze made more frightening by a roach haircut that spiked upward down the center of his otherwise shaved head. A blue Army tunic emblazoned with sergeant's stripes provided a semblance of a uniform, but beneath the tunic he wore an Indian breechclout instead of Army trousers. His thighs and knees were bare, his calves encased in fur-skin leggings extending to his leather moccasins. Wrapped around his tunic, a beaded belt held a revolver, a large hunting knife, and a tomahawk. He balanced a Spencer carbine over the saddle in front of him.

The sergeant smiled. "How can I help the nephew of Sean Corcoran?"

"You know my uncle?"

"All Pawnee know Sean Corcoran. Fine man. Fair and brave."

His uncle certainly was well respected out here. He'd have to work hard if he ever hoped to match such a high standard.

The two rode in silence for a while, then Will pulled the broken arrow shaft from his saddlebags and handed it to Coyote. "I was shot with this. We think it's Cheyenne."

The sergeant scrutinized the arrow, turning it in his weathered hand to examine the feathers and the markings on the shaft. He spat on the ground. "Cheyenne, for sure."

He handed the arrow back to Will and pointed at the sling. "Shot?"

"It was painful to have that rip through my arm."

"Hurt for sure, you bet." Coyote laughed. "You lucky it hit arm."

Will nodded. He was glad he hadn't been shot in the butt like Bullfrog Charlie. He felt the eagle talon's scratch beneath the front of his shirt. "I also had a run-in with a young Cheyenne mixed-blood not long ago."

Coyote looked at Will and raised an eyebrow. "You attract Indians?"

"Maybe."

"You lucky for sure." Coyote's broad grin revealed crooked teeth. "Most Indians stay away from white man."

"That Cheyenne told me I should learn sign language."

Coyote nodded.

"I was wondering. We'll be riding together for a few days . . . could you teach me?"

"Good idea learn sign language. All Indians understand. Sure, I teach you."

Chapter 28

The resupply wagons had started up Lodgepole Creek on the ninth of July. Late on the afternoon of the sixteenth the mule teams topped the rise above the beautiful valley of the new town of Cheyenne. From this elevated position, Will could see survey stakes extending up and down the creek banks and outward from there in perpendicular lines. General Dodge and his uncle had been busy laying out the city plat while he'd been gone.

A cry arose from the camp and a band of mounted Pawnee Scouts raced up the slope to greet Sergeant Coyote and his detachment. Dodge, Rawlins, and his uncle stood along the creek bank to await the arrival of the resupply wagons.

Will reined in beside Dodge and handed him the saddlebags of mail.

"Welcome back," General Dodge said. "Word reached us a few days ago about your run-in with the Cheyenne." Dodge pointed to Will's sling. "How's the arm?"

Will raised his left arm shoulder high. He fought to hide the discomfort. "Soon be normal, General."

"Hm. We'll have Doc Parry look at it . . . he'll decide if you'll be able to work." Dodge turned his attention to the lead wagon and gave instructions to the mule skinner on where he wanted the wagons parked.

Will's spirits fell. Maybe Dan Casement was right. Maybe he wouldn't be able to work for the railroad. Then what?

Will's uncle approached Homer, who had dismounted, and pulled him to one side. Will stepped down from his saddle, but his uncle held up a hand, indicating Will was to stay put. His uncle and Homer talked for several minutes. They were too far away for Will to hear.

Homer walked back to where Will stood beside his horse. "I'll take Ruby and unpack her. You go talk to your uncle."

Will followed his uncle into the team's wall tent, where they sat on opposite bunks. Beside his uncle lay Judge Sampson's package of documents. Will told his uncle about the encounter with the Indians and the ambush attempt by Paddy O'Hannigan.

"You're one lucky boy . . . ah, fellow. The same day you and Homer were attacked, a band of Cheyenne jumped the Mormon wagon train and killed two of their track graders."

The thought of Jenny's wagon train making its way into Cheyenne territory flashed through Will's mind.

"The West is a dangerous place," his uncle said. "Not only are the Indians out to stop the railroad, but as you've experienced, Paddy O'Hannigan is out to get us personally. Are you sure you want to stay out here?"

Of course he did—he didn't want to do anything else. "Yes, Uncle Sean. I want to work for the railroad. I want to stay out here with you. You're the only family I have left."

His uncle held up the judge's papers. "Your wound may preclude you from working on the railroad, but you could still hammer away on a blacksmith's anvil with your good arm. I can sign Judge Sampson's order and you can return to Burlington where life is safer."

"Uncle Sean, please don't sign those papers. I don't want to go back, even if I can't work on the railroad. I'll stay out here and take care of myself. Maybe find a job in Hell on Wheels."

"Hell on Wheels is certainly no place for a decent person to work, even though Homer says you proved yourself capable of taking care of yourself. He told me you didn't panic, even with an arrow sticking through your arm." A smile crept across his uncle's face. "He tells me you're a heck of a shot with a carbine."

Will shrugged and grinned.

"General Dodge wants Doc Parry to confirm there's no permanent damage to your arm before he'll agree to giving you a job as a construction worker on the railroad. Doc's out checking on the wounded at the Mormon wagon train right now. He may be back tomorrow." His uncle dropped the papers back onto the bunk. "Then we'll decide."

After the supper meal, Dodge's party gathered around the campfire, puffed on pipes and chewed on cigars, and watched the sun set beyond the mountains. Dodge motioned for Will's uncle to join him. Will sat beside them on the log.

Dodge spoke softly to his uncle, but Will heard what he said. "You're aware that we're leaving the easy part of the tracklaying behind. We're fortunate that Blickensderfer has agreed the Rocky Mountains start just to the west of where we're sitting. The government will pay more for each mile of track laid from here on. And that's as it should be . . . construction costs will escalate through the mountains."

Dodge pulled an unburned twig from the fire and pointed to the west with it.

"Sherman Summit in the Laramie Range yonder is the highest point to be crossed by the Union Pacific. And Dale Creek, just beyond the summit, is the deepest gorge we'll have to bridge. I want you to see if you can find any better route before the graders start up that slope. I want your team to head out in the morning."

Will's head bobbed up, his eyes widened. In the morning? What if Doc Parry didn't return from the Mormon wagon train by morning? What if his arm was too seriously injured to work on the railroad? Was he going to be left behind when his uncle's team departed? Would his uncle send him back to Burlington?

Chapter 29

"Rise and shine, Will." Out of the corner of one eye Will watched his uncle step out of the tent and survey the brightening sky. "Get a good night's sleep?"

"Yes, sir." Actually, he hadn't slept a wink. All night his mind had churned over the direction his life had taken since he'd run away from home less than two months ago, with the dream of becoming part of the team building the first transcontinental railroad.

He'd chosen to sleep under a tree last night, rather than in the tent with the four survey inspection team members. Tossing his blanket aside, he stood and ran fingers through his tangled hair. He settled the old slouch hat on his head, strapped on his pistol belt, and slipped his left arm into the sling.

"Let's get packed up, boys," his uncle said. "Time we hit the trail."

Homer, Otto, and Joe emerged from the tent, exchanged morning greetings with Will, and set to work dismantling their sleeping quarters.

"Ah," his uncle said, "here comes General Dodge with Doc Parry."

Will's heart beat faster. He took slow, deep breaths.

"Morning, Sean," Dodge said. "Morning, Will. Doc's going to take a look at that wound."

The doctor stepped in front of Will. "Arrow shot, was it?" he asked. "Get your shirts off and let me see."

"Yes, sir." Will slipped his arm out of the sling and dropped his shirt and undershirt to the ground. The sling hung empty around his neck.

The doctor pointed at the eagle talon strung on the leather thong. "Interesting-looking adornment. What is it?"

"Just an eagle talon."

The surgeon shrugged. He grabbed Will's arm and studied the wound. He pressed his thumb near the scab that'd formed where the arrow had penetrated the bicep. The tissue there was tender. Will gritted his teeth. The doctor turned Will's arm over and poked around the exit wound. That was the most painful spot. He fought not to show his discomfort. He didn't want to make a sound.

Doctor Parry raised Will's arm above his head and pulled upward. Wow! That hurt. The doctor jerked the arm down and yanked it toward the ground.

"Mm!" Will couldn't help himself. So much for not making a sound. He squeezed his eyes shut trying to suppress the forming tear.

The doctor asked Will to grasp two of his fingers and squeeze hard. Will exerted every ounce of energy in his hand. He managed to make the doctor wince.

"You can let go now." The doctor massaged his fingers.

"Well, Doc?" Dodge asked.

"The wound's going to leave nasty scars. The muscle's not badly damaged, but it'll be months before he can comfortably do heavy lifting. He'll recover the use of his arm . . . given time. Still, I can't in good conscience recommend him for a job as a tracklayer at this time."

Will felt his shoulders slump.

The doctor lifted the sling off Will's neck. "I'll take that. You don't need it anymore. The more you use the arm, the faster it'll recover strength."

Will put his shirts back on and turned to his uncle.

His uncle stared at him. "Doc's assessment doesn't sound good. Guess I'd better sign the guardianship transfer papers. By the time you make it back to Burlington you should be healed enough to work in Klaus Nagel's blacksmith shop."

"Uncle Sean, wait." Will took a deep breath. "I really don't want to be a blacksmith. I have an idea. Let me work as a hunter. I can bring fresh meat to the fire for you and the crew. I can help Homer with the camp chores. I'll wash the dishes. And you don't have to pay me anything. I just *have* to stay out west, Uncle Sean. Don't send me back. Please."

His uncle looked at Homer.

Homer shrugged. "Sounds like a plan to me. I can use some help."

"If you don't have a paying job," his uncle said, "how're you going to repay the railroad for a dead horse and two busted carbines? Klaus Nagel will have to pay you apprentice wages and you'll be able to send some of it to pay off your debt to the UP."

"I'll shoot antelope for General Dodge. Maybe he'll give me credit."

His uncle turned to Dodge.

"Your decision, Sean," Dodge said. "If he's as good a shot as reported, you might appreciate another rifle in your camp. These bloody savages aren't going to stop their attacks."

Will's uncle stared at Will for several seconds, then sighed. "All right. I'll tell you what. I'll give you a temporary position as Homer's assistant. But you'll have to prove that you're a good hunter to stay on. If you do, I'll think about wages later. Agreed?"

"Agreed! Yes, sir! Agreed! I won't let you down, Uncle Sean. I promise."

"I'll count on that, William Braddock." His uncle held up the package containing Judge Sampson's papers. "I'll hold onto these. If this job doesn't work out, I may have no choice but to sign these. Understand?"

"Yes, sir."

"All right, boys." His uncle motioned to his team members. "Time to get moving."

"Will," Homer said, "how 'bout you go fetch Ruby. Pack the tent on her. You knows how. Since you're part of the team, you'se got to start pulling a share of the load." A smile lit up the black man's face.

"Sure thing." Will grinned. He had his first official task. He raced down the slope to the picket line.

Buck and Ruby stood tied side by side in the shade of the trees. Will slipped in between them, patted the Morgan's neck, and caressed one of the mule's ears. The horse snorted and tossed his head, shaking his black mane.

Will stroked the white star on Buck's forehead. The Laramie Range loomed to the west. Somewhere north of here, Lone Eagle rode with the Cheyenne. Off to the south Jenny McNabb trudged beside her family's covered wagon. Behind him to the east lurked Paddy O'Hannigan.

Will ran a hand across his chest and felt the scratch of the eagle talon. "I'm heading west, Buck. Wish me luck."

Chapter 30

Will dropped to his belly behind a stunted juniper. The Indians rode single file over the ridge. He drew the carbine up beside him, laid his thumb on the hammer and waited. If he cocked it now they might hear. They passed fifty yards away—too close to be careless.

He glanced over his shoulder to where he'd tied his horse in a stand of ponderosa pine, farther down the slope. He wished the animal would stand still and stop swishing his tail. A sharp-eyed brave might spot that. Fortunately, a strong wind blew over the ridge from out of the west and carried his horse's scent and shuffling sounds away from the sensitive Indian ponies. He hoped he was far enough away that the ponies couldn't smell him.

Will counted ten braves. He saw only two rifles. The others carried bows. The lead rider looked toward his hiding place. Black paint obscured the lower half of his face. Will puckered his lips and exhaled. The same warrior who'd led the Cheyenne band he'd battled just a few days ago, resulting in his arm wound.

The blackened-faced leader raised his rifle over his head and motioned those following to keep moving. He turned his pony aside, reined in, and stared down the slope. He looked right at the spot where Will was trying to bury himself in the ground. Two eagle feathers dangled from a black band encircling the warrior's head. He wore a breechclout and leggings. His moccasins rested in rope stirrups suspended from a blanket saddle. His white pony's flanks bore the black imprints of a wolf's paws.

Clouds scudded overhead. Will shivered from the chill mountain air, even though he wore a wool shirt. Surely this brave felt the cold, but he showed no sign of it. None of the spartanly dressed warriors did. They rode by stoically.

Will wished he could crawl into the earth behind his skimpy shelter. He kept his head low, peering beneath his hat brim to watch the brave. His thumb twitched on the hammer.

He wouldn't be able to hold off all of them if they charged him. He had seven shots in the Spencer carbine, and six more in his Colt revolver. He'd take out several before they overran him. If they did try, at least his firing might alert his uncle and his companions.

His uncle's five-man survey inspection team had ridden up into the windswept Laramie Range six days ago, out of the newly founded town of Cheyenne, which lay thirty miles to the east. General Dodge had sent them to determine if a better route could be found over the steep mountain range. The team was due to report their findings to Dodge at Fort Sanders, fifteen miles farther west, in three days.

The sun stood directly overhead. Will's flattened body wouldn't cast any revealing shadow. Only sparse vegetation grew along the ridge. Any tree or bush could conceal an enemy and that undoubtedly was what drew the attention of the Cheyenne leader. Danger might lurk there and he wouldn't want to be surprised.

Half the riders passed behind the leader before he jerked on the pony's reins and kicked it in the ribs. He trotted back to the front of the band. Now if the others would just ride by.

Will jerked his head up and quickly dropped it. The last rider surprised him so much he forgot to keep his head down. Lone Eagle rode with this band.

The eagle talon Lone Eagle had given him scratched his chest where he pressed down against the ground. He was convinced the talon had saved his life before, but the wound wasn't completely healed and the muscle ached when something reminded him of it. If he didn't need to keep his hand poised on the carbine, he'd reach across and rub his throbbing arm right now.

He thought about the other talon he'd given to Jenny. He hoped her talon was bringing her good luck. Jenny's wagon train would be plodding along the Overland Trail south of where he now lay and should reach Fort Sanders about the same time he and his uncle's team arrived there. He looked forward to seeing her again.

Pay attention! Will chastised himself for letting his mind wander.

Lone Eagle brought up the rear of the file. Even at this distance, Will could make out the broad stripes of yellow and vermillion painted on Lone Eagle's chest. The young brave's cheeks bore similar distinctive stripes. Lone Eagle rode past without looking to either side.

The column of warriors disappeared over the ridge heading southwest. If they continued as they now traveled they'd pass well to the north of the Dale Creek canyon where his uncle's team worked. The Indians would know that crossing the creek at that location on horseback was difficult. The railroad, unfortunately, was going to have to bridge that canyon in order to maintain the minimum grade up the slope that allowed locomotives to make the climb. His uncle's team had not found an easier route than the previously plotted grade that led straight to the canyon's rim.

Will waited several minutes to ensure the warriors didn't double back. He eased out from under the juniper and skidded down the slope. He leaped onto his horse and kicked him into a gallop. He had two miles to race to reach the team.

"Uncle Sean!" Will cupped his hands around his mouth and shouted down into Dale Canyon from the rim. "Uncle Sean!"

Will watched his uncle lean forward and sight through the telescope of the transit. The surveyor raised a hand and signaled to Otto Hirsch, who steadied the measuring rod farther up the canyon. Joe Quinn adjusted the chain that marked off the distance between the transit and the rod. His uncle stepped back from the transit and scribbled in his notebook.

"Uncle Sean!" No response from below. Even though he wasn't a good whistler he puckered up and tried. Still no response.

The wind blowing across the canyon rim carried all sound away. The men working a hundred twenty feet below didn't know he was there. Homer wasn't visible. He must be in the tent preparing the noon meal.

He guided the horse down the rocky cliff, doglegging back and forth. It was too steep to descend straight ahead. If he had a more sure-footed horse like Buck, he'd try it—but the Morgan was back in Cheyenne with General Rawlins. Will didn't trust this old saddle horse issued by the railroad. He'd just have to ease his way down.

"Uncle Sean!" He called again halfway to the canyon floor. His uncle looked up and waved, but returned to looking through the transit. Will would have to get all the way to the bottom to tell his uncle about the danger.

Loose rocks dislodged by his horse clattered down the slope. His shouting, or more likely the noise of the falling rock, got Homer's attention. The black man stepped out of the tent, looked up and waved. Will returned the salute.

Five minutes later Will halted before the tent.

"Where's the game?" Homer asked.

"Didn't get any."

"You don't usually come back empty-handed. Why?"

"Indians. A Cheyenne band passed by, only a couple of miles from here. I was tracking an antelope and moving into position for a shot, when they rode over the ridge right in front of me."

Homer's eyes got so wide the crow's-feet wrinkles around them disappeared.

"They were the same band that attacked us on Lodgepole Creek. I recognized the leader . . . the one with the blackened face."

Homer lifted his old hat and ran his fingers through his short-cropped salt-and-pepper hair. "I 'spect I best be packing this gear up. We needs to get out of here."

"That's what I intend to suggest to Uncle Sean." Will looked up at the steep walls of the canyon. Indians along the rim would have easy shooting from there—even if they were only equipped with bows and arrows.

Will rode to where his uncle worked with his transit.

"Hey, Will. Get us something good to eat?"

"No, sir. I got chased back by a band of Cheyenne."

His uncle looked up. "Chased by Indians?"

"Not chased, actually. I stayed out of sight. I hightailed it back here as soon as they were gone. They passed about two miles to the north of here."

"Not headed in this direction?"

"No, they rode southwest, in the direction of the Overland Trail."

"We'd better finish up and get on to Fort Sanders. We're right in the middle of the Cheyenne hunting grounds here." He signaled to Otto and Joe to come back to him.

"Homer said he'd start packing up the gear. I'd best go help."

"No," his uncle said. "You get back up to the rim of the canyon and keep a lookout. We don't want to be surprised, if that band circles back."

Chapter 31

"Jenny, why aren't we getting into place?" Her mother sat beside her on the jockey box of their Conestoga watching the long line of wagons move single file along the Overland Trail past Virginia Dale, the last Wells Fargo stagecoach station in Colorado.

Jenny laid a hand over her mother's. "Mama, we're going to rest here a few days."

"But, we should be going on with the others."

"You're too weak to go on now, Mama. Papa thinks you need to get your strength back. That nasty bout of diarrhea and vomiting yesterday means you haven't really recovered from the bilious fever. You need rest."

Her mother sighed, her shoulders slumped even more.

"Don't worry, Mama. We caught up to the wagon train before. We can do it again."

"Yes, we can, Mama," Duncan said. Her younger brother stood beside the wagon looking up to where Jenny sat with their mother. "Can't we Elspeth?"

Elspeth stood in the wagon bed behind Jenny. "I just want to get to California," she said. "Or Oregon. Or wherever we're going."

Her mother reached over her shoulder and took one of Elspeth's hands. "We'll be there before you know it, dear. The promised land is just ahead. Then everything will be fine."

"It certainly can't get any worse," Elspeth muttered.

Dryden Faulkner rode up to their wagon, leaned forward in

his saddle, and lifted his hat. "Ladies. Young man. My compliments to the McNabb family. Is Alistair around?"

Jenny's father stepped around the wagon and faced the wagon master across the back of one of his oxen. "Right here, Dry."

"Alistair, sorry I can't hold the wagon train here longer. There's not enough water and forage for all the animals. Fort Sanders, up on the Laramie River, is the next place where a wagon train can find grazing for a herd this big. And the sutler at the fort will have supplies to sell the folks. Even though this is one of Wells Fargo's home stations, they only have enough supplies to take care of their passengers' needs."

"How much farther to Fort Sanders?" Alistair asked.

"Thirty miles. Couple of days . . . maybe three."

The McNabbs' wagon stood in front of the one-story, hewn-log station that stretched atop a knoll alongside the trail. Behind the station Jenny could see stables and corrals for the stage horses, along with a smattering of small outbuildings. Jenny watched smoke curl lazily upward from the station building's stone chimney. "Why do they have a station in this place? There's nothing here."

"When the stage company laid out the trail years ago," Faulkner said, "they built stations every twelve miles, or so. That's as far as they can run a team pulling a loaded coach before having to change horses."

This was the sixteenth stage station she'd counted since Faulkner's wagon train had left Julesburg, two hundred miles back. Jenny held a hand above the brim of her bonnet to better shield her eyes from the sun. Stretched out before her, the row of wagons struggled up the narrow, rocky trail. Drivers shouted and cursed at their yoked oxen teams for greater exertion. Outriders on horseback trotted up and down the line urging everybody to keep moving. A fine cloud of dust hung suspended axle high around the squeaking wagon wheels.

"No Indian trouble on the Overland Trail, Mr. Faulkner?" Jenny asked.

"Army claims they've suppressed the trouble through here. That's not to say there can't be any."

Alistair laid his good right hand and the stump of his left arm on the back of the ox. "I want to thank you again, Dry, for slowing the pace the last few miles so we could get here to Virginia Dale with you."

Jenny looked at the straggling pine and scattered pinion trees dotting the rolling hills. She shook her head. "Doesn't look much like the Virginia I know."

Faulkner laughed. "It's named for Jack Slade's wife. He built this station and named it for her, not for any dale in the Old Dominion state."

Jenny's father laughed too. "Guess that explains it. Anyway, thanks for taking it easy for a while. Mary can't seem to get her strength back. We'll rest here a day or so and then press on."

"I'll hold the wagons at Fort Sanders for a few days to let the teams rest and the stock graze," Faulkner said. "We'll refit there and make repairs at the fort's blacksmith shop before pushing on over the Continental Divide. I can't wait there too long though."

"Understood."

"You come along as fast as you can, McNabb. When you do hit the trail, keep a sharp eye out. They say it's been quiet through these parts for a while . . . but that's no guarantee."

"I guess the Cheyenne are especially riled up over the construction of the railroad," Alistair said.

"Well, that shouldn't surprise anybody. We ain't paying the savages anything for digging up their hunting grounds. They never cottoned much to the stage line cutting through their lands, but the railroad's worse. Buffalo can walk across a stage road, but they often balk at crossing steel rails."

Faulkner turned his horse away and raised his hand against the brim of his hat in a salute. "See you in Fort Sanders, Colonel." Faulkner used McNabb's former Confederate Army title, even though Jenny's father didn't use it himself.

Percy Robillard strode up the slope, his red curls streaming from beneath his hat. "Sir?" Percy addressed Jenny's father. "If you don't mind, I'd like to travel with you to Fort Sanders. My folks say they'll do fine without me for a while. Perhaps I can be of assistance to you and your family."

Jenny chuckled. "Your interest wouldn't be in staying close to a blonde-headed sister of mine, would it?"

Jenny watched Percy blush and shuffle his feet. Elspeth swatted at her, but Jenny ducked the blow.

"We'd be pleased to have your help, Percy," her father said. "You can assist me with the oxen. That'll free Jenny to spend time with her mother."

The McNabb family and Percy watched until the last wagon passed over the far ridge and dropped out of sight. Now they were alone again.

Jenny climbed down from the jockey box and walked toward the rear of the wagon. She lifted the gold ribbon she wore around her neck, withdrawing the eagle talon from beneath the front of her dress. She ran her fingers over the talisman.

"Thinking about that boy again?" Elspeth had slipped to the back of the wagon and confronted her from the tailgate.

"Hush up, Elspeth!"

"You're sure sweet on that *boy.*" Elspeth's cultivated Southern accent caressed the word "boy" with sarcasm. "Bet you'll never see him again."

"Pooh!" Jenny returned the talon beneath the neckline of her dress, spun around, and walked away. Why did her sister have to be so mean? Maybe she was right about never seeing Will Braddock again. But why did it give her sister such pleasure to rub it in?

Chapter 32

Will, his uncle, and Homer stepped out of the sutler's store into bright sunlight on the parade ground of Fort Sanders. Each held a small, cloth sack of food items.

"Them wagon train folks done bought out the store," Homer said. "Nothing left. Not one sack of flour."

"A disappointment, to be sure," Will's uncle said. "We'll have to go easy on biscuits until we can buy flour." The team had hoped to replenish its supplies before they proceeded west. It was two hundred and fifty miles to Fort Bridger, the next place they could buy supplies.

"Will?"

Will was staring across the dusty parade ground and didn't hear his uncle address him.

"Will." His uncle repeated. "I'm sorry your friends had to remain behind at Virginia Dale. Don't worry though. You heard that wagon master say he'd rest the group here for a couple more days. He expects the McNabbs to rejoin the wagon train before they press on."

Will nodded. But he did worry about Jenny, no matter how much his uncle advised him not to. She and her family would have to make the trip from Virginia Dale to Fort Sanders alone. He recalled the difficulties the McNabbs had with a broken wagon wheel when he'd first encountered them east of Julesburg. They were traveling alone then.

Maybe he should go south to help them—but that could

jeopardize his newly won position on his uncle's team. He still had to prove himself worthy of full-time employment. Besides, the wagon master had said a fellow named Percy Robillard had stayed behind to help them. And the Army patrol that'd ridden in last night said they'd encountered no signs of Indian activity along the Overland Trail south of Fort Sanders. Maybe that band of Cheyenne he'd spotted above Dale Canyon hadn't gone that far.

"Sergeant of the Guard!" The shout came from the parapet walk next to the two-story blockhouse on the far side of the parade ground. The blockhouse was built into the middle of the north side of the ten-foot-high wooden palisade wall that surrounded the fort.

"Cavalry coming." The sentry called down to a sergeant who'd stepped out of the blockhouse.

"Open the gate!" the sergeant ordered. Two sentries at the gate lifted a wooden beam from iron brackets and swung the heavy doors inward.

Lieutenant Luigi Moretti led a column of horsemen at a slow trot through the gate. Behind Luey rode General Dodge and General Rawlins, followed by a dozen dusty cavalry troopers. Trailing the troopers came Sergeant Coyote and half a dozen Pawnee Scouts. Rawlins held his reins tight to control a prancing Buck. The Morgan arched his neck, pricked his ears, and shook his mane.

Will laughed. "Buck, you show-off."

Moretti returned a salute from the sergeant of the guard, then looked back to his own column. "Sergeant Winter, get the men and the horses fed."

"Yes, sir." Sergeant Winter saluted.

"Sergeant Coyote." Moretti called to the rear of the column. "You and your scouts are dismissed."

"Yes, sir." Coyote saluted the lieutenant.

Moretti reined in at the sutler's store and raised his hand in another salute. "Major Corcoran. Good day."

Will's uncle smiled and waved at his forehead in a halfhearted return of the salute. His uncle usually brushed aside military courtesy since he was no longer in the Army, but Moretti was an old friend and the salute was offered partly in jest to an old comrade in arms. "Hey, Luey. How was the ride from Cheyenne?"

"No Indians, if that's what you mean. But ask the generals."

"Good morning, General Dodge," Will's uncle said. "Morning, General Rawlins."

Dodge and Rawlins dismounted and passed their reins to Moretti. "Morning, Sean," Dodge said. Rawlins nodded his greeting, coughing into his bloodstained handkerchief. Will shook his head. The Western climate didn't seem to be helping Rawlins's tuberculosis.

"Good ride?" his uncle asked.

"Not bad." Dodge rubbed his backside. "And more comfortable now that those dignitaries have gone back to Julesburg. Wouldn't you say so, John?"

Rawlins stifled another cough. "More comfortable indeed. I understand the necessity of catering to the officials for the benefit of the railroad, but it is a relief to be able to ride through these beautiful Laramie Mountains without the interruption of their constant chatter."

"Couldn't have said it better myself," Dodge said.

Will stepped up and patted Buck's neck. The black horse nickered and nuzzled Will's cheek. "Good to see you again, too." Will ran his fingers through the long mane to untangle the glistening hair.

Dodge brushed the trail dust from his jacket sleeves. "Have you had your dinner, Sean?"

"No, sir. We were picking up some meager supplies from the

sutler's store and then heading back to our tent to fix something."

"I need to stop by headquarters first and pay my respects to the commanding officer, then we'll go to the Officers' Club. My treat."

"That would be greatly appreciated, General," Will's uncle said.

"Have you ever met General John Gibbon?"

"No, sir."

"Well, come with me. I'll introduce you to the hero of Gettysburg. It was his division that repulsed Pickett's Charge, you know. Good soldier. A colonel now. Had to revert to a lower rank to stay on active duty though."

"Most professional soldiers did." Will's uncle looked at Moretti.

"After we eat, I want to go over some plans with you. We can use one of club's tables to spread out the map."

"Very good, General."

"You come with us too, Will," Dodge said.

"Thank you, sir." Will gave Buck a final pat.

"I'll see to the horses, sir." Moretti led the generals' horses away.

"Thanks, Major." Dodge used Moretti's old wartime rank.

"Mr. Corcoran," Homer said. "Let me take the sacks. I'll get these skimpy goods back over to the tent."

"Thanks, Homer."

Dodge and Will's uncle headed toward the headquarters building. Will fell in beside Rawlins.

Dodge pointed up at the large Union flag streaming stiffly in the breeze from a flagstaff that rose a hundred feet above the parade ground. "That's got to be the most impressive flagpole this side of the Missouri."

"I agree," Will's uncle said. "We could see it for miles when we approached. The staff looks like a ship's spar. Saw lots of those in New York harbor. I wonder whose ship they stole it from."

Dodge laughed. "More than likely some former ship's carpenter joined the Army and was pressed into service to build it."

"It's nice to see that you and Buck are still on good terms," Rawlins said to Will. "I have a proposition for you. We'll discuss it after General Dodge goes over his plans with your uncle."

A short time later Dodge pushed his chair back from the table. "That wasn't bad for Army food, was it?" he said.

"No, sir," Will's uncle replied. "Better than what we could've fixed over a campfire."

"Did that fare meet with your approval, Will?" Dodge asked.

Will opened his mouth to speak, but closed it when he realized he was still chewing on a piece of steak. He quickly swallowed the juicy beef. "That's the best meal I've eaten since the Fourth of July celebration in Cheyenne, General."

"He's right about that," Rawlins said. "Too bad we had to send that good cook back to Julesburg with the dignitaries."

Dodge motioned to an attendant to clear the table. "Let's spread out the map."

When they'd entered the Officers' Club, several of the garrison's officers were present, but they'd eaten and returned to their duties. Dodge and his party now had a private room in which to discuss railroad business.

"I'm going to establish another railroad town right outside Fort Sanders here. I'm calling it Laramie, since it's located along the Laramie River. I want you, Sean, to lay out the plat for the new town just like you did for Cheyenne."

Dodge didn't ask Will to leave the table, so he sat quietly across from the three older men and studied Dodge's map.

"That's a steep climb over the Laramie Range out of Cheyenne," Dodge said. His finger traced the route on the map. "As hard as we look, we can't seem to find an easier way. You have any luck?"

"General," Will's uncle said, "my team searched all through this region the past couple of weeks and haven't found a better route."

Dodge placed his finger on a spot on the map. "When we get the tracks laid over Sherman Summit we'll be at eight thousand two hundred forty-two feet above sea level, higher than anything the Central Pacific has to contend with in the Sierra Nevada."

"William Tecumseh Sherman will be mighty pleased you've bestowed his name on that pass," Rawlins said. "Good thinking to keep him appeased. Never know when you'll have to call on the Army to drive off these pesky Indians."

"Just a little tribute to my old commanding officer," Dodge said.

While the two generals and his uncle talked, Will memorized the terrain features marked on the map. Knowledge of the territory would be useful as he worked to prove his worth to the Union Pacific. Geography had been his favorite subject in school. He understood what he was looking at.

"I wish there were a way around Dale Creek though," Dodge said. His finger pointed to another spot on the map, a few miles west of Sherman Summit. "You can step over that brook at the bottom of that canyon . . . but it's so far down, we're going to have to bridge it."

"That's going to be some bridge, Grenville," Rawlins said.

"I've had plans drawn up for a wooden trestle," Dodge said. "Like the ones we built during the war, but several times bigger. What do your calculations show, Corcoran?"

"The bridge will have to rise a hundred twenty-six feet above the creek bed and extend at least fourteen hundred feet to span the ravine."

"I hope I live long enough to see that bridge, Grenville," Rawlins said. He coughed harshly.

"You will, John," Dodge said. "You will."

"Thanks for the vote of confidence in my life span, Grenville." The two generals looked at each other. Neither smiled.

Dodge sat back and folded his hands over his stomach. "Listen to that," he said.

"Listen to what?" Will's uncle asked.

"Nothing. Quiet. Except for the occasional hoofbeat on the parade ground, it's downright peaceful here."

Rawlins coughed again, then held the handkerchief away from his mouth. "Hell on Wheels reached Cheyenne just before we rode out, Corcoran. The calm of that lovely valley is gone forever. They're planning a big celebration this coming Sunday in conjunction with the sale of the first lots in the new town. And that brings me to my proposition, Will."

Will looked up from the map where he'd been studying the lay of the mountain ranges, the flow of the streams, and the routing of the trails. "Sir?"

"Mort Kavanagh is offering a large purse for the winner of a horse race through the town of Cheyenne and around the surrounding hills," Rawlins said.

"Humph!" Will's uncle snorted. "That no-account Kavanagh still around?"

"Oh, yes," Rawlins said. "Still fancies himself the mayor of Hell on Wheels. He made a point of issuing the challenge directly to me. He says he has a horse that can beat any other in the territory, including Buck."

"Buck's not a racehorse, sir," Will said.

"He's not a thoroughbred, I'll grant that. But he's the fastest horse I've ridden. And I rode a lot during the war. I have yet to see a horse on the plains or in the mountains that can match Buck."

Will nodded his agreement.

"And that's where you come in, Will. I can't ride Buck in the race. I originally thought to get Private Skelly from Moretti's detachment to ride him. Skelly was a jockey before the war. Quite well known in Kentucky. One of the best of his day. Trouble is, Skelly's disappeared."

"Disappeared?" Will said.

"Luey told me the last anyone remembers seeing Skelly was near the Lucky Dollar Saloon the night Hell on Wheels opened shop in Cheyenne. He was seen drinking behind the saloon with that Irishman with a scar down his left cheek."

"Paddy O'Hannigan!" Will and his uncle spoke at the same time.

"Fits his description," Rawlins said. "I've never seen the man myself."

"O'Hannigan undoubtedly works for Kavanagh," Will's uncle said. "Both of them were involved in the New York draft riots in sixty-three. The connection makes sense. This whole thing sounds suspicious. Kavanagh challenging you to a horse race, and then your jockey disappearing. Could be dangerous."

"Could be," Dodge said. "But Colonel John Stevenson . . . he's constructing Fort D. A. Russell outside Cheyenne . . . has promised me he'll have his Thirtieth Infantry on guard to keep down any mischief during the celebrations."

"What do you say, Will?" Rawlins asked. "Buck likes you. He responds to your direction. You're bigger than a professional jockey, but that won't matter. You and Buck make a good team."

Will looked at his uncle, then back to Rawlins. "General Rawlins," he said, "I'm a member of Uncle Sean's survey inspection team. I can't do it unless my uncle says it's all right."

"Will," his uncle said. "If you think you can ride Buck in the race, and if General Rawlins thinks you're the best man for the job, then the survey inspection team can do without your services for a few days."

Will beamed. "I know I can ride Buck. That's for sure."

"Looks like the boys and I'll be busy laying out the plat for Laramie here for a few days," his uncle continued. "And since we can eat here at the fort, I can send Homer along with him."

"I'll agree to that plan," Dodge said. "That's settled then."

Will and his uncle left Dodge and Rawlins in the Officers' Club and walked across the parade ground.

"Uncle Sean," Will said. "You go on. I want to ride over to Big Laramie Stage Station and ask the evening Wells Fargo driver a question. I'll be back soon."

"All right, Will. I think I know your question." His uncle flashed a grin at him.

It was a five-mile ride from the fort to the stagecoach station on the Laramie River, but Will wanted to see if he could learn something about Jenny's status before he went to Cheyenne for the race.

By keeping his horse at a gentle trot he reached Big Laramie Station in less than an hour. The evening stage arrived a few minutes after he did. He rode up beside the driver who was wrapping the bundle of reins around the brake lever on the coach.

"Pardon me, sir?" Will asked.

"What, son?"

"You come from Virginia Dale today?"

"Yep."

"Did you see a one-armed man and his family in a covered wagon pulled by a team of oxen?"

"Yep. Passed 'em on the trail 'bout twenty mile back."

"They're headed this way?"

"Yep. At their pace, I 'spect they'll reach Fort Sanders in a couple a days."

"Any sign of Indian trouble on the way, sir?"

"Nope."

"Thank you, sir."

Jenny and her family were on their way. They should join up with their wagon train before Dryden Faulkner led them west again. And they were safe—so far.

Chapter 33

Paddy O'Hannigan looked up and down the alleyway behind the Lucky Dollar Saloon. The alley was empty except for a drunk railroad worker sleeping it off beside the rear entrance to the dance hall.

Paddy knelt beside the passed-out worker and rifled through his pockets. Only a few coins. He'd obviously spent all of his wages on the rotgut whiskey that had been his undoing. But here was what Paddy really wanted. He slid a long plug of tobacco from the fellow's inside coat pocket. Paddy had been needing a fresh plug and this was almost a complete twist.

The drunk moaned and shifted against the wall. Paddy pulled his Navy Colt revolver from its holster. "Sure, and ye don't need to be seeing me, old-timer." He whacked the drunk over the skull.

Paddy stepped through the back entrance of the circus tent that covered the packed-dirt floor of the interior. He glanced at the gaming tables and the upright piano, then tipped his bowler hat to Randy Tremble. Kavanagh's burly, bearded bartender ignored Paddy's greeting and continued polishing glasses on top of the long wooden bar.

Paddy crossed the expanse of dirt floor and stepped up onto the wooden floor of the false front. He knocked on a door and waited. A gruff voice invited him in. He entered Mort Kavanagh's office and sat in the straight-backed chair in front of his boss's desk.

"You have a job for me, Mort?" Paddy asked.

"Have Randy give you another case of whiskey to take to Chief Tall Bear," Kavanagh said. He blew a smoke ring from his cigar. He leaned back in his swivel chair and plopped his shiny boots on his desk.

Paddy leaned back in his chair and lifted his feet onto the desk.

"Get those dirty boots off my desk!" Kavanagh kicked Paddy's feet aside.

Paddy lunged forward to keep the chair from tumbling over. The kick had startled him and he nearly swallowed his tobacco chaw. He righted the chair and looked down at his worn boots. They were covered with trail dust and horse manure. He looked at the soles of Kavanagh's fancy polished ones, which had probably never been near a corral.

Kavanagh drew on his cigar. "I've got a man working on getting that ammunition for Chief Tall Bear. A little bribe to one of the storekeepers in Casement's warehouse should do the trick. The railroad's got so much ammunition they won't miss it. I expect to have it here tonight. As soon as it's delivered, you get on out to that Cheyenne camp."

"Aye, Mort. It's not so long a ride from here . . . maybe a day. Sure, and it's faster than from Fort Sanders."

"Don't let them pesky redskins steal a horse from you like you lost that Army one the last time you rode out to that camp." Kavanagh glared at him and puffed on his cigar.

Paddy dropped his eyes. Hopefully Sergeant Lunsford would continue to cover up that loss. He'd paid the drunken sergeant at Fort Sanders extra for his promise to do so. That'd reduced the amount of Kavanagh's money Paddy had hoped to skim off to send to his mother. When he'd returned to Hell on Wheels he'd tried to get Kavanagh to reimburse him, pretending he'd used his own money. Kavanagh had refused. It was another festering point in Paddy's relationship with his godfather. He wasn't sure how much longer he'd be able to put up with the abuse his relative heaped on him. If he didn't feel an obligation to provide money to his mother and sister in Brooklyn, he'd cut out now.

"Those Indians proved good on their promise to attack the railroad," Kavanagh said. "That ambush of the Mormon track graders scared the pants off the bunch of them . . . not to mention that two of them got killed. Attacks like that'll slow down the UP's construction. Those workers will be looking over their shoulder all the time to see if another attack is coming."

Paddy nodded. When he'd arrived in Cheyenne with Kavanagh a few days ago to set up the latest version of Hell on Wheels they'd ridden past the new cemetery where the two Mormons were buried. They were the first occupants of what was a necessity for any new Western town.

"Tell the chief I want that black Morgan stolen for sure this time," Kavanagh said.

"Sure, and I'll take care of it."

"You'd better." Kavanagh pointed his cigar at O'Hannigan. "And you tell the chief if he pulls this off real proper like, I'll see he gets more ammunition. And whiskey, too."

A soft knock drew Paddy's attention away from Kavanagh. He looked over his shoulder at the door.

"Come in," Kavanagh said.

Paddy smiled. It'd been the dainty hand of Sally Whitworth that'd knocked. She was always a pleasant sight.

Sally carried a silver tray on which she balanced a bottle and two glasses. She swished by Paddy's chair, avoiding eye contact with him. She shook her head from side to side, her red curls swinging. She wrinkled her nose to show Paddy that the foul smell wafting up from his clothes weren't to her liking.

"Here's your special whiskey, Mort." She smiled brightly at her boss.

"Thanks, honey. That'll be all for now."

She placed the tray on the edge of the desk and sneered at Paddy. "You've got the rottenest teeth and the foulest breath of any man alive," she said. "Don't smile at me and don't breathe in my direction either, if you please."

Kavanagh laughed, the cigar clamped tightly between his teeth. He popped the cork out of the whiskey bottle.

Paddy's grin broadened. "Well, and d'ye see now Miss Whitworth. It don't please me to not be smiling at ye."

"Humph." She snorted and sashayed out of the office.

Kavanagh poured a full tumbler in one glass and a short shot in the second. He pushed the second glass to Paddy. "You did a reasonably good job in your last trip to Tall Bear's camp. That raid on the Mormon wagon train was successful. So I'm rewarding you with two fingers of the good whiskey. If you're successful in arranging the theft of the Morgan during the race, I might even consider giving you a whole bottle. It has to be a permanent theft, mind you."

Paddy picked up the glass. He spat the tobacco chaw into the spittoon at the corner of the desk. He brought the glass up to his nose and inhaled the smooth aroma of the Irish whiskey. My, that was good. He couldn't afford this quality on what Kavanagh paid him. This stuff came from the old country. It certainly wasn't the cheap liquor the Lucky Dollar served its customers. Paddy looked forward to earning a bottle of this. Yes, sir. He'd ensure the black Morgan was stolen this time.

"Here's to success." Kavanagh raised his glass. "If Rawlins loses that horse permanently, he'll report back to General Grant that this railroad construction is very dangerous and the Union Pacific needs to proceed with more caution."

Paddy raised his glass before his face and nodded to

Kavanagh. Paddy thought he might even be able to entice the prissy Miss Sally Whitworth to share a drink with him if he offered her this quality. He tipped the tumbler back and swallowed the fiery liquid in one gulp.

Chapter 34

In the waning light, Jenny trudged up the slope above the Overland Trail. She walked on the balls of her feet to keep the heels of her high-button dress shoes from sinking into the soft soil. A heavy rain earlier in the day had soaked her work shoes and she'd left them beside the fire to dry.

When she reached the top of the ridge she looked south with the hope she could still see Virginia Dale, but they'd come too far. Two days ago they'd buried her mother in the station's tiny cemetery, below a rocky outcropping.

She leaned close to a ponderosa pine and inhaled the sweet, vanilla aroma of the bark. It reminded her of the cookies her mother used to bake at Christmas time. The rain clouds had pushed off to the east earlier, leaving a crispness to the air. The blustery weather made her glad she'd tucked her hair beneath the confines of her bonnet. She imagined that the breeze soughing through the boughs of the trees was her mother's voice whispering to her.

Jenny was thankful they'd been able to provide her mother a decent burial place. When Mrs. Casper had succumbed on the trek across Kansas the wagon master insisted they bury the old woman in the middle of the trail. He had all of the wagons drive over her grave to compact the site to make it impossible for animals to dig up the remains. He'd refused to allow the family to erect a cross. He said it would be an obvious marker for the Indians to rob the grave.

Alistair McNabb wanted to make it hard for animals to disturb his wife's final resting place too, so Jenny had helped her father, her brother, and Percy Robillard pile rocks atop the grave. Elspeth said she was too distraught to help. The grave lay close enough to the station that a marker on it wouldn't attract potential grave robbers. Her father had chiseled a brief inscription on a wooden cross: *Mary McNabb RIP.*

They hadn't lingered after her father pounded the cross into the ground. They'd yoked the oxen to the wagon and headed up the steep trail that led through this pass to Fort Sanders. The oxen managed ten or twelve miles a day on level ground, but this uphill grind was too much to expect that pace.

A Wells Fargo stagecoach had passed them earlier today heading north and a cavalry patrol out of Fort Sanders had ridden by the day before on its way south to Virginia Dale. Other than those brief encounters they hadn't seen another soul. Jenny gazed down the slope to where they'd stopped the wagon. She'd prepared the evening meal, as she did every night, before climbing the hill. Below her, she could see the oxen grazing on the sparse grass that grew alongside the trail.

She watched her father and Duncan carry buckets back to the far side of the wagon after watering the oxen. There was no stream in this mountain pass and the McNabbs shared the water from their barrels with the animals. Elspeth was busy stowing the dishes and cooking utensils into the back of the wagon, which she'd agreed to do as her share of the chores, while she chatted with Percy. Her sister had suppressed her rebellious ways after their mother's death. The presence of her boyfriend was undoubtedly a factor in improving her attitude.

Percy chopped branches into firewood with a hand ax. Even though it was late July, it would be cold tonight here in the foothills of the Front Range of northern Colorado Territory. The five travelers would wrap themselves in their blankets and sleep close to their campfire.

Jenny touched her chest and felt the eagle talon. She lifted the gold ribbon and its amulet from beneath the front of her dress. She caressed the talon, felt the roughness along its length, and the prick of its tip. Where was Will Braddock tonight?

"Mmphm!" Jenny gasped.

A hand clamped across her mouth, jerking her head back sharply. A strong arm wrapped around her waist and pulled her slender body back against her attacker. The odor of rancid animal grease assailed her nostrils from the hand that muffled her. She couldn't see her attacker around the edge of her bonnet, but she knew she was in the grasp of an Indian.

The bushes on either side of her rustled. A dozen other Indians, most of them armed with bows and arrows, slipped silently past.

"Hwm!" She screamed a warning into the hand over her mouth, but the hand tightened and drowned out the sound.

The Indians crept to the bottom of the slope. They broke their silence opposite the wagon. *"Aiyee, aiyee, aiyee!"*

Percy raised his ax. "Run, Elspeth! Run!" he shouted.

Elspeth dropped the dish she held and dashed around the wagon. Percy threw the ax at his attackers. They deftly dodged it. He reached for his Enfield rifle that he'd leaned against the wagon. Two Indians unleashed arrows at his back. Percy crumpled.

Jenny blinked furiously. Tears clouded her vision. What was this horror happening below her? An Indian jerked Percy's head back by his long red hair and sliced a knife around his scalp.

"Aiyee, aiyee, aiyee!" The Indian turned in Jenny's direction and hoisted Percy's bloody scalp. The scalper's face was painted black from beneath his eyes to below his chin.

Jenny caught a glimpse of Elspeth's blonde hair as her sister disappeared into the trees beyond the wagon. She couldn't see her father or brother.

The Indian removed the hand from her mouth. He shifted her to stand beside him, but kept an arm firmly around her waist.

"Let me go!" Jenny hissed. She wriggled, but couldn't free herself. The Indian lifted the ribbon that hung in front of her—the eagle talon dangling before her eyes.

"Who gave you this?"

She was so shocked to hear English, she blurted out her answer without thinking. "Will Braddock."

"Humph." Her captor grunted. "I did not give the talons to him to give one to you."

What'd he mean? How'd he know about the talons? She studied her captor. He was taller and lighter skinned than the others. Streaks of vermillion and yellow highlighted his high cheekbones. Stripes of the same color banded rough scars on his pectoral muscles. On a leather thong around his neck hung six eagle talons. He'd spoken English. Of course—he was the mixed-blood Cheyenne Will had saved from the quicksand.

"Lone Eagle, why are you doing this?" she asked.

"Quiet. No talking."

He hadn't acknowledged he was Lone Eagle, but she was certain he was.

From where they stood on the hilltop, her captor kept looking to the south, toward Virginia Dale. Was he aware that a cavalry patrol should be coming from that direction? Where was that patrol? The lieutenant had told her family they would pass back this way today on their return to Fort Sanders.

She watched the Indians throw her family's possessions out the back of the wagon, whooping loudly when they held up something appealing.

The Indian with the blackened lower face held Percy's Enfield rifle aloft with one hand and swung the scalp with the other. Blood dripped from the long red locks. Another Indian discovered her father's Springfield rifle, which he kept in the foot well of the jockey box. Shouts erupted from all of the attackers when the second rifle was brandished. *"Aiyee, aiyee, aiyee!"*

Jenny averted her view from the gruesome sight below her and looked to the south again, wishing for a miracle. She could tell Lone Eagle kept shifting his concentration from his companions at the wagon to the trail leading back toward Virginia Dale.

She gasped. At the same time Lone Eagle emitted a grunt. Emerging above a rise in the road not more than a mile away a red-and-white-striped guidon appeared. Following the tiny flag a dozen soldiers topped the rise two by two and trotted toward them.

Lone Eagle hoisted her up against his side and carried her quickly down the slope. Her bonnet tangled in a bush and ripped off her head. Her loose hair caught in the branches, but he didn't stop.

When he reached the wagon he dropped her facedown beside Percy's body. Percy's open, unseeing eyes stared at her. Congealing blood from the ghastly wound oozed down the side of his face. She rolled away and sat up. Lone Eagle kicked her back down. He flipped her onto her stomach and tied her hands behind her.

She watched Lone Eagle engage in a heated discussion with the blackened-faced lead warrior, who continued to clutch Percy's scalp. Lone Eagle motioned repeatedly down the trail as his voice grew more insistent.

The leader finally made a sweeping motion up the hill with the rifle and shouted at the other Indians.

Jenny heard hoofbeats and first thought they might be the approaching cavalry, but then she saw two more Indians ride down the slope leading several ponies.

The Indians who had been engaged in the looting jumped down, grabbed firebrands, and tossed them into the wagon bed. The canvas cover blazed. The wooden bed smoldered briefly, then burst into flames. A roaring inferno engulfed the wagon.

The Indians mounted the ponies and herded the oxen up the slope.

Lone Eagle heaved himself onto a pony, reached down and grabbed her by the hair, jerking her up and dumping her in front of him, belly down.

"Ahh!" she screamed. Tears filled her eyes, as much from the horror of what she'd witnessed as the pain of being hoisted by her scalp. Her eyes searched the brush behind the burning wagon, but she saw nothing of her family. Lone Eagle rode up the slope with her. She looked a last time at Percy's body.

Had she been spared because of the eagle talon? Maybe it had brought her luck. But what about her family?

Chapter 35

Will and Homer had departed Fort Sanders early the previous day with a detachment of Pawnee Scouts led by Sergeant Coyote. The scouts were riding to the new Fort D. A. Russell carrying reports from General Dodge. The small column had ridden as long as there was daylight, but twilight faded rapidly in the mountains and the waning moon kept hiding behind scudding clouds. Sergeant Coyote didn't want to ride into an ambush in the dark, so they'd camped overnight in the hills halfway to Cheyenne.

They'd arisen early this morning enshrouded by dense low-lying clouds that hugged the hilltops of the Laramie Range. They followed the railroad's survey stakes down the gentle ridge and when they broke out of the fog they got their first glimpse of the new Hell on Wheels. Sergeant Coyote and the Pawnees parted ways here with Will and Homer and rode cross-country toward the new Army post visible along the north bank of Crow Creek, two miles to the west of the town.

What spread out before him wasn't the Cheyenne Will remembered when he'd ridden out with his uncle's team just two weeks ago. The peaceful meadow on which General Dodge had hosted the Fourth of July celebration no longer existed. Hell on Wheels had moved to the junction of Crow Creek and Clear Creek.

Will and Homer continued down the long ridge and two hours later rode up the new town's dusty main street, already rutted from traffic. Will led Buck, to keep him fresh for the race. Homer led Ruby.

"Homer, when General Rawlins said there was to be a horse race in Cheyenne, I didn't expect to see this." Now approaching mid-morning, some all-night drunks were still sleeping it off on the boardwalks. "It looks just like Julesburg."

"I 'spect that's the way it's gonna be all the way west till the railroad gets built. These rascals are gonna stay right close to the workers so's they can steal their wages."

Will pointed to Benjamin Abrams General Store. "After I collect the prize money for winning the race we'll stop in and buy cigars for Uncle Sean . . . and jawbreakers for me." He laughed at the face Homer made.

The Lucky Dollar Saloon occupied a prominent spot in the center of the new town. Strung between the saloon and a livery stable on the opposite side of the street a banner flapped in the morning breeze. Painted letters in black proclaimed it to be the START–FINISH.

"That'd be the livery stable where the general tole us to go for the startin' of the race," Homer said.

"Right. We've got a little over an hour before race time, since it's supposed to start at noon."

Will and Homer dismounted in a corral that abutted the livery stable. Will fed and watered Buck. He curried Buck's coat until it shined and combed out his mane, ridding it of tangles. After he'd groomed Buck, Will munched on hardtack and jerky while waiting on the starting time.

Spectators gathered in clusters along both sides of the street. Greetings and challenges flew back and forth across the road. Hucksters peddled food and drink. A burly bartender stepped out of the Lucky Dollar and chased the overnight drunks off the boardwalk. A piano banged away in a nearby dance hall.

" 'Bout time to head to the startin' line," Homer said.

"Yes, it's time." Will settled the McClellan saddle on Buck. He'd stripped it of all its accoutrements and given his carbine and revolver to Homer. He didn't want Buck burdened with unnecessary weight.

Will tightened the cinch and spoke softly to the Morgan. "Buck, we're going to show these folks how fast you can run today, aren't we?"

Buck whinnied and shook his mane causing it to glisten in the sunlight. Will laughed and patted the horse's neck. "That's right, boy. We're going to win this race."

He looked across the saddle and froze. Peering back at him from alongside the Lucky Dollar Saloon was a scrawny man in a bowler hat. A scar ran down his left cheek.

Will turned quickly to Homer. "You see that?"

"See what?"

When Will looked back the face was gone. Maybe he was imagining things. He could've sworn he'd seen Paddy O'Hannigan.

Will climbed into the saddle and gathered up the reins. He pulled his slouch hat squarely down onto his head—didn't want it blowing off during the race. Homer opened the gate and Will guided Buck out into the street and took up a position under the START–FINISH banner.

While he sat there, he assessed the competition. The only horse out of the other five capable of giving Buck a race was a bay that stood slightly taller than the Morgan. This was Kavanagh's thoroughbred—a fractious stallion. The horse's rider was a small man, decked out in a yellow silk jockey's shirt emblazoned with the black letters *LD*. The Lucky Dollar's jockey swished a riding whip and sawed the bridle to keep the thoroughbred in line. The horse backed and sidestepped, and bumped into Buck.

Buck whinnied and reared his head. "Can't you control that

animal?" Will hissed through gritted teeth, holding Buck's reins firmly.

"Ah, now, could it be that this is just too much horse for that little Morgan, sonny?" The jockey's brogue confirmed that he was one of Kavanagh's Irish flunkies. "Sure, and that horse of yers don't stand no chance, boy!"

"We'll see," Will said. He leaned forward and patted Buck's neck to calm him.

"Ladies and gentlemen!" A booming voice drew Will's attention to the boardwalk in front of the saloon. A stocky man in a fancy suit stood beside Sally Whitworth—the same man he'd seen talking with Sally in Julesburg the day he'd encountered her in Abrams General Store.

"I'm Mayor Mortimer Kavanagh. Welcome to Cheyenne and the big race!" He shouted so the gathered crowd could hear him. "Someday folks will come from all over the world to enjoy frontier festivities in Cheyenne. Today you're witnessing the first of many to come."

Shouts and jeers erupted from the spectators. People waved wads of paper bills above their heads indicating their willingness to make a bet.

Kavanagh stepped to the edge of the boardwalk and spoke in a normal voice directly to Will. "I'm glad that General Rawlins accepted my challenge. But I don't think that Morgan has a chance, young fellow."

Kavanagh stepped back and raised his voice again. "That bay stallion is my thoroughbred and I'm covering all bets against him."

Will returned Kavanagh's glare.

"Attention, riders," Kavanagh continued. "The course is a five-mile circuit. When I give the signal, you'll ride east and circle around that low hill yonder to the north." He pointed to the northeast. "On the far side of that hill, you swing west and proceed until you reach the main gateway at Fort Russell. There you turn south and descend to the bed of Crow Creek, where you turn east and race back into town. Every half mile are two red flags, where I have stationed an observer. Any rider fails to pass between the flags is disqualified. The first one to pass back under the banner here is the winner. Are you ready?"

The crowd roared. Kavanagh raised a revolver. "I'll fire on the count of three."

The horses edged close together under the banner. Some riders turned to stare at the upraised revolver. Will and the Irish jockey kept their eyes straight ahead. They would go on the sound of the shot—not be distracted watching the starting gun.

Kavanagh began his count. "One!"

Will spoke softly to Buck. "Five miles. That's a piece of cake, Buck. That's where Kavanagh has made his mistake. His thoroughbred may be fast in the beginning, but he won't have your stamina."

"Two!"

Will leaned forward in the stirrups and took a deep breath.

BANG!

Will gave Buck a kick with his heels and the horse leaped forward. The Morgan and the thoroughbred were first across the line—the others a pace behind.

The racers galloped down the center of the main street of Cheyenne amid cheers from the crowd. Men tossed hats into the air. Women waved scarves above their heads.

The Irish jockey set a face pace with the thoroughbred. Will held Buck in check, but stayed well ahead of the other riders. Will knew the race would be between Kavanagh's horse and his. And Will intended to win.

The red flags made following the course easy. After the riders made the turn to the north and headed for the back side of the hill they left behind any vestige of a prepared road. From here on the course was a cross-country ride. Here was where the Morgan would gain on the thoroughbred.

Will leaned over Buck's neck and urged him to go easy. "Wait, Buck. Wait." He stayed within striking distance of the thoroughbred, allowing the Irish jockey and the bay stallion to set the pace.

Will looked back. The other horses were falling behind.

When the thoroughbred approached the main gateway into Fort D. A. Russell, Will released his tight hold on the reins. He touched Buck's flanks with his heels. "Now, Buck. Go!"

The Morgan lengthened his stride and pulled alongside the thoroughbred. Both horses made the turn at the fort neck and neck. Dozens of soldiers were gathered near the gate shouting and waving encouragement to the lead riders.

Will and the Irish jockey raced south toward the bank of Crow Creek. Both horses slowed as they dropped down the steep embankment to the creek bottom. They were now out of view of the soldiers and the other four racers. Two red flags at the creek's edge marked where the course turned east for the final leg back into Cheyenne.

Buck had learned early to pass between the two flags, and Will didn't have to haul on the reins to effect the sharp turn to the left at the creek's edge. The thoroughbred and Buck raced neck and neck over the soft ground along the creek bed. Here was where Will knew that Buck's sure-footed gait would pull them in front.

Small trees and scruffy brush lined the creek's edge. The two horses swung wide in a dogleg to the left to get around a large clump of trees that grew farther up the bank.

Without warning the Irish jockey lashed out at Will's face with his whip. The leather quirt cut into his forehead.

"Ow!" He raised his hands reflexively to protect his face. In doing so he pulled up on the reins and Buck slowed his pace.

The thoroughbred surged ahead. Blood trickled into Will's eyes from the cut made by the whip.

Will swiped across his eyes with his shirt sleeve to clear his blood-blurred vision. That's when he saw a half dozen Indians on ponies surge out of the clump of trees and dash against Buck, jostling him sideways. A familiar-looking Indian with a blackened nose and chin raised a tomahawk. Will ducked. The blow glanced down his temple and knocked him from the saddle. He hit the ground hard, the wind forced out of him.

Blood oozed into his eyes. He squinted and reached for his revolver. It wasn't there—he forgot he'd left it with Homer.

"Kill him!" Will knew that Irish brogue—Paddy O'Hannigan.

"No killing!" Will recognized that voice too—Lone Eagle.

"Sure, and Kavanagh don't care what happens to the rider," Paddy said.

"You said steal the black horse," Lone Eagle said. "You did not say kill the rider."

"Then I will," O'Hannigan said.

"No!" Lone Eagle said. "Leave him. Black Wolf counted coup. We have the horse. We go."

Will felt the eagle talon under his shirt digging into his chest.

Chapter 36

Will opened one eye. His head throbbed. He opened the other eye. His ears buzzed. "Hwm," he groaned.

"Easy, Will." Homer's voice sounded far away. "Doc say you have a mighty bad concussion."

"Hwm." Will groaned again and raised up onto his elbows.

"Easy," Homer said. "Doc say you gonna be all right. Jest have a bad headache for a while."

"He's got that right." Will reached up and explored the bandage wrapped around his head. He winced when he touched the lump behind his ear. He was thankful his reflexes had made him duck, otherwise the tomahawk would've fractured his skull.

"Where am I?"

"Fort Russell hospital."

"How'd I get here?"

"When them four trailing racers dropped down to the creek they seen the Indians racing away with Buck and seen you sprawled on the trail. They fetched the soldiers from the fort who brung you here."

"Buck's gone?"

"I reckon so. Leastwise that's what them other racers say."

Will lay on a cot along one wall of a spartanly furnished room. Homer sat opposite him on a matching cot. Between the cots, beneath a window, a nightstand held a pitcher of water, a glass, and a white towel. A single doorway entered the room opposite the window. A soldier stood in the hallway—a carbine on his shoulder.

"How long have I been here? How'd you get here? Who won the race?"

Homer chuckled. "One question at a time."

Will grinned, but wished he hadn't. It hurt to move the muscles in his face. He gritted his teeth. "All right, one question at a time."

"Kavanagh declared hisself the winner when his thoroughbred crossed the finish line alone. That made everybody in Cheyenne, including me, suspicious. No other racers showed up at the finish line. Them other racers knowed they'd lost, so why continue. Weren't no prize for second place. When them racers never showed up for the longest time, I gots real worried. I grabbed my horse and started back down the course looking for you. I passed them other racers heading back to Cheyenne and they tole me what happened."

Footsteps echoed in the hallway. The soldier stepped aside and brought his carbine to present arms. Will raised up far enough to see two men stop outside the open door.

"I tell you, Doc, General Dodge isn't going to take this well." The man who spoke wore an officer's blue uniform jacket with silver eagles on its shoulder boards. The other man wore the white uniform coat of an Army surgeon. "Dodge counted on the Army to maintain order during the race. To have Indians attack one of the riders, almost within sight of the fort, and steal General Rawlins's horse is too much. Dodge's not going to like it. Rawlins isn't either. I remember from the war Rawlins has a short temper. No sir, Doc, neither one of them is going to like this one bit."

The officer who'd spoken stepped into the room. His flowing mustaches blended into long side whiskers that touched his shoulders on either side of a bare chin. The doctor followed.

"Afternoon, son. I'm Colonel John Stevenson, commanding

officer of the Thirtieth Infantry and commandant of Fort D. A. Russell. The doctor tells me you're Major Sean Corcoran's nephew. That right?"

"Yes, sir."

"I know your uncle. Knew him during the war. Good man. I've sent a courier to Fort Sanders to inform him and General Dodge about the . . . accident."

The doctor stepped up to Will's cot. "We sent word to your uncle that your injuries are neither fatal nor lasting. Nasty blow to the temple, to be sure, and a slash across the forehead that may leave a scar. Not a bad one, I don't think. After a few days of bed rest you'll recover."

"Days?" Will asked. The doctor nodded.

"Your man's welcome to stay here with you," Colonel Stevenson said, "unless we need the other bed for a soldier."

"He's not my *man*," Will said. "My friend's a member of my uncle's survey inspection team."

"Well, whatever." Colonel Stevenson inclined his head toward Homer. "You can stay."

"Thank you, suh," Homer said.

"You rest here for a few days, son. And when the doctor says you're fit to travel, you can return to Fort Sanders."

"Colonel?" Will asked.

"Yes, son."

"You're sending troops to retrieve General Rawlins's horse?"

"No, son. I'm too shorthanded to send men chasing after a horse. Shame to lose such a fine animal. With all due respects to Generals Rawlins and Dodge, I've got better things to do with my men right now. Cheyenne is a lawless town."

The doctor adjusted the bandage that encircled Will's forehead. "You took quite a blow. Your concussion may make you unsteady on your feet for a while. The headache will persist for a day or two. I'll check on you from time to time. Your man

. . . I mean, your friend can bring you meals from the dining hall until you're able to go there on your own."

"Thank you," Will said.

"Another thing. When I examined you I saw that you've had a recent wound to your left bicep."

Will described how he'd received the arrow wound.

"Seems like you've had your share of hard luck, young man," the doctor said. "The arm is healing nicely. You won't suffer any permanent damage."

"Son," Colonel Stevenson said. "Sorry about your . . . incident. I must return to my duties now. When I receive any dispatch back from your uncle, I'll inform you. In the meantime, you rest here in the hospital as our guest."

The officers left the room. The soldier with the carbine stepped back in front of the door.

"We're more prisoners than guests," Will said.

Will swung his feet off the cot and sat up. He hunched forward, his elbows on his knees, his chin in his hands. He touched the bandage gingerly with his fingertips.

"Worried 'bout your headache?" Homer asked.

"That's not what worries me."

"What'd you mean?"

"I mean General Dodge is going to be so upset that I let Buck get stolen. He'll think I'm not responsible enough to work for the railroad."

"General Dodge'll think no such thing."

Will looked at Homer. "I have to get Buck back. Colonel Stevenson isn't going to send any soldiers to get him. I don't know what might happen to Buck in the hands of those Cheyenne . . . not to mention that rascal Paddy O'Hannigan."

"Paddy O'Hannigan?"

"Yes. He was with the Indians. He would've killed me if he'd had his way. But Lone Eagle stopped him." Will touched the front of his shirt. The scratch of the eagle talon against his chest felt comforting.

"Lone Eagle?" Homer asked.

"Yes. He was with them—the band that attacked us down on Lodgepole Creek—the same ones that raided the train. It was the blackened-faced one that clubbed me with a tomahawk. I think Lone Eagle called him Black Wolf."

"Hmmm," Homer said. "Well, I reckon yore even with Lone Eagle now."

"Even?"

"He tole you he owed you his life after you saved him from that quicksand. Now he saved you from that no-account Irishman and them other Indians. That 'bout makes you even on saving lives, way I sees it."

Homer was probably right. Will pushed himself off the cot and extended a hand to the windowsill to steady himself. Through the window he saw there were no buildings behind the hospital. He had a clear view of the Laramie Range to the west. "There's no stockade," he said.

"They don't need no walls 'round this fort," Homer said. "With a entire regiment of infantry here, any Indian would be a fool to attack this place."

Will swayed slightly, but remained standing. His head kept spinning.

"You needs to lie down and rest," Homer said.

"No, I need to go get Buck back."

"You ain't gonna do no such thing." Homer rose from the cot and stood before Will. "Yore in no condition to be going anyplace, much less out yonder to find a horse that you got no idea where it is."

"I do have an idea where he is."

"How you know?"

"I studied General Dodge's map at Fort Sanders. He'd

penciled in the location of an Indian encampment along Lodgepole Creek, just north of Cheyenne Pass."

"Cheyenne Pass! That's thirty miles from here."

"Just a day's ride."

"Jest a day's ride if you was in good condition . . . and if you had a horse."

"You've got a horse. You said you rode out here to find me."

Homer shook his head. "Don't do it, Will. How'll I explain to your uncle if you go off and try this fool thing in the condition yore in?"

"Homer, I'm going. Uncle Sean will understand. I'll be letting him down, as well as General Dodge and General Rawlins, if I don't get Buck back. So you either let me have your horse, or I'll start walking."

"Aw," Homer sighed. "If yore that determined, I'll fetch my horse."

"Thanks. And I need you to get rid of that soldier guarding the door."

"I don't like this, one bit. You're as stubborn as your uncle when it comes to wanting your way."

Will grinned. He liked being compared to his uncle.

"You can't just walk out the front door of the hospital and ride out of the fort. We'll wait till sundown when the soldiers have to stand to attention on the parade ground 'round the flagpole. When they's lowering the flag I'll bring the horse 'round to the window here. Then I'll come back in and distract the guard so's you can climb out."

"Good," Will said.

"Then, I'se got to get back into Cheyenne and pick up that other horse and Ruby and hightail it back to Fort Sanders to tell your uncle what yore doing."

★ ★ ★ ★ ★

A few hours later, a bugle call summoned the soldiers to assemble on the parade ground. Will could hear the officers calling the troops to attention for the daily ritual of lowering the flag. The Army called the ceremony "retreat." Strange name, Will thought. He didn't think the Army liked to retreat.

The front door of the hospital banged open and he heard Homer shouting and cursing from the entrance. The guard stepped away from the door to investigate. Now was the time.

Will pulled the night table away from the wall and pushed opened the window. He swung a leg over the windowsill. The drop to the ground was farther than he'd hoped. He swung the other leg outside, took a quick look back inside the hospital, then launched himself off the sill with a shove. He landed feet-first with a jolt. "Hwm!" A stab of pain shot through his head.

His sudden appearance startled the horse and it pulled back hard on the reins which Homer had wedged into a loose board on the hospital wall. "Easy, boy," Will said. He caught the reins and patted the horse's neck.

Homer had left his saddlebags on the animal's flanks. Hopefully they contained a canteen and some food. Maybe even a revolver. Will didn't have time to check.

Another bugle call sounded from the parade ground on the other side of the hospital. "Dismissed!" The command announced the end of the assembly. Will had to move.

He mounted the horse and rode away from the hospital, dropping down the steep embankment to Crow Creek. He was beneath the view of anyone at the fort. He turned southeast and rode parallel to the creek.

The sun was setting behind him over the Laramie Range, the sky streaked with reds and yellows. Even in the diminishing light he easily identified the spot where he'd been ambushed. Broken bushes and tree branches revealed where the Indians had hidden before their ambush. Will reined in and dismounted.

He examined the trail where the grass was heavily trampled and found what he was looking for. The clear impressions of two shod horses and the markings left by half a dozen unshod ponies led away from the trail and down to the creek's edge. Paddy O'Hannigan would've ridden one of the shod horses. The other was Buck.

Will led his horse through the brush and down to the creek. Broken bushes on the opposite bank revealed where they'd raced to get away. They hadn't bothered to conceal their route. Will mounted and rode across the creek.

On the opposite bank he found the tracks of the Indian ponies and the two shod horses heading northwest. He was right. They were heading for Lodgepole Creek.

CHAPTER 37

Paddy had ridden with the Cheyenne to their village following the theft of the horse. The last couple of hours of the ride had been especially difficult. After the sun set there'd been no moon to illuminate the trail, but that hadn't slowed the braves. A sixth sense seem to guide them. Paddy simply trusted his horse to follow the Indian ponies.

At the village Paddy had to sleep outside. The Cheyenne neither offered him the hospitality of a tepee, nor the nourishment of food. Fortunately, he'd strapped a blanket roll behind his saddle. He'd wrapped himself in the blanket and laid on the ground beneath a cottonwood tree.

He thought about the first time he'd seen Will Braddock's face looking down at him from the stable loft over the barrel of a revolver. His failure at stealing the horse that night always made him seethe. When he'd failed the second time at getting the horse during the train raid, and had convinced himself it was Braddock's fault, he'd become doubly infuriated. That's when he'd sworn vengeance against Corcoran's nephew.

He'd missed killing Braddock when he'd shot at him a few weeks back in Julesburg, and when he'd had the chance to make good on his promise during the horse race, that bloody half-breed Lone Eagle had stepped in and stopped him.

But at least this time, he'd finally been successful in stealing the Morgan. Kavanagh would be proud of him for that. He smiled, snugged the blanket under his chin, and fell asleep.

★ ★ ★ ★ ★

Paddy squinted and rubbed his eyes. The morning sun felt warm on his face. Where was he? Oh yes, on the ground under a cottonwood outside the Cheyenne camp. He got up and took a dozen steps to Lodgepole Creek where he splashed cool water on his face. He cupped his hands and slated his thirst with the refreshing stream water.

He watched the encampment as one by one the women slipped out of their tepees and poked at the coals to restart cook fires that had cooled overnight. Several of them walked past him to the creek to fill buckets, skins, or gourds with water to prepare the morning meal for their menfolk. Few looked at him. None said anything.

He returned to the tree, gathered up his blanket and shook it.

"You're a white man." The English-speaking voice startled him. He spun around. A pretty, black-haired white girl dressed in buckskin held a battered tin bucket. A rawhide thong dangled from around her neck.

"Sure, and I am," he said, "and who're ye?"

"Jenny McNabb. They've kidnapped me. I need your help to get away."

"Get away?"

"Yes. What's your name?"

"Paddy O'Hannigan's the name . . . but why would I want to help ye get away?"

"Because we're both white. I don't belong here."

"Well, do ye see now, that's beside the point. These redskins would slit my throat if I raised a hand to help ye."

The girl glanced back to the ring of tepees. "I don't have much time. I've got to get this bucket of water back right away or Small Duck will be after me." She nodded back toward an old crone that stood between two tepees in the outer ring.

"Small Duck?"

"Chief Tall Bear's wife." She lifted the rawhide thong. "Small Duck only lets go of this thing when I come to fetch water because she's too lazy to walk out here herself. I'm her slave."

"Ah, now, darlin'. If that be true, I sure don't want nothing to do with helping ye escape. Chief Tall Bear is not one to trifle with."

A tear trickled down her face. She turned from him and walked to the creek. He felt sorry for her, but what could he do in the midst of a band of Cheyenne warriors? She filled the old bucket and headed back toward the tepees.

"Miss McNabb. There is one thing I might be able to do."

She stopped and looked at him. "What?" Her blue eyes flashed.

"Well, d'ye see, I might be able to get my boss to buy ye from the chief."

"Your boss? Buy me?"

"Sure, and he's Mortimer Kavanagh. Owns the Lucky Dollar Saloon. If ye'd agree to go to work for him as a dance hall lady, he might buy ye."

"And become a slave to a dance hall? Humph! I may as well remain a slave here."

A few hours later, Paddy sat cross-legged on the compacted dirt floor of the buffalo hide council tepee. Chief Tall Bear sat opposite him, across a small fire that burned in the center of the circle of warriors. Paddy pointed at Lone Eagle. "Well, d'ye see, the half-breed protected the boy what was riding the black horse. Sure, and we should've killed him."

The chief spoke to Lone Eagle, obviously asking for a translation. The chief and Lone Eagle spoke for a moment in Cheyenne, then Lone Eagle faced Paddy. "Killing the rider was not in the deal. I said so yesterday. Chief Tall Bear says so today."

"Well, don't ye see, that boy can identify the lot of ye who stole the horse." Paddy made a sweeping gesture at the braves who were participants in the theft. "And by all the saints, he might identify me. Sure, and he may not have seen me. But he may've recognized my voice, it being such a lilting Irish accent I have, don't ye know."

"You told the chief that Kavanagh wanted a horse stolen," Lone Eagle said. "You did not say Kavanagh wanted the rider killed. We stole the horse. The deal is done."

Paddy sighed. "Aye, but letting that rider live may bring big trouble down on all the Cheyenne . . . and me."

"How can one rider bring big trouble?"

"Well now, did ye not know, he's the nephew of Sean Corcoran." Paddy spat his enemy's name out with particular venom.

"Sean Corcoran." Chief Tall Bear said the name in English.

Lone Eagle and the chief conversed, then Lone Eagle explained. "The chief knows Corcoran works for Dodge. Now he knows the rider is the nephew of Corcoran."

Chief Tall Bear spoke to Lone Eagle again. Lone Eagle interpreted once more. "The chief says Cheyenne will not kill Corcoran's nephew. That will make the railroad boss mad. That will bring big trouble."

Paddy sighed. Further protest wasn't going to gain him anything. He'd have to find another way to take care of Will Braddock—and Corcoran—and the nigger.

"You bring the bullets?" Lone Eagle asked. "You bring the whiskey?"

"Now how would I be doing that? Isn't it that I rode straight here with ye? Sure, and I'll have to return to Kavanagh to get the ammunition and whiskey."

"You bring the bullets and whiskey. Then we will give Kavanagh the horse."

"Well, Mayor Kavanagh, he don't want the horse, don't ye see. Sure, and he gives Chief Tall Bear a gift of the horse."

Lone Eagle translated and spoke again to Paddy. "Good. Chief keeps the horse. He is a strong racehorse. You can leave now. Chief will wait for the bullets and whiskey."

The chief stood and waved a hand in dismissal at Paddy.

"Sure, and I will. That's a promise, ye might say."

Chief Tall Bear ducked low when he exited to keep from dislodging his eagle feather headdress against the opening in the tepee.

Shortly thereafter, Paddy led his horse toward the edge of the camp. Lone Eagle walked silently beside him. "Humph." Paddy snorted. They didn't even trust him to leave by himself. Maybe they thought he'd steal something. He grinned. They were right. If he had half a chance he'd grab something of value just to pay them back for their rudeness.

He walked beyond the circle of tepees with Lone Eagle, where they stopped. They watched a rider approach from the south. Paddy identified him at the same time Lone Eagle apparently did. The rider wasn't an Indian. It was Will Braddock.

Paddy drew his Navy Colt, but before he could cock it, Lone Eagle grabbed it out of his hand.

"No!" Lone Eagle hissed. He held the revolver out of reach with one hand and gripped Paddy's shoulder tightly with the other. Paddy winced from Lone Eagle's strong grip.

"Well now, Chief Tall Bear may've ordered ye not to kill that rider," Paddy said. "But seeing as how I don't take orders from no Indian chief—"

"You take orders from Chief Tall Bear when you are in his village."

Lone Eagle released his grip on Paddy's shoulder. He flicked the percussion cap off each chamber and jammed the disabled revolver into Paddy's holster. "Mount," he said. "Ride straight down the creek, Irishman. When you can no longer see tepees, turn south."

Lone Eagle pushed Paddy toward his horse. Paddy knew he couldn't overpower the Indian. Even if he had his Bowie knife out, he probably couldn't take the half-breed. Lone Eagle was taller and stronger. Without a loaded gun Paddy was helpless. He jammed a foot into a stirrup and heaved himself up.

"Leave Will Braddock alone," Lone Eagle said. "You kill him . . . I will kill you."

Paddy glared at Lone Eagle. "Someday, half-breed. Someday." Paddy kicked his boot heels into the flanks of his horse and rode down the creek bed.

Chapter 38

After riding away from Fort Russell the evening before, Will had followed the trail left by the Indians until the diminishing light made tracking impossible. While the light had lasted it'd been easy to identify the hoofprints left by the two shod horses. Had he been tracking the unshod ponies alone, the task would've been difficult.

He dismounted by a lone tree on the open grassland, wrapped the reins around a branch, and leaned against the tree. He wadded up his hat to cushion his bandaged head against the rough tree bark and tried to sleep. But the throbbing in his skull, and the horse shuffling around beside him, made for a restless night.

Before he knew it, the rays of the rising sun streamed into his eyes. The eastern sky was devoid of clouds. If stormy weather were to develop, it would come later in the day from the west, from over the Rocky Mountains. Time to get started.

Will rose and adjusted the bandage that had drifted askew from rubbing against the tree. He touched the lump behind his ear and winced. Shaking the wrinkles out of his slouch hat he eased it down over the bandage.

He picked up the trail of the horses and ponies easily in the daylight and followed it northwest, keeping the Laramie Range off to the left. By visualizing General Dodge's map, he felt fairly certain he was on the right path. He stopped every hour to rest the horse and nibble on the hardtack he'd found in Homer's saddlebags. Homer had also left a revolver and a canteen in the bags.

Mid-afternoon the undulating prairie abruptly gave way to a steep decline into a wide basin carved over thousands of years by the erosion of a meandering stream. A mile ahead lay Lodgepole Creek. The lush vegetation along the water course etched a dark-green swath through the broad valley, contrasting sharply with the lighter green of the short grass that stretched away on either side. On the far bank of the creek, a cluster of tepees fanned out in a large semicircle. He'd found the Cheyenne village.

He rode down the slope and across the basin. He watched a mounted man with a bowler hat ride east away from the camp along the north bank of the creek. "Humph," Will snorted. "Paddy O'Hannigan, dang your hide."

On the opposite bank of the stream, outside the ring of tepees, a solitary figure stood with his arms folded over his bare chest. A single eagle feather hung from a beaded head band.

Will urged the horse through the shallow water and reined to a halt in front of Lone Eagle. "You didn't have to come out to meet me." Will chuckled and then winced when his attempt at a joke caused his head to throb.

"Head hurt?"

"Yes." Will touched the sore spot behind his ear. "Thanks for saving my life."

"We are even now. A life for a life."

Will nodded. Homer was right.

Lone Eagle stared at him. "You are either one brave fellow, or one dumb one. Why do you come here alone?"

"I came to get my horse back."

"Buck?"

"You remember his name. I'm impressed. You and those other braves, along with that no-account Paddy O'Hannigan, stole him from me."

"You ride into a Cheyenne camp unarmed?"

"I have a revolver in the saddlebags."

Lone Eagle grunted. "Do you a lot of good in the saddlebags."

"I thought it best to ride in without a weapon. Show I come in peace."

Lone Eagle shook his head, turned and walked into the village. Will followed on horseback.

They passed through the outer edge of a double ring of tepees. The flapped openings on all of the lodges faced east, no matter where the tepee was pitched in the circle. The broad opening in the ring of tepees also faced east. The Cheyenne obviously paid homage to the rising sun.

Children ran alongside and swatted at Will's legs with switches. Dogs nipped at the horse's heels. Lone Eagle spoke harshly in the Cheyenne tongue and the children backed away, but the dogs continued their yapping.

Will looked straight ahead and guided his horse behind Lone Eagle. From the corner of his eye he spotted the warrior who had clubbed him with the tomahawk. He turned his head to stare at the warrior with the blackened face. A scalp of tangled red hair hung from his belt. At least Will thought it was a scalp. He'd never seen one before. The warrior returned Will's stare.

Will turned his attention back to following Lone Eagle. In an open area in the midst of the central ring of tepees, Lone Eagle stopped. Will reined in.

A stately, elderly Indian approached riding Buck. His warbonnet trailed eagle feathers from two red bands that flowed down his back and touched the ground on either side of the horse. The Indian drew up in front of Will. Buck whickered and tossed his head, letting Will know he recognized him.

Lone Eagle spoke in Cheyenne to the mounted Indian, then spoke to Will. "This is Chief Tall Bear, my grandfather. My mother, Star Dancer, was his daughter."

Will dropped his head as a sign of respect, but kept his eyes on the chief.

"Chief Tall Bear knows your uncle," Lone Eagle said. "Now he knows you. Tell him why you have come."

Will sat straight and cleared his throat. "Chief," he said. He swept his right index finger in a long arching loop in front of him to indicate that the chief was above all others. "Tall." He raised his right arm to its full extent above his shoulder. "Bear." He placed both hands alongside his forehead with his palms open and quickly clasped his fingers together into the shape of claws.

Will glanced at Lone Eagle, who smiled and nodded his approval.

Will turned back to the chief. "I." He pointed to his own chest with the thumb of his right hand. "Take." He pointed his right index finger at Buck and repeatedly hooked his finger back toward himself. "Horse." He held his left hand before him with his fingers pressed together and placed the index and middle finger of his right hand atop his left to signify a person sitting astride a horse.

The chief laughed and spoke to Lone Eagle.

"Chief Tall Bear admires your sign language." Lone Eagle translated. "But you will not take the horse. It is his now."

Will's shoulders slumped. He wasn't sure what else he expected riding alone into the Cheyenne camp. He certainly had no authority over Chief Tall Bear. He could call him a horse thief he supposed. But he knew it was considered an honor among Indians to steal horses from other tribes. Why should they care about a white man's law that arrested horse thieves?

The chief spoke at length to Lone Eagle, then turned Buck to the side and rode away. Will slid off his horse and stood beside

Lone Eagle.

"Chief says you are a brave fellow. He says you can live. He knows your uncle surveys for Long Eye Dodge."

"Long Eye Dodge?"

"White men call him General Dodge. Cheyenne call him Long Eye Dodge. When he surveyed our mountains many years ago he looked through a transit. Is that right . . . transit?"

"Yes."

"Cheyenne knew that Long Eye Dodge could see a long way through the transit."

Will doubted he would ever call the general Long Eye Dodge. He wondered if Dodge knew the Indians called him that?

"The chief says he is glad you were not afraid to come here alone. He says you should eat before you walk."

"Walk?"

"He keeps your horse. You walk back."

Will followed Lone Eagle through the camp leading his horse. They stopped near the creek's edge, outside the circle of tepees, and added Will's horse to a herd of a dozen others that were corralled behind rawhide rope strung around several trees.

"Chief Tall Bear keeps his horses here near the village. The special horses . . . racehorses. The warriors' ponies are out on the prairie, to graze." Lone Eagle motioned to the north of the camp.

Will counted a half dozen young boys watching the horses. Obviously their job was to ensure the horses didn't stray. Buck was in the herd and trotted up to Will.

"Hello, Buck." Will reached across the rope and stroked the horse's forehead. Buck whickered and nuzzled Will's cheek.

"I'll get you out of here," he whispered. "I promise."

"Come," Lone Eagle said. "We will eat."

Lone Eagle led Will to a tepee in the outer ring. He motioned Will to join him on a log in front of a cook fire. Will removed his hat and laid it on the ground, revealing the white bandage wound around his scalp.

Lone Eagle raised his eyebrows and grinned. "You need an eagle feather in that bandage and you will be Indian."

"Maybe a turkey feather. To show how gullible I am in thinking I could walk in here and get Buck back."

An old woman hunched over an iron pot that rested on a bed of coals in the fire pit in front of Lone Eagle and Will. She stirred the pot's contents with a long-handled wooden spoon.

"Lone Eagle," Will said. "When I rode in I saw the brave that hit me the other night . . . the one whose lower face is black. Was that a scalp tied to his belt?"

"Yes. That is Black Wolf . . . leader of the Crooked Lances. I want to join the Crooked Lances someday."

"Crooked Lances? What's that?"

"White men call it a military society."

"Like the Dog Soldiers? The ones that burned Julesburg?"

"Yes."

A young girl skipped up to the old woman and handed her two hollowed-out gourds, then turned and raced away. She wore a pair of black, high-button shoes. Before Will could say anything about the girl's unusual footwear, the woman handed each of them a gourd filled with a gruel of some unidentifiable nature.

"Eat," Lone Eagle said.

Will forced himself to eat the strange-smelling stew. It'd been more than a day since he'd eaten anything other than hardtack. If he was going to walk back to Cheyenne, he needed nourishment. His plan hadn't included a long walk. He wasn't sure he ever had a plan.

Chapter 39

Paddy sat across the desk from Mort Kavanagh. Sally Whitworth stood beside Kavanagh's swivel chair, her hand on his shoulder.

"Twice I could've killed him," Paddy said. "Twice. Sure, and both times that half-breed Lone Eagle stopped me."

"Forget about killing Will Braddock," Kavanagh said. "That wasn't what was important. Stealing General Rawlins's horse was the objective, and you finally managed to pull that off. Maybe now General Grant will get the message that pushing the construction of the railroad too fast is not a good idea."

"Sure, and I'll be avenging my pa someday by killing that surveyor's nephew." A night seldom passed that Paddy didn't wake from the recurring dream of his father dying from Sean Corcoran's saber thrust. Paddy ran his fingers along the scar on his cheek. "Aye, I'll get that boy someday, and that's the truth of it."

Sally sneered. "Why do you call him a boy? You're not much older than he is."

"Humph," Paddy snorted. "Maybe not age-wise, but I grew up fast after my pa died. That be four years ago, Sally, my sweet." He flashed his rotten-toothed grin at her.

Sally wrinkled her nose. "I'm not your sweet! I'm not your anything and don't you forget it."

"Enough bickering," Kavanagh said. "Tell us more about this white girl that's captive in the Cheyenne camp."

"Aye, pretty she is," Paddy said. "A real bonny lassie. But a scared one, for sure. Said her name was McNabb, Jenny McNabb."

"McNabb. McNabb." Kavanagh repeated the name, reaching for a newspaper on his desk. "That sounds familiar." He shook open the *Cheyenne Gazette* and scanned the columns. "Here it is. That's the name of the family the cavalry brought into Fort Sanders after their wagon had been ambushed. It says here that Alistair McNabb, a former one-armed Confederate cavalry officer, his daughter Elspeth, and son Duncan survived the attack. Another daughter was captured . . . Jenny McNabb."

"I think I know that family, Mort," Sally said. "Ben Abrams said he sold the ribbon I wanted to buy to a girl accompanied by her one-armed father. That was the day I met Will Braddock in Julesburg."

Kavanagh read more of the article. "Says a Percy Robillard was killed and scalped."

"Well now, sure, and that'd be the fresh scalp I seen sported 'round by Black Wolf," Paddy said. "A redheaded scalp, it was."

"What are the Cheyenne doing with this white girl?" Kavanagh asked.

"Well, such a charming girl, don't ye know. She's a slave to the chief's old wife, Small Duck. Least ways that be what she told me. The bonny lassie asked me to help her escape. I told her that'd be mighty dangerous and would get me skinned alive if I tried, to be sure. I said I'd try to get you to buy her from the chief if she'd agree to come work for you. She said she might as well be a slave to the Cheyenne."

"It's not like the Cheyenne to keep a slave," Kavanagh said. "They usually sell them to the Blackfoot or the Sioux."

"Well, do ye see, this Small Duck leads the lassie about with a leather thong tied 'round her neck. Makes her do the cooking and scrubbing, she does."

"Ben Abrams described the girl who bought the ribbon as pretty," Sally said. "He may be just an old Jewish merchant, but if she was pretty enough to impress him, then she must be a beauty. We could use another girl. Maybe you could buy this Jenny McNabb from the chief."

"If the old chief's wife has her doing chores," Kavanagh said, "she's not likely to part with her. But this other girl. There's a possibility. The newspaper says this Alistair McNabb plans to spend the winter in Fort Sanders in the hopes he can locate his missing daughter."

Mort laid the newspaper on the desk. "Railroad won't get to Fort Sanders until spring. It's going to be a boring winter for a girl stuck there in the meantime. I've been meaning to ride over and scout out a place for moving Hell on Wheels after the tracks cross the Laramie Mountains. I bet I can entice this Elspeth McNabb into joining our establishment, Sally."

Sally stroked the back of Mort's hair. "That'd be a welcome addition. I could teach her the business and she could take some of the pressure off me so I could spend more time with you, dear Mort."

"Phew," Paddy snorted. "Sure, and ye don't do nothing now, sweetheart."

Sally launched herself around the end of the desk at Paddy. She slapped him across the face. "How many times do I have to tell you, that I'm not your sweetheart, you slimy Mick. And I do a lot more work around here than you do!"

"Ah, now, darlin'. If ye're talking about drinking weak tea with the customers and pretending it's whiskey, I'd agree." Paddy grinned and rubbed the scar on the side of his face where she'd slapped him.

"Stop it!" Kavanagh said. "Both of you. We've got work to do. I've got to ride over to Fort Sanders. Sally, dear, you've got to get downstairs and entertain our guests. And you, Paddy O'Hannigan, need to take that liquor and ammunition out to Chief Tall Bear."

Chapter 40

Lone Eagle walked Will to the edge of the village. "Return the same way you came." He pointed south, across Lodgepole Creek. "Stay alert. The buffalo herd comes late this year because of the railroad. Our village needs food, so a hunting party went out that way a day ago to hunt antelope. They will return soon. Not good if they find you."

Will stepped into the creek, stopped, and looked back. "So we're even now, Lone Eagle?"

Lone Eagle nodded. "Even."

Will hefted the canteen. "Thanks for the water and hardtack." Lone Eagle had kept the saddlebags and revolver. Will waded through the creek and struck out across the basin toward the escarpment that rose a mile away. Once he climbed that ridge he'd be out of sight. It was late afternoon and he still had several hours of daylight ahead of him for a trek back to Cheyenne.

But he had no intention of returning to Cheyenne.

It didn't take long to reach the top of the ridge. Will walked far enough to be sure he wasn't visible from the village, stepped several paces off the trail, and crawled into a tangle of bushes. He would rest here in a bit of shade until sunset.

He nibbled on the hardtack and sipped water. Where was Jenny today? Had the McNabbs reached Fort Sanders? The warmth of the afternoon made him drowsy and he nodded off to sleep.

Voices and the trod of ponies roused him from his nap. The

hunting party Lone Eagle had cautioned him about was approaching. He flattened himself under the cover of the bushes and pulled his hat firmly down on his head to hide the white bandage.

Three braves rode along the trail leading to the village. They were in a jovial mood, chattering and laughing. Two of them sat astride a single pony together, since one pony was burdened with the carcasses of two antelopes. They would be welcomed by the Cheyenne encampment for bringing in fresh meat.

All three were armed only with bows. Will rubbed his arm where the arrow had pierced his bicep. He had full use of the arm now, but the muscle ached from time to time. He knew how good the Indians were with bow and arrow.

After the Cheyenne hunters passed, the rest of the afternoon dragged. He watched the sun descend beyond the hills. When the burning disk dropped out of sight he rose and walked west into the fading light. He remained away from the edge of the cliff, careful to stay out of sight of the village. He planned to approach the camp from a different direction. He knew where Buck and the chief's horses were corralled. That was his objective.

He trudged along the ridge toward the base of the Laramie Range. The clouds strung above the mountains reflected vivid shades of red, orange, and yellow, from the setting sun. When he reached the base of the hills he turned north and descended to Lodgepole Creek, where it rushed out of a canyon onto the plain. He was a half mile upstream from the camp. He turned east and followed the south bank of the stream back down to the village.

The tremolos of women added to the chanting and singing of men, all accompanied by the steady thump of drums. The noise from the camp masked any sound he made. Still, he approached the area opposite the corral with stealth. He didn't want to alert the boys who watched the herd. He crept through the brush, slipping from tree to tree, trying not to shake the branches. He knelt beside a large cottonwood and studied the village. Light from cook fires cast shadowy figures on the walls of the lodges. The antelopes brought in by the three hunters had provided a reason for a feast and the entire camp was enjoying the celebration. Nothing indicated to Will that he'd been spotted.

A light evening breeze blew from the west, down from the hills, parallel to the creek. That should keep his scent from drifting across the stream to the horses. He wasn't so sure that the Indian boys didn't also possess a heightened sense of smell. He'd heard that an Indian could smell a white man a mile away. He hoped the wind didn't shift.

He eased close to the creek's edge. By the glow of the campfires on the opposite side he counted the silhouettes of six herd boys clustered along the farthest reach of the rope corral. Good. They were observing the festivities—probably wishing they were participating. He was pretty sure it was six boys he'd counted earlier. The horses were congregated near the boys too.

Will stepped off the bank into the fast-moving water. He felt carefully for stones that could shift under his weight. "Dang it." His left boot tangled in a branch concealed beneath the surface. He stopped and looked around, hoping his ill-considered curse hadn't been heard.

The stream was deeper here than he'd anticipated. He blew through his pursed lips when the water spilled into his boots. There was no help for it. His feet would just have to be wet and cold. He refilled his canteen and slung the strap over his head and shoulder, tucking the canteen under his armpit to keep it secure.

He continued across the creek, crouched so that only his head extended above the bank, and studied the corral. No horse moved. No herd boy shifted.

Will climbed out of the creek behind a tree around which was tied the rawhide rope that formed one side of the corral. He unwound the bandage from his head and tucked one end into his waistband. He struggled to untie the rope. The knot was so tight his fingers couldn't budge it. He pulled the eagle talon from beneath his shirt, inserted the sharp tip into the knot, and picked at it until it loosened. He untied the knot and clasped the two ends of the rope in his hand, holding it in position.

He pursed his lips and whistled. *"Tseeeee, Tse, Tse, Tse!"*

Buck whinnied, whirled away from the other horses, and trotted toward him. The herd boys jerked their heads around and shouted. *"Aiyee!"* They raced toward him.

Will dropped the ends of the rope as soon as Buck reached him.

"Stay, Buck! Here, boy!" He grabbed Buck's mane and flung himself onto the horse's back.

"Hiyah! Hiyah!" Will shouted. He swung the bandage wildly above his head. The white cloth flashed in the reflected light of the campfires. The other horses spooked at the flailing bandage and Will's shout. They wheeled and raced through the opening in the corral rope, jumped into the creek, and leaped up the far bank. The herd boys chased after them. Will dropped the bandage. No need to attract the attention of pursuers with a white flag.

Having no halter rope with which to guide Buck, he grabbed a handful of mane and leaned over the horse's neck. "Let's get out of here, Buck." Buck snorted and jumped into the creek.

Will tugged Buck's mane and guided him up the middle of the creek. He wanted to stay in the water to conceal any tracks from Buck's shod hooves. Perhaps the Indians weren't good enough trackers in the dark to realize Buck was no longer with the other horses.

He'd decided earlier in the day not to ride to Cheyenne. That'd be the direction they would expect him to go. That was the direction the other horses were now running. From his memory of General Dodge's map, he'd decided to cross the Laramie Range by way of Cheyenne Pass and ride for Fort Sanders.

It was late afternoon the next day when Will and Buck reached the fort. Dryden Faulkner's wagon train, which had been circled outside the fort a few days ago, was gone. Will felt certain that Jenny's wagon would have rejoined the train before it had headed west. He felt sorry he hadn't returned in time to see her again.

He rode through the front gate, crossed the parade ground, and tied Buck to the white picket fence in front of the Officers' Club. He'd spotted his uncle's horse hitched there as soon as he'd entered the fort.

Will stepped into the open doorway of the club and removed his slouch hat. The four men he sought were standing in the center of the room. Homer stood with his back to him talking to the other three. "I tried to talk him outta going, suh." Homer spoke in an apologetic tone. "Honest, I did."

The three men facing Homer looked over his shoulder. Homer turned to see what had drawn their attention. "Well, speak of the devil." A broad grin spread across Homer's face.

Dodge, Rawlins, and his uncle looked at him. Will's uncle broke their silence. "You'd better have a good explanation, young man."

Will stepped aside so they could see Buck tied to the fence. They all laughed.

"I expect you're hungry," Dodge said.

"Yes, sir. All I had to eat was hardtack."

"Let's get you something."

Dodge insisted that Homer join them at the table while Will ate cold chicken and a plate of stale biscuits. While he ate he told them what had happened since he'd left Homer.

"That's quite a tale, Will," Rawlins said. He paused to cough into his handkerchief. "I'm grateful you got my horse back, but I wish I hadn't asked you to ride in the race. I'm sorry you had to undergo that painful ordeal."

"Oh, don't be sorry, sir. Buck and I would've won that race if it weren't for Paddy O'Hannigan's conniving."

"Mortimer Kavanagh was more than likely behind all of it, I imagine," Dodge said.

Will's uncle had sat silently through Will's telling of his story. "Will," he said. "I have some unpleasant news for you."

He stopped chewing on a chicken leg and looked at his uncle.

"The McNabb family was attacked by Indians between Virginia Dale Station and here. A Percy Robillard traveling with them was killed and scalped . . . Jenny is missing."

Chapter 41

Will excused himself and dashed outside. He almost knocked Lieutenant Moretti off his feet. Moretti grabbed him and steadied them both.

"What's the rush, Will?" Moretti asked. "And welcome back, by the way."

"Uncle Sean told me Jenny's missing."

"Ah, that's so." He twisted the end of a waxed mustache.

"Are the McNabbs still here?"

"In a tent behind the stables."

Will hurried in the direction Moretti pointed. He found an Army wall tent and called out as he approached. "Mr. McNabb! It's Will Braddock."

Alistair McNabb stepped through the tent's open flap. The one-armed Confederate veteran looked haggard, his features drawn. He clasped the stump of his missing arm in his good hand. "Hello, Will," he said.

"Jenny's missing?"

"True."

"What happened?"

Elspeth and Duncan came out of the tent and joined their father.

"My sister's gone," Duncan said. He hugged his father's waist. His lower lip trembled. "We don't know where she is."

"And they murdered my Percy." Elspeth blubbered. "The savages scalped him."

McNabb placed his good arm around his daughter's shoulders. "Now, now, Elspeth. Crying won't change the facts. Try to control yourself."

"I can't help it, Papa."

"Come in, Will," McNabb said. "I'll tell you what happened."

The four of them sat on cots in the tent while McNabb told Will that after they'd buried his wife they'd set out alone from Virginia Dale. He'd thought they'd be safe because reports had indicated no recent Indian trouble, but when they'd stopped the second night along the trail they were attacked. "Indications are they were Cheyenne," he said.

Will frowned. "Cheyenne?"

"Percy evidently tried to fend off their attack, but there were too many," McNabb said.

"It's awful." Elspeth sputtered. "They scalped Percy of his beautiful red hair."

Red hair. Black Wolf had been wearing a red-haired scalp in the Cheyenne camp.

"There, there, Elspeth. Dry your tears." McNabb handed his daughter a handkerchief.

Elspeth sobbed and settled her head against her father's shoulder.

"We three got away," McNabb continued, "and hid in the woods until the Indians rode away and the cavalry patrol arrived." McNabb fell silent.

Will waited a moment before prompting him. "Go on, sir."

"We made our way back to the wagon. It was destroyed. All our possessions burned. The only recognizable things were the cast-iron stove and the tires and hubs of the wheels. Percy was beyond help. And the oxen were gone."

"And Jenny?" Will asked.

"Jenny had walked away from the wagon after we'd finished supper. She wanted to see if Virginia Dale was still visible from above the trail. She probably hoped to get one last glimpse of where we'd buried her mother. Elspeth, Duncan, and I climbed the slope where we'd last seen Jenny. We could follow her trail going up the hill because the heels on her shoes made a distinct depression in the soft soil. It'd rained earlier and she'd gotten her work shoes wet. The only shoes she had to wear were her high-button ones."

High-button shoes! Will leaned forward. Could that be?

"At the top of the slope her tracks were obliterated by those of the Indian ponies that'd evidently surrounded her. We found her bonnet tangled in a bush, but no other trace. I fear she's been taken by the savages. I just hope she's still alive."

Will closed his eyes and recalled the vision of Jenny's feet tapping to the music—the shape of her ankles contained in the high-button shoes had captivated his imagination and drawn Jenny's chiding. He pictured the high-button shoes he'd seen the Indian girl wearing in the camp. Of course. They had to be the same shoes! Why hadn't he recognized that!

McNabb finished his story. "After the troopers helped us bury Percy, they brought us to Fort Sanders."

Will couldn't bring himself to tell the McNabbs that Jenny had probably been in the Cheyenne camp while he was there. And he'd done nothing about it. Would she still be there?

He left the McNabbs' tent and went to look for his uncle. He found him talking with Homer outside the Officers' Club.

"Homer," Will's uncle said. "General Dodge plans to press on tomorrow. He wants to get to Salt Lake City and talk with Brigham Young about the Mormons providing contract labor for grading in Utah. He wants us to go along and check the surveying that's been done across the Red Desert."

Will stood silently beside the two men. He only listened to half of what his uncle said. He kept visualizing a red-haired scalp and high-button shoes. Jenny had been in Chief Tall Bear's village. He was sure of it.

His uncle acknowledged Will's presence with a nod, but continued talking with Homer. "Get the gear packed. Find Joe and Otto and tell them to be ready to head out at first light tomorrow."

"Uncle Sean," Will said.

"Just a minute, Will." His uncle placed a restraining hand on Will's shoulder. "Did the sutler get any flour?"

"Yas, suh. Not much. I bought all he had . . . two bags. That won't last long."

"When you find Joe tell him I need his help to calibrate the transit this afternoon. Otto can get the horses ready."

Homer nodded.

"I think that's everything, Homer. On your way."

Homer headed across the parade ground and his uncle turned to his nephew. "You find out what happened to the McNabbs?"

"Yes, sir," Will answered. "I'm pretty sure I know where Jenny is, Uncle Sean."

His uncle cocked his head and raised an eyebrow. "Oh?"

"She had to have been in Chief Tall Bear's camp while I was there. She's probably still there."

"Well, at least you got away from the Cheyenne safely."

"But I can't leave her there."

"What do you mean? You don't know for certain she's there. And what can you do about freeing her from a camp full of hostile Indians?"

"I have to try."

"Forget it, Will. We're leaving Fort Sanders in the morning. We have to accompany General Dodge. This may be the most important assignment that the survey inspection team has been given. Don't you want to be part of it?"

"Yes, sir, I do. But—" Will couldn't think of anything else to say to his uncle. He wanted to be part of the team. He didn't want to lose his job with the Union Pacific. But he couldn't forget Jenny.

"Well then, help Homer get packed up. We're leaving in the morning." His uncle turned and strode across the parade ground. Will stood with slumped shoulders and watched him go.

Lieutenant Moretti rode his horse across the parade ground. That's it, Will thought. The Army can get Jenny back. Colonel Stevenson had refused to rescue Buck, but that was a horse. This is a human being—a white woman. The Army can't refuse to act.

Will intercepted Moretti's path. "Luey," Will called.

Moretti reined in his horse. He pulled on one end of his mustache. "Will, I guess you travel west tomorrow with your uncle."

"I'm supposed to," Will said, "but first I have to do something to help Jenny McNabb."

"Jenny McNabb?"

"Yes. I know where she is." Will explained what he'd seen in the Cheyenne camp. "Luey, you have to take some soldiers to the camp and get Jenny."

"Will, that's not going to happen. Colonel Gibbon's not going to issue orders to attack an Indian camp. Even if he did, I don't have enough men to fight a whole Cheyenne village. It would be suicide to approach that camp with my small detachment. Remember Captain Fetterman last year. You know what happened to him . . . and he had a full company."

Will dropped his head.

"Sorry, Will." He flicked the reins and his horse walked away.

His uncle wouldn't help. The Army wouldn't help. There was nobody else to turn to. He had to do it himself.

Throughout the afternoon, Will helped Homer pack the supplies and equipment. Homer fussed at him each time he placed an item in the wrong pack or accidently spilled the contents that had been carefully assembled.

"Pay attention, Will. Where your mind be, son? You ain't done this bad afore."

"Sorry, Homer. I can't stop worrying about Jenny. I should've helped her while I was there."

"Now, you stop fretting. Ain't nothing you can do 'bout it. Nothing! And don't you go getting foolish ideas 'bout trying something, neither."

Will shook his head and returned to the job of packing. Yes, there was something he could do about it. He would take Buck back to Chief Tall Bear and trade the Morgan for Jenny.

They finished the packing and Homer left to say goodbye to friends. Will's uncle had not yet returned from calibrating the transit. While he and Homer had worked in silence, Will had formulated his plan.

He had to get Buck out of the cavalry stables and through the front gate of the stockade without being stopped. Getting Buck out of the stables was easy. He simply told the corporal on duty that he'd been sent by General Rawlins to exercise the horse. The necessity to lead the horse had enabled him to put a bridle on Buck, but he'd have to ride bareback. A saddle would've been suspicious.

He led Buck out to the parade ground. The sun was setting and the Army's patrol from the Overland Trail was due to return. The fort's gates would be opened to admit the patrol, but only for a few minutes. He had to be in position at the right time.

He walked Buck back and forth across the parade ground. Buck was restless, tossing his head and shaking his mane. The horse seemed to sense something unusual was about to happen.

Will kept one eye on the sentry pacing the wall near the blockhouse. Finally the sentry lowered his rifle and called down to the sergeant of the guard. “Patrol coming! Open the gates!”

The gates opened and the half dozen cavalrymen rattled through. They had barely cleared the entrance when the guards shoved on the gates to close them.

Now! Will swung onto Buck’s back and kicked him hard in the flanks. The Morgan jumped forward and raced through the closing gates.

Darkness descended across the Laramie Plains behind him as Will galloped away from the fort. He urged Buck up the steep western slope of the Laramie Range. When he neared the top of the ridge he halted. “This is as far as we go tonight, Buck.” He looked at the blackening sky. “There’ll be no moon tonight. Too dark to go on.”

He’d hoped to cross over the crest of the ridge and down the other side as far as the headwaters of Lodgepole Creek so he could get water for himself and Buck, but night had come on too fast. He dismounted and let the bridle rope trail on the ground. The horse could graze on patches of the short grass and gain some moisture from the vegetation. As for himself, he’d have to suffer his stomach grumbling through the night.

Will wasn’t worried about Buck wandering off, so he left him unhobbled. He found a pile of boulders to crawl among to shelter himself from the wind, turned the collar up on his shirt, and buried his hands beneath his armpits to keep them warm. The day had been strenuous and he soon nodded off to sleep.

Will jerked awake. The squeaking of a leather saddle grew more pronounced. Someone rode close by. There was no moonlight, but his night vision was aided by a clear sky filled with sparkling stars. He watched the silhouette of a horse and rider appear in front of his concealed position. Trailing them was another horse without a rider. Abruptly the rider stopped.

“Howdy, Will,” a hoarse voice said.

Will let his breath out. "Bullfrog Charlie. How'd you know it was me?"

"Oh, I see right good in the dark. Helped me keep my scalp all these years." Bullfrog dismounted. "Besides, my horses scented yours and they knowed it weren't no Indian pony."

Bullfrog unbridled his riding horse, loosened the cinch on his saddle, and lifted it from his horse. "Mind if I join you in the shelter of them rocks?"

Will shifted to the side. "Help yourself."

Bullfrog dropped his saddle in the space Will vacated. "What's for supper?"

"Nothing." Will groaned.

Bullfrog laughed. "Thought so. Didn't see no fire. We can fix that though." He stepped back to his trailing horse and removed its pack. "What you doing out here by yourself?"

"I'm taking Buck back to Chief Tall Bear to trade for Jenny McNabb."

Bullfrog built a small fire and boiled coffee. The two of them shared a simple meal of jerky and hardtack. "Now," Bullfrog said, "tell me more about this plan of yours."

Will told Bullfrog about his suspicions that Jenny was being held captive in the Cheyenne camp and that the only way left to him to rescue her was to take Buck back to the chief.

"I reckon it's not my place," Bullfrog said, "but I question the wisdom of riding into that village alone. You got away with it once, but I'd be mighty careful if it was me going in there again."

"I have to try to free Jenny."

"I reckon I can understand that." Bullfrog raised his cup of coffee. "Here's to luck."

Will touched his chest. Beneath his shirt he felt the scratch of the eagle talon.

Chapter 42

Jenny flipped the rawhide thong back across her shoulder to keep it from trailing in the pemmican she was making. Small Duck had tied the water-soaked thong around her neck the night she'd been brought into the Cheyenne village. Once the leather dried, there was no way Jenny could untie it with her fingers. It may as well be an iron collar. She could cut it off, but the old woman never left her alone with any of the knives.

Kneeling on a buffalo hide beside a cook fire, she placed strips of dried meat, from her father's oxen, on a large flat stone and ground it into a pulp with an elk bone. Then she mixed the pulp with an equal amount of bone marrow and blended in a handful of dried, crushed berries. She patted the pemmican into compact cakes about six inches square and wrapped each one in thin strips of damp parchment.

She stared into the fire and wished it were the cook fire next to their wagon. But there no longer was a McNabb wagon. She'd watched it burn the night she'd been captured. She frequently pictured her father, sister, and brother running into the trees behind the wagon. At least she kept telling herself she'd seen them get away. Anything else was unimaginable.

She licked her fingers. The pemmican tasted good, but she felt guilty about eating it. The poor oxen had never been abused. Even when her father lashed out his bullwhip it was above their backs. The sharp crack of the whip was enough to get them moving. The oxen had simply let the Indians herd them away.

How'd they know they were to be butchered?

Jenny shook her head. She had to stop reliving those horrible memories. She had nightmares every night. She didn't need to think about it during the day. She would not, however, stop saying a prayer that her father, Elspeth, and Duncan were still alive. She reminded herself how her mother had persevered through the war. She had to be as strong as her mother had been.

A week had passed since she'd arrived at this village along the pretty creek. If it'd been under different circumstances, she would've found the place charming. She might even have liked the people. But she was a slave. Plain and simple. She was their prisoner to do with as they chose. Thankfully they hadn't physically abused her. At least not yet.

Black Wolf sauntered past and shook Percy's scalp at her. She dreaded each time she had to look at the strong warrior who painted the lower half of his face black.

"Go away," Jenny hissed.

"Forget about Black Wolf." Lone Eagle stepped up beside her. "Ignore him. He will stop."

Jenny sighed, stood, and brushed her hands down the front of the soft buckskin dress to smooth its folds. It was beautifully decorated with blue trade beads and multicolored porcupine quills. Its skirt brushed the tops of her soft moccasins. A young Cheyenne girl now pranced around the camp wearing her high-button shoes. Actually, she was glad she wore the moccasins. They were far more practical than high-button shoes for the life she now led.

She was thankful for the times she could talk with Lone Eagle. He showed her more respect than the others. He spoke good English and understood what she was saying. He'd told her about his education at the boarding school in Saint Louis. She knew his father was a white trapper and his mother was the chief's daughter. She was able to relax in Lone Eagle's presence, something she couldn't do when Black Wolf came around. Lone Eagle kept a respectful distance and never touched her.

"Lone Eagle." She had to look up. He was much taller than she. "How much longer do I have to endure this? I've been here for seven days."

"You are fortunate you have not been sold to the Blackfoot or Sioux. Chief Tall Bear sells white captives fast. It is not wise to keep slaves here . . . too close to white man's eyes."

"I don't want to be a slave! I want to be free!" She felt a tear trickle down her cheek. Lone Eagle's face revealed no sympathy.

"It could be worse. Black Wolf offered ten ponies for you. Black Wolf would take you for his wife."

Jenny shuddered. Yes, that would be worse.

"You are lucky Small Duck likes you. My grandfather lets her keep you. She does not let others whip you. You have it good."

Jenny lifted the leather thong from her neck. "This is good?"

Lone Eagle did not answer.

"I know Chief Tall Bear is your grandfather," Jenny said. "Is Small Duck your grandmother?"

"No. Small Duck is grandfather's second wife. My grandmother died long ago."

"Small Duck's not so small," Jenny said. "She's twice my size. She drags me around by this rope. I don't like it."

"Chief Tall Bear offered you freedom."

"Sure, he offered me freedom. He demanded a large ransom from my family. I told him we were poor. Even if I were certain my family were still alive, they have no money to ransom me."

"Then you remain a slave."

"Lone Eagle, you and I have talked about your time at the school. You told me how you felt confined there . . . how you missed these prairies and mountains." Jenny searched Lone Eagle's eyes. "Did they tie you up at night so you couldn't move, like that old squaw, Small Duck, ties me up in that wikiup prison of mine?"

Lone Eagle shook his head once.

"But you felt enslaved. They locked you in your room. You felt you'd been deprived of your freedom. You ran away. You returned to your freedom."

He stared at her.

"What chance do I have? How can I ever achieve my freedom? It's not right for one person to make another his slave."

"You sound like Will Braddock." Lone Eagle turned and walked away, leaving her alone.

Jenny glanced around. No one was near. She knelt and pulled her eagle talon from where she had secreted it beneath a seam in a small, beaded parfleche she wore tied around her waist. Lone Eagle had allowed her to keep the talon, but the yellow ribbon on which she'd worn it was gone. It, like her high-button shoes, was now the proud possession of a Cheyenne child. She unwrapped one of the parchment packets and cut the center out of the pemmican block with the sharp talon. Slipping the mushy substance into the soft leather parfleche, she returned the talon to its hiding place beneath the seam. Then she scooped sand into the hole left in the pemmican and rewrapped it.

"Aiyee, aiyee, aiyee!"

She jerked her head up. Had someone seen her steal the pemmican? No, the sharp cry came from the far edge of the camp. The warning passed quickly from one tepee to another. Small Duck waddled up and grabbed Jenny's thong from behind. The old woman pulled hard on the thong.

Jenny tripped and fell forward onto her hands. Small Duck yanked the thong. Jenny choked. "Agh." She reared back onto her knees and clutched at her throat, sliding her fingers beneath the biting leather to keep it from crushing her windpipe.

Small Duck jabbered in Cheyenne. Jenny couldn't understand. The old woman dragged her to her feet and down to the wikiup beside the creek where she was secluded each evening. Small Duck forced her through the narrow opening into the shelter constructed of branches and twigs surrounding the trunk of a cottonwood sapling that had been incorporated into the back portion of the wikiup. Jenny obeyed Small Duck's pointed directions and sat with her back to the tree trunk.

Small Duck kicked her in the ribs and pushed her in the chest to force her back tightly against the trunk. Jenny stretched her feet out in front of her. The woman pulled Jenny's arms behind the sapling and tied her hands with a length of rawhide. Jenny winced. The old squaw certainly wasn't gentle with cinching the knot. Small Duck took three turns with another rope around Jenny's waist, trussing her snuggly against the cottonwood. Then, she stuffed a rag into Jenny's mouth and tied a strip of rawhide around the rag to secure it. Small Duck had never done this before. Why now?

Small Duck tugged on the thongs to ensure that Jenny couldn't move freely. Then she left the wikiup, dropping the flap door and tying it closed behind her.

Jenny struggled to find a comfortable position. The rawhide binding her hands bit into her wrists. The one around her body dug into her ribs and limited her ability to breathe. But the most painful was the thong that cut into the corners of her mouth where it passed over the rag. She was afraid to swallow. She might draw the rag deep into her throat and choke on it.

Chapter 43

Will reached Lodgepole Creek opposite the Cheyenne village in the late-afternoon sun. His clothes were almost dry. He'd been soaked by an unusual early-morning rainstorm that had pelted the Laramie Range. As a result, the creek flowed swifter than the last time he'd been here. He urged Buck into the strong current. The water rose to the horse's chest. Will swung his feet to the side to keep his boots out of the water.

He rode slowly through the outer ring of tepees. The camp's dogs growled and yapped. Buck pranced to fend off the nipping dogs. Will faced straight ahead. His eyes shifted from side to side to check out the gathering crowd. The Cheyenne hemmed him into a narrow passageway, forcing him toward the central circle.

Will reined in at the circle's outer edge. Opposite him stood Chief Tall Bear. Will raised his hand in the peace sign. Lone Eagle stepped up beside his grandfather.

Will inhaled deeply, squeezed his fists tightly, then exhaled to calm himself. He hoped not to convey his nervousness. He jabbed his thumb into his chest. "I," he said. He next pointed to the chief. "Bring you." Then he placed two fingers of his right hand astride the imaginary horse formed by his left. "Horse."

The chief held up a hand and waved his palm back and forth. "Stop," he said in English. He continued speaking to Lone Eagle in Cheyenne. Lone Eagle translated. "Chief says you cannot give him the horse. The Irishman already gave him the horse. You stole it."

"Paddy O'Hannigan and your braves stole the horse from me!" Will hadn't meant to speak so angrily—his temper got the better of him.

The chief folded his arms across his chest and stared at Will.

"I return horse," Will said, "in exchange for Jenny McNabb. She is your captive."

Lone Eagle translated for his chief. "Chief says there is no Jenny McNabb here."

"Jenny's father told me their wagon was attacked by Cheyenne." Will pointed to Black Wolf. "That brave wears the scalp of Percy Robillard on his belt. Percy was with the McNabb wagon when Jenny was kidnapped."

Through Lone Eagle, Chief Tall Bear spoke. "Scalp could be anyone's. Why do you think it belongs to someone you call Percy?"

"The scalp has red hair. Percy Robillard had red hair."

Lone Eagle translated again. "Chief says many white men have red hair. This does not prove Cheyenne attacked the wagon."

"I have more proof," Will said. "When I was here two days ago I saw a Cheyenne girl wearing high-button shoes. They are Jenny McNabb's shoes. She was wearing them when your braves brought her here."

The chief spoke through Lone Eagle once more. "Chief says many white women wear these shoes. This does not prove anything."

"I recognized those shoes," Will said. "I have seen Jenny wearing them."

Lone Eagle again conversed with the chief. "Chief says high-button shoes are all alike. Could be any white woman's shoes."

Will had exhausted his line of reasoning. He couldn't think

of any other way to convince the chief he knew Jenny was in the camp.

Chief Tall Bear spoke to two braves standing next to Black Wolf. They crossed the circle. One of them grasped Buck's reins and the other pulled Will off the horse. They led Buck away.

The chief spoke to Lone Eagle, turned and left. The crowd dispersed. Only Lone Eagle and the snarling dogs remained facing Will.

"Chief says you have a long walk again. You are lucky you are not dead. Chief still thinks you are a brave fellow. Not wise . . . just brave." Lone Eagle spread his hands open before him. "You come empty-handed. No saddle. No saddlebags. No food. No water. No gun. Come, chief says to feed you again. Then you can rest before you have to walk tomorrow."

Will slumped. He'd failed. Not only had he not rescued Jenny, he'd lost Buck again.

The cottonwood and willow trees along Lodgepole Creek faded from green to gray. Then the grays dimmed into shadowy blacks. Only a matter of minutes passed after the sun disappeared behind the Laramie Range until night engulfed the camp.

Will stared into the fire. A log snapped. The flames blazed up momentarily, then the burning pile settled to fill the void created by the explosion of a knot in the log. Red and gold sparks flitted fitfully into the air.

Will and Lone Eagle sat beside one another. "Lone Eagle," Will said. "The cavalry patrol that rescued the McNabb family and took them to Fort Sanders found signs at the site of the burned wagon that identified the raiders as Cheyenne."

"Hmm," Lone Eagle said.

The two sat silent for a time.

"Lone Eagle, we have saved each other's lives. Is that not so?"

"That is so."

"That means we should have a trust, a respect, for one another. Is that not so?"

Lone Eagle hesitated, then answered. "That is so."

"People who respect one another should tell each other the truth. Right?"

"Hmm." Lone Eagle grunted.

"Why do you say Jenny is not here? Why do you say the high-button shoes I saw that girl wearing are not Jenny's shoes? I know those shoes. I've seen Jenny wearing them. Why do you deny she is here?"

"*I* did not say Jenny was not here. The chief said Jenny was not here. I only told you what the chief said."

"What?" Will grasped Lone Eagle's arm. He felt a sharp prick against his neck. Lone Eagle had drawn his knife so quickly that Will had not even seen the blade's movement.

"Never touch a Cheyenne," Lone Eagle said, "unless you plan to kill him."

CHAPTER 44

The saliva in Jenny's throat made it hard to breathe. She wanted to swallow, but she was afraid she would choke on the gag. The leather thong cut into the corners of her mouth, making the edges of her lips raw.

The Cheyenne hadn't treated her like this before. Small Duck had always tied her hands each night to the cottonwood inside the wikiup. But they'd always been tied in front of her, and she'd had some freedom of movement. Before, she'd been able to slide her hands down to the bottom of the trunk and curl up. When she'd gotten cold, she could stretch out and sidle closer to the embers of the small fire that Small Duck allowed her to build in the center of the wikiup during the day. The little warmth that remained from those coals provided enough heat that she could sleep a few hours. Now she was forced to sit upright, her back lashed tightly to the small tree, her legs extended before her.

"It's not right, Lone Eagle. And you know it."

Jenny eye's widened. That was Will Braddock's voice!

"Jenny should not be held here as a captive. She did nothing to deserve being made a slave."

Jenny heard Will's words clearly.

"Slave? What does a white man like you know about slavery? You kept African men as slaves for years."

That was Lone Eagle speaking. Will Braddock and Lone Eagle were right outside her wikiup.

"My family never owned slaves," Will said. "My father died in the war to free the Negros. Don't include me with other white men who owned slaves."

"Arggh." Jenny yelled into the gag. It came out as a whimper.

Will would never hear her. She had to get his attention somehow. She twisted against the thong that bound her. If she could just loosen it . . . She stomped her feet on the ground. If Will couldn't hear her voice, maybe he could hear the drubbing. She may as well be pounding with bare feet, no more sound than her moccasins made.

She blinked fiercely to squeeze away her tears. She looked around the wikiup, searching for something that could aid her.

There. That gourd held buffalo fat she used for cooking. It should still be liquid because she kept it near the fire during the day. Her feet hadn't been tied. She stretched a leg as far as she could reach. If she could drag that gourd into the embers of the fire she might get a blaze started with the fat. Then she could kick the burning embers against the bottom of the wikiup and set the branches from which it was made on fire.

"Come," Lone Eagle said. "We will sleep now. You have to walk to Fort Sanders in the morning."

"Arggh." Jenny shouted against the gag. No! Don't leave! She had to get Will's attention. She hooked her toes around the gourd and pulled it toward the coals. The gourd wouldn't slide on the dirt. She had to hurry. She pulled again, harder. The gourd tipped over. The fatty contents ran out and seeped into the ground—far from the embers.

No! No! She choked on her gag. Tears streamed down her cheeks.

Chapter 45

Will felt a toe poke him in the ribs. He rolled over and looked up at Lone Eagle.

"Time you get up," Lone Eagle said.

Will sat up and rubbed his eyes. Lone Eagle had given him a buffalo robe last evening and he'd rolled up in it under a cottonwood beside the creek. He looked around the small clearing where he'd spent the night. The first rays of light streaked the eastern horizon with yellows and reds. He tossed the robe aside and stood.

Lone Eagle handed him a strip of jerky. "Breakfast."

"Humph, thanks." Will took a bite out of the dried meat and stuffed the remainder into his pants pocket.

"Last night," Lone Eagle said, "when we talked about slavery." Lone Eagle paused.

"Yes, what about it?"

"I thought all night about what you said."

"And?"

"You are right. Jenny should not be a slave."

"You know where she is?"

Lone Eagle nodded. "In that wikiup down by the creek bank . . . where we stopped yesterday and talked about slavery."

Will turned and stepped toward the creek. Lone Eagle grabbed his arm and held him. The Cheyenne's grip on his bicep dug into the arrow wound. It hurt. Will gritted his teeth. He glared into Lone Eagle's eyes. Will resisted the urge to pull away—although he was tempted to try. In truth, he probably couldn't get away from Lone Eagle without a weapon.

"If I had a knife I would probably try to kill you right now," Will said. "You told me that one warrior doesn't touch another unless he intends to kill him."

"I am saving your life." Lone Eagle released Will's arm.

"Saving my life?"

"If someone sees you go to that wikiup, they will kill you. If the chief had wanted you to know Jenny was here, he would have told you. Chief does not want the soldiers to know a white woman is here. He would not let you go, if you knew she was here."

Will dropped his head and sighed. "How can I save her?"

Lone Eagle was silent for a moment. "There is a way."

"There is?"

"Knock me out."

"What?" Will wasn't sure he'd heard correctly. "Knock you out?"

"Yes. Then I do not know when you rescue Jenny. I do not know that you escaped up the creek. The village will think you overpowered me." Lone Eagle flashed Will a broad grin.

Will smiled too. "Me overpower you?"

"Surprise me. From behind."

"You really want me to knock you out?"

"It is the only way."

Will stooped and picked up a sturdy limb. He weighed its feel in his hand. It was solid enough.

"When I turn, you hit me."

Will nodded.

"Take my knife." Lone Eagle pointed to the sheath at his waist. "Jenny is alone in the wikiup, but she is tied to the tree."

Will nodded.

"Do not steal a horse. The herd boys are alert now. They

were punished when you stole Buck last time. They will not let it happen again."

Will held out his hand. "Thank you."

Lone Eagle looked at Will's hand for a moment before grasping it. "Good luck, Will."

"We are no longer even, Lone Eagle. I owe you."

"Someday you will repay me."

"That's a promise."

Lone Eagle turned his back. Will studied the club. It was the size of a baseball bat.

"Why are you waiting?" Lone Eagle asked.

Will tightened his grip. He swung hard. Lone Eagle groaned and slumped to the ground.

Will knelt over the prostrate body. "Whew. Bet that hurt." He felt Lone Eagle's neck for a pulse. It beat strongly. He ran his hand over the back of the skull. It wasn't broken, nor was there blood, but a lump swelled on the back of the mixed-blood's head.

"Sorry, Lone Eagle." Will pulled the mixed-blood's knife from its sheath and slipped it into his own waistband.

He crept through the surrounding trees past the outer ring of tepees until he came opposite the spot where Lone Eagle had said Jenny was captive. At least he hoped he had the right spot. He could only see one wikiup from here. It must be the one. He crouched behind a cottonwood and studied the tepees in the outer ring. The camp was still quiet. He needed to make his move before the Indians awoke, though. And light was increasing in the east.

A large dog lay beside one of the tepees. It growled, baring its teeth. He might be able to kill the dog with the knife. On the other hand, the dog might bark an alarm before he could do it. He slipped the piece of jerky out of his pocket and tossed it over the head of the dog as far as he could. The dog ran to fetch it.

He darted across the space between the outer ring and the creek bank. He squatted next to the wikiup that was his target. It'd better be the right one. He didn't want to wind up inside with a startled warrior.

"Jenny," he whispered. No response. He whispered louder. "Jenny." He heard scuffling inside the wikiup. Was it Jenny? Or some brave? Was he at the right place?

He used Lone Eagle's knife to cut the thongs that tied a buffalo skin covering over the wikiup's entrance. He lifted the covering and stuck his head inside. "Jenny," he whispered.

A thump answered him. "Arggh." He heard a strangled grunt.

Good heavens it was dark inside there. He crawled through the doorway to keep his profile small against the outside sky. "Jenny?"

"Arggh." More thumping. Louder this time.

He crawled close to the embers of a fire that provided the only bit of light inside the wikiup. "Jenny, I think that's you. If it is, stomp once."

Thump!

"Good. Give me a minute to let my eyes adjust."

"Arggh."

"I hear you. I'll get you free in a minute."

He made out the shape of a person hunched against the trunk of a slender tree that seemed to grow up through the roof of the wikiup. Lone Eagle had said she'd be tied to one. He crawled closer. It was Jenny. He ran his hands up her side and located the thongs that bound her waist to the sapling. He sliced the bindings. When Jenny didn't move he pulled on her arm. "Come on. We have to go."

"Arggh."

"Say something, Jenny."

"Arggh." Feet pounded fiercely.

He reached up and felt the gag covering her mouth. He untied it.

"How do you expect me to say anything, Will, with that gag in my mouth?" She spit onto the ground.

Will traced his fingers along her face and felt the cuts where the leather had sawed into the side of her mouth. His fingers came away sticky. He couldn't see it, but knew it was blood.

"My hands, Will. My hands are tied behind the tree."

He cut the leather thong that secured her hands.

She brought her hands forward and pounded on Will's chest with her fists. "Mmm." She grunted.

Will could hear her frustration and didn't stop her. She slumped forward, leaned her head on him, and cried.

"Thank you, Will. I'm sorry I hit you. I'm just so angry."

"It's all right. You'll be all right now." It felt strange, yet comfortable, to feel her face pressed close against his shoulder.

"How'd you know where to find me?"

He told her Lone Eagle had pointed out her prison. Will told her that her family was safe and explained how he'd pieced the clues together about her whereabouts.

"We have to get out of here, Jenny. Are you ready?"

Her head nodded against his shoulder.

Will untangled the remains of the leather thongs that had bound her to the tree. His hand caught in a strap that encircled her waist and he reached to cut it.

"No," Jenny said. "That's my parfleche."

Will stuck the knife in his waistband and led her toward the light that filtered into the wikiup through its entrance.

"We've got to get away from here before the camp awakens."

Chapter 46

"Aw, now, ye danged old nag." Paddy swatted the swaybacked horse with the reins. "I swear to tell ye, if I'd known ye were gonna throw a shoe I'd a made ye the packhorse. Sure, and if it weren't so much trouble I'd switch the load off the packhorse now. Come on, giddup."

He spat a stream of tobacco juice onto the ground. "Sure, and I ain't got all the time in the world to deliver this liquor and ammunition to Chief Tall Bear."

Paddy had ridden out of Cheyenne early the previous morning anticipating that a day's ride would bring him to Lodgepole Creek. He hadn't bargained on the shortage of riding horses in Cheyenne and had to settle on leftovers from the livery stable's meager herd. Folks kept flocking into the new town to buy lots and take up residence. That meant good business for Hell on Wheels and Mort Kavanagh's saloon, but the demand for horses was greater than the stable could handle.

He'd sold two of the bottles of liquor to the stable owner at a bargain price to get the last two horses in the place. He patted his vest pocket and jingled the coins. He'd send the money to his mother and sister. Chief Tall Bear wouldn't know he was being shorted on the amount of liquor Kavanagh was sending. Paddy had gotten away with cheating the Indians before—he could do it again.

When the saddle horse had thrown the shoe late yesterday he was forced to slow his pace and finally wound up camping for the night, short of his destination. He'd not wanted to ride into the Cheyenne village after dark. Might get his scalp lifted. So he'd waited until morning before setting out again.

Paddy hadn't thought he'd be able to lift the heavy liquor and ammunition boxes back onto the packsaddle if he took them off, so the animal had stood all night with its load in place. This morning the tired packhorse, as well as the shoeless one he was riding, slowed his progress.

"Ah, come on, now, ye no-account nags. We're almost there. I can see the camp from here." He'd reached the ridge above Lodgepole Creek's broad valley. The horses smelled the water a mile away and both picked up the pace, slightly.

Paddy watched the village come to life in the early-morning sunlight. Off to the west he saw two figures creeping through the tall grass beside the creek. Now, sure, and what would that be? That don't look right. Why would Indians sneak away from their own camp? Wait. Something was different about those two. Sure, and they're not Indians. One wore buckskin, but the other didn't.

They're white! Bloody hell! He knew those two. Jenny McNabb and Will Braddock. "Hey!" he yelled. He spit out his tobacco chaw to keep from choking on it. "Hey, ye bloody Cheyenne! Wake up!"

He pounded his heels into his horse's flanks and slapped the reins back and forth trying to get more speed. The horse ambled along at a trot, more to reach the water than in response to Paddy's wishes.

"Hey! Look alive ye mangy savages." He forced the horse across the creek and up the far bank. The old horse fought the bit, wanting to stop in the creek to drink, but Paddy pulled up hard on the reins to keep its head out of the water. The packhorse, tied to Paddy's saddle horn, had to follow.

The camp's dogs barked and howled in response to Paddy's

shouting. Soon several Cheyenne were attracted by the commotion and came out to watch his approach. Since he'd been in the camp before, he was recognized and not challenged.

"They're escaping! They're getting away!" He pointed up the creek. "Sure, and ye're letting Jenny and Will escape, and that's the truth of it." The Indians ignored him.

He rode as quickly as his old horse would go into the center of the camp and slid from the saddle. "Chief Tall Bear!" he shouted. "Where's the chief?"

The elderly Cheyenne emerged from the council tepee. He held a hand out to stop Paddy's approach.

Paddy excitedly waved his arm toward the creek. "Over yonder," he pointed. "Well, d'ye see now, it's that Will Braddock and that captive girl, Jenny McNabb, that are escaping. They're sneaking off, don't ye see?"

The chief shook his head.

"Well, now, where's that half-breed Lone Eagle?" Paddy asked.

The chief spoke to a brave nearby. Paddy recognized the Cheyenne word for Lone Eagle. He'd heard it before. Hopefully the old chief was summoning the one person in the village who could speak English well enough to understand him.

The brave had been gone only a moment when he came racing back. He spoke excitedly to the chief, who followed the brave back through the ring of tepees. Paddy shrugged and trailed along. What's going on?

Lone Eagle sat against a tree holding his head in his hands. While Chief Tall Bear and Lone Eagle were talking, Small Duck rushed up. She held out a shredded leather thong and screamed something that Paddy couldn't understand.

Chief Tall Bear shouted instructions to several braves who had joined him. They dispersed rapidly.

Paddy looked at Lone Eagle. “Sure, and now what’s happening?”

“Will Braddock and Jenny McNabb have escaped.”

Paddy threw up his hands in disgust. “Well, sure, and if that’s not what I been trying to tell everybody.”

“Chief told the braves to find them.” Lone Eagle struggled to stand. He rubbed the back of his head. “I will go with them.”

“Aye, and I’m going too.”

Chapter 47

Will gripped Jenny's hand tighter and brought her to a stop. He held a finger to his lips. "Sh." Cupping a hand around his ear, he turned his head down the creek toward the Cheyenne village.

"That's Paddy O'Hannigan all right. I thought that's who rode into the camp shouting."

"You're right," Jenny said. "I recognize that Irish brogue, even though I only talked to him one time."

"He must've seen us and given the alarm. They'll be after us now."

Will helped Jenny climb up the creek bank. "It's too slow going down there. It would've provided better cover, but since we've been spotted it won't matter. We need better footing to put some distance between us. They'll be riding ponies and catch up fast. We've got to run a while, Jenny. You up to it?"

"I think so. Rocks bruise my feet in these moccasins, but they're better for running than high-button shoes."

"I'll hold your hand," Will said. He looked into her eyes—they were definitely blue. He felt a flush creep up his face. "If that's all right?"

"Yes, Will." She squeezed his hand and smiled. "That's all right."

They ran hand in hand through the short grass at an easy trot, alongside the creek.

The way grew steeper as they approached the base of the

Laramie Range. They were soon panting from the effort. Will felt Jenny dragging on his hand. He stopped.

"Let's catch our breath," she said.

Looking back, he saw a dozen ponies emerge from the trees that ringed the camp. He pulled Jenny down and they squatted in the deep grass. "Here they come."

Will and Jenny watched the Indian ponies mill around along the bank of the creek half a mile away. One brave slid off his pony and inspected the grass. He pointed up the creek. He'd found their tracks.

"We're making it too easy for them," Will said. He closed his eyes for a moment to refresh his memory of the details on General Dodge's map. "The last time I came up this creek, I turned south along the base of the range here until I reached Cheyenne Pass. They'll either expect us to do that or go straight up Lodgepole Creek. Those are the two most direct ways across the range. But we'll go up the North Fork. Hopefully, we can gain some ground while they check out the two more obvious routes."

Will watched the tracker remount. The band of braves turned upstream to follow their trail. Paddy's bowler hat looked out of place among the feathers.

"Let's walk in the water again to conceal our tracks," Will said.

"All right."

He stepped off the bank and held out a hand to help Jenny into the creek.

"Oh!" she exclaimed. "That's colder than it was farther down."

Will's boots shielded his feet for a few moments before the water soaked through the seams, then he felt the cold that had shocked Jenny when the water had filled her moccasins.

The stream was heavily silted, the water opaque, making it

hard to see the bottom. Will walked in front of Jenny, holding her hand behind him. Frequently he lost his footing, but her grip was strong enough to keep him from falling.

He stopped from time to time to look back. The Indians were obviously confident their quarry couldn't outrun their ponies, because they came on at a leisurely pace. They shook their weapons above their heads and called back and forth to one another, laughing loudly. They were probably boasting about what they'd do to the two escapees when they caught them.

"Here's North Fork," Will said.

Lodgepole Creek passed through a defile straight ahead of them. A narrow branch joined the main creek here. It flowed from around the northern end of a pyramidal peak that rose abruptly four hundred feet above them.

They turned into the smaller stream. It was harder to maintain balance in the swiftly moving water. The pleasant murmur of the water that had flowed past the Cheyenne village was now a rushing, tumbling chatter.

They followed the narrow stream around the north end of the peak. Will halted and Jenny bumped into him. "Sorry. I was watching my feet."

"We have to get around this," Will said. He nodded to a dam of logs and branches that blocked their path. It rose five or six feet high and stretched thirty feet or so across the width of the narrow valley.

"What is it?" Jenny asked.

"Beaver dam."

"Aiyee, aiyee, aiyee!" The cries were distant, but distinct.

"They've reached the junction of the creeks," Will said. "It won't be long before they've discovered we didn't go straight or turn south. We've got to hurry."

They trudged up the slope to the end of the dam where it was anchored against the south side of the valley. Here they broke into a trot along the shore of a pond that stretched a hundred feet behind the dam.

In the center of the pond, Will saw a mound of logs and debris. He stopped abruptly and Jenny ran into him again.

"Mmphm," she said.

"That's it!"

"What's it?"

"The beaver lodge. We can't outrun them. We have to get inside the lodge."

"The lodge? That thing in the middle of the pond? How?"

"Swim."

"Swim?" Jenny stared at Will. "I can't swim."

"You don't have to. I'll do the swimming."

"But what if there are beaver in that thing?"

"There won't be. Bullfrog Charlie said beaver were trapped out of here years ago." He surveyed the tree stumps near the pond. They didn't look like they'd been chewed recently. He wasn't positive there weren't beaver around, but they didn't have a choice.

The shore along the artificial lake was rocky, so footprints would be concealed. Will stepped into the pond. "Wait here," he said. "Try not to disturb the gravel. We don't want to leave scuff marks." He waded out behind the dam, pulled a log out of the jam, and pushed it to the shore in front of Jenny.

"Sorry, but you're really going to get cold now. I want you to wade into the water and hug the log with your arms while I swim us out to the lodge."

Jenny looked at the log—then at Will. "Will, I told you. I can't swim."

"I know. All you have to do is hold onto the log. The water's cold. Don't let the shock cause you to let go."

Will steadied the log with one hand and reached for Jenny with the other.

She stepped into the icy water and blew out her breath. "Whew! That's really cold!" She let Will lead her waist-deep into the pond.

"Now," Will said. "Grab the log with both arms, and hang on tight."

Jenny dropped to her chest and wrapped her arms tightly around the log, lacing her fingers together. Will shoved the log ahead of him and laid out fully in the water behind it. He drove the log forward with strong kicks of his legs.

He was soon breathing hard from the exertion. The weight of his water-filled boots made swimming difficult. He was thankful he had the log to hold on to. "You all right?" he asked.

Jenny shivered. "Barely."

"We're almost there. It's deep here. Don't let go."

"What makes you think I'm going to let go?" She hissed through clenched teeth.

Will grinned. He liked her spunk. A final strong kick drove the log into the base of the beaver lodge. He climbed onto the lodge and pulled Jenny up beside him.

Will shoved his hat between some branches in the surface of the lodge. "Stay here while I find the way in."

"I'm not going anyplace." She was shivering so badly Will could hear her teeth chatter.

Will dove into the water and swam beneath the lodge. He and some schoolmates had dived into an old wreck on the bottom of the Mississippi once. He'd held his breath for a quite a while then, but he didn't know how long he could hold it. He searched for the opening that would lead up into the center of the lodge. There it was. He swam back out from under the lodge and kicked hard to drive himself up.

He came up gasping. "Found it."

He held a hand out to Jenny. "Into the water once more. I'll take you to the opening. It's under water."

"Under water?" She shook her head, but slid into the water next to him.

"You'll have to put your face in the water, Jenny. In fact, you'll have to put your entire head under water. Can you do that?"

He could see the fear in her eyes—they were gray now. She nodded once, slowly.

"We're going to dive straight down to the bottom of the lodge and swim beneath it a short distance to reach an opening that leads up into the center. We'll be safe once we get in there."

Jenny shivered. Her teeth chattered.

"When I tell you, take a deep breath and hold it. Close your eyes tight and don't open them until we're inside the lodge. You'll have to trust me on this. Understand?"

"Yes." She gritted her teeth. "Let's get it over with."

"Aiyee, aiyee, aiyee!" The cries came from below the dam. The Cheyenne knew Will and Jenny hadn't gone the easier ways.

Will wrapped an arm around Jenny's waist and pulled her close. "Eyes closed. Deep breath. Hold it. Now!"

He pulled Jenny under the water. He fought his way down the face of the lodge, using his feet and free hand to force them deeper. He could feel panic take hold of Jenny. She struggled against him. He knew she wanted to get back to the surface. He pushed down one final time and turned them forward beneath the bottom of the lodge. He held Jenny tightly against him with one arm and used the other to pull them forward, bumping along beneath the jumble of logs and branches. At the opening, he turned them upward, kicked hard, and they shot up inside the lodge.

"Oh," Jenny gasped. She gulped air. Her hands flailed the water. Her black hair obscured her face.

"Easy." Will spoke to her as if she were a frightened horse. "Easy. We're safe now."

Inside the lodge, the beavers had fashioned a small shelf on which they would have raised their young. "We have to crawl up there," Will said, "to get out of the water."

He heaved himself onto the shelf, lay on his side and scooted back against the outside wall of the lodge, then helped Jenny scramble up and curl her body in front of his.

"Cold," she said. "So cold."

He pulled her hair off her face. She shook all over.

"Don't be such a prude, Will. I'm cold! Put your arms around me."

He reached around her waist and pull her snugly against himself.

"Aiyee, aiyee, aiyee!" The Cheyenne's ponies pounded along the bank of the pond.

"Well, and where'd they go?" Paddy O'Hannigan's shout came from the edge of the pond. "Sure, and they can't have gone far. They must be up the trail a piece, wouldn't ye be thinking?"

Jenny sneezed. Hopefully the sound had been contained by the walls of the lodge and hadn't carried to their pursuers. Will wished he could transfer more of his body heat to her—but he was shivering, too.

The chatter of the Indians and the snorting and stamping of ponies faded away. They'd ridden up the trail beyond the pond. Perhaps they were gone.

Then the sound of the ponies' hooves returned.

"Why are we turning round?" Will heard Paddy shout.

"Black Wolf says no tracks." It was Lone Eagle who answered. "Black Wolf is a good tracker. If he says no tracks. Then there are no tracks."

Will heard the Indians calling to one another while they searched for signs.

"Maybe they're in the lodge," Paddy said.

"Maybe," Lone Eagle said. "I will check."

"Sh." Will cautioned Jenny. If Lone Eagle actually came close to their hiding place they would have to be quiet. She nodded against his shoulder.

A pony snuffled. Will listened to the animal splash into the pond.

"Sure, and I'll go with ye," Paddy said.

The sound of the wading pony stopped.

"You swim?" Lone Eagle asked.

"No," Paddy replied.

"Too deep here for the pony. I will swim there."

Will heard the pony splash back out of the water, its hooves clattering on the gravel. He heard a gentler swishing of water as Lone Eagle waded into the pond. Then he heard the splash when the Indian plunged forward into the water. He listened to the rhythmic stroking as the swimmer drew closer.

Will searched for an opening in the side of the lodge to look out, but the beavers had been good constructors and had packed the logs and branches with mud. Even though the lodge had probably not been used for some time, they'd built a structure that would last.

He took his arms away from Jenny and scraped at the mud chinking with Lone Eagle's knife until he'd dislodged a chunk. He worked at the opening, enlarging it enough to see out.

The swimming strokes ceased and Lone Eagle climbed out of the water. Branches shifted in the pile, rustling against each other. The shelf beneath Will and Jenny shook.

"Ah, now, see anything?" Paddy called.

"No," Lone Eagle answered.

The lodge swayed as Lone Eagle climbed onto it. Will hoped Lone Eagle didn't dislodge the whole structure and send it crashing to the bottom of the pond.

A face appeared directly opposite the opening Will had

fashioned and peered in. Will locked eyes with Lone Eagle.

"Sure, and do ye see anything now?" Paddy called.

"No."

Lone Eagle placed a foot over Will's slouch hat, where it was stuck in the jumble of branches, and pushed the hat deeper into the tangle with a shove of his toe.

"Well, d'ye see anything, half-breed?" Paddy called.

Lone Eagle looked back toward the edge of the pond. "This Cheyenne finds nothing. The next insult from you and I will slit your throat."

Shouting from below the dam announced the arrival of another Indian. Ponies stamped on the gravel along the shore and the chatter among the Cheyenne increased.

"And what be all this ruckus, Lone Eagle?" Paddy asked.

"Chief Tall Bear calls us back. A buffalo herd nears the village. He wants all the braves for a big hunt."

"Buffalo?" Paddy said. "Ye are giving up the hunt because of some mangy old buffalo?"

"Buffalo means food and shelter for the Cheyenne this winter. Not many buffalo come now that the iron horse blocks the way and the white man slaughters them. Our village needs the buffalo to survive."

Lone Eagle retreated from the top of the lodge. He disappeared from Will's view. A splash indicated he'd plunged back into the pond. The logs and branches ceased swaying. Will blew out the breath he'd been holding. The splashing of water ceased after a couple of minutes. Lone Eagle had reached the shore.

"Well, now," Paddy said. "For sure, and that don't beat all. I'm betting them two are close to hand, and you savages are giving up the pursuit to go hunt buffalo."

"Today we hunt buffalo," Lone Eagle said. "Maybe tomorrow we can hunt for Will and Jenny."

"Aiyee, aiyee, aiyee!" The braves' ponies pounded away from the pond.

Jenny shivered fitfully. Will rubbed her shoulders. "We've got to wait a bit," he said. "After we're sure they haven't returned, we'll go. I'd like to get over the top of the range and start down the far side toward Fort Sanders before dark."

"Will," Jenny whispered. "I'm so cold."

Chapter 48

Will hadn't heard any sounds of horse or man alongside the beaver pond for what he thought must be a couple of hours. After Lone Eagle and the braves had departed, he'd heard a single horse, which must have been Paddy, riding back and forth a few times, but that had ceased.

Through the hole he'd made in the beaver lodge Will had tracked the path of the sun. The morning had remained clear, and the sun shining on the pile of logs and branches had warmed the interior of their shelter.

Their clothing had partially dried—Will's wool shirt and trousers better than Jenny's buckskin dress. Jenny's teeth had stopped chattering.

"Will," Jenny said, "I'm hungry."

"Me too. I threw the only food I had at a dog to keep it from giving an alarm last night."

Jenny raised the parfleche that she wore around her waist. "I have some pemmican here. I stole a piece yesterday. Maybe I had an inkling something was going to happen."

She opened the parfleche and withdrew a handful of mush. "Oh, no. It's water soaked, and falling apart. What a mess."

"We can still eat it," Will said. "It's all we have."

They picked pieces of meat and berries from the fatty mass.

Jenny withdrew her eagle talon from the parfleche and held it up. "Maybe it did bring luck, Will. Not sure why Lone Eagle let me keep it, but he did."

Will grinned. "Told you it'd be lucky."

"This parfleche is ruined. It's soaked with grease from the pemmican. I'll never get it clean. But I can use the thong to restring the talon. Can you do it?" She untied the parfleche and handed it to Will.

He cut the leather thong off with Lone Eagle's knife, then strung the eagle talon on it and knotted the thong around Jenny's neck. She slipped the talon beneath the neckline of the buckskin dress.

After the sun passed beyond the zenith of Will's observation point, he decided it was time to leave. He wanted to find shelter before nightfall and build a fire to dry their clothes. He knew they wouldn't be able to make it all the way to Fort Sanders. They were going to have to get wet again, but at least they wouldn't have to dive beneath the water this time.

Will scratched at the opening with the knife to widen the hole he'd made in the mud-covered structure, then set about dismantling the intertwining branches. He pulled the maze apart until he had an opening big enough to squeeze through.

"Come on, Jenny. Let's get out of here."

Will wriggled through the hole and reached back to help her. He pulled his hat out of where Lone Eagle had shoved it, slapped it on his head, and slid into the water. He found the same log they'd used earlier and pushed it into position for Jenny.

"Sorry, but you have to get wet again."

She shivered, slid into the water, and grasped the log. "Whew." She blew through her pursed lips.

After leaving the pond, it'd taken them the rest of the afternoon to hike to the crest. The Laramie Plains stretched out before them. Far in the distance the sun dropped behind the Medicine Bow Range of the Rocky Mountains.

"This is as far as we go today, Jenny. It's steep and barren on the way down from here. Won't be any moon tonight. Too risky to go on in the dark. Besides, we'll stand a better chance of not being discovered if we shelter here in the trees. And we need the wood to build a fire."

Will surveyed the land on either side. "Over there." He pointed along the ridge. "That stand of pines."

Will led Jenny along the hillside. They slipped on the loose footing. If it were going to be daylight much longer he'd brush out their tracks, but it'd be dark soon and he didn't think anyone could track them tonight. He didn't plan to be here in the morning when their tracks became visible.

They stepped into a stand of ponderosa pines. Will chose a spot between two large ones. "Wait here," he said. "I want to take a quick look around to be sure this is a secure place."

Jenny sank down on a pile of pine needles and leaned against the trunk of a tree. Will climbed the slope above the trees and looked back down the eastern side of the range from where they'd come, then turned and looked back to where he'd left Jenny. This should do. Anyone coming over the ridge wouldn't be able to see through into the center of the clump of trees. They should be safe here tonight.

Now to build a fire. The problem would be to keep smoke from curling up above the pines. That'd give them away.

He gathered up loose branches as he worked his way back down the ridge. He dropped the firewood beside Jenny, then trimmed the branches with Lone Eagle's knife, separating the smaller ones from the larger.

"Jenny, see that lone tree over there? The one that's been struck by lightning?"

She nodded.

"See if you can find dead moss on the trunk and some pine needles on the ground. Those needles should be plenty dry. A handful of each will do. That'll get the fire started."

"I know how to select dry buffalo patties," she said, "but I'm not sure about dead moss."

Will pealed some green moss off the tree next to him. "This stuff. Make sure it's brown, not green."

While Will whittled a stack of kindling, Jenny went to the dead tree. He scraped aside pine needles until be reached bare ground and erected a tiny tepee with the wood. Jenny returned with both hands full—one of dry, brown moss and the other of brittle, pine needles.

Will fashioned a nest from the moss and cradled the needles in it. "Now comes the hard part," he said.

He fished the arrowhead from his pants pocket. "I'm not much good at this. Homer can start a fire with flint and steel with a couple of whacks." He struck the flint against the back of the knife blade, sending a shower of sparks into the nest he'd fashioned. It smoldered, but by the time he gathered it up, it'd died out. He tried a second time without success.

"The breeze is blowing it out as fast as you get it started," Jenny said. "Duncan provided a shield with his body when I tried to light a fire, even though I used lucifer matches."

She knelt and spread out her skirt. Will struck the flint against the steel, and sparks dropped into the nest. He gathered up the smoldering pile and held it close between himself and Jenny's skirt. He blew gently on the nest and almost dropped it when the flame ignited. He shoved it beneath the kindling of the tepee and the whole stack burst into flames.

"Hey! We did it. Thanks, Jenny." He slipped the knife into his waistband at the small of his back to keep the blade from stabbing his legs while he knelt to build up the fire.

Jenny smiled. She backed away from the fire to keep her skirt clear of the flames. "That feels good, Will. But I'm cold. Let's make it bigger." She tossed a branch onto the fire. The tepee collapsed and the fire sputtered.

Will snatched the branch out of the fire and used it to push the kindling back together to get the blaze started again. "Too soon for one that big," he said.

"Sorry. We didn't have that trouble with buffalo chips."

"Don't worry about it. We just need to feed the branches in slowly, from smaller to larger."

Typically the afternoon breeze would calm down at sunset, but that hadn't happened today. A cold westerly wind gusted up the slope. The fire danced wildly. The flames flared up with each gust, then died back with each lull.

"It's getting colder, Will. This buckskin dress never has dried. I wish I could hang it by the fire." Jenny clasped her arms across her chest and held her shoulders. She crouched close to the fire.

Will took off his wool shirt and handed it to Jenny. "Here, mine's dry. If you don't mind seeing me in my undershirt, this'll keep you warm."

Jenny stood and took the shirt. "Thanks. I don't mind your undershirt. But are you going to be warm enough?"

"Pooh, I'm fine."

Jenny grinned. "Then turn around while I get out of this dress."

Will faced away and listened to the rustling of clothing.

"Finished," she said.

Will turned. His mouth dropped open. The shirt only reached her knees.

"There you go again, looking at my ankles." She giggled.

He felt his face flush. "That's not all I can see."

"Why Will Braddock. Even in the firelight I can see you're blushing."

"We're going to need more wood to keep the fire going all night. I'll get some."

He headed up the slope, picking up branches until he had an

armload. When he turned to go back, he saw the flickering of their fire through openings in the stand of pines. He stepped back into the shelter of the trees and froze.

Paddy O'Hannigan held Jenny—a Bowie knife pressed against her throat.

Chapter 49

Will cradled the armload of wood against his chest. Where had Paddy O'Hannigan come from? How'd he find them? Will gritted his teeth, angry with himself for being careless.

Jenny looked at Will. Her eyes wide. He could see fear in them.

"Well now," Paddy said. "Sure, and I thank ye for building such a nice fire. Made finding ye much easier, don't ye know."

"Let her go." Will tightened his eyelids, intensifying his glare.

"And why, pray tell, would I be doing that?" Paddy pulled his arm more tightly around Jenny's neck.

She stretched her head up, trying to ease the choking grip. Her hands, which had been along her side, inched up her front toward Paddy's arm. What was she doing? If she tried to grab Paddy, he'd stab her. Will moved his head slowly from side to side trying to signal her not to move.

Paddy pricked Jenny's neck with the tip of the Bowie knife.

"Ow!" She winced and tried to pull away from the blade.

"Stand still, lassie." Blood trickled from where he'd nicked her.

Jenny's hands froze beneath the swell of her breasts, her knuckles touching. Will watched her take a shallow breath, then her hands resumed their crawl upward. He could see the eagle talon hanging suspended on its leather thong, just in front of the second button on his shirt that she wore. She was reaching for the talon.

"Ye've been a big problem for me, Will Braddock." Paddy's sneer wrinkled the scar on his cheek. "Twice ye kept me from stealing that black horse. Twice."

"Well, you finally stole him."

Jenny's fingers touched the talon. She eased it away from the front of the shirt and turned it so the sharp tang pointed up and toward her body.

"Sure, and ye're going to pay now."

"What are you going to do?" Will moved his eyes up from the talon to look into Jenny's eyes. They were cold gray.

"I'm going to slit the lassie's throat while ye watch, then I'm going to blow yer brains out with my pistol." Paddy cackled. The Irishman's harsh laugh revealed broken, rotten teeth.

"Now!" Will shouted.

Jenny ripped the talon across Paddy's hand.

"Agh!" Paddy screamed and loosened his grip. The hand that held the Bowie knife jerked aside.

Jenny slipped beneath his grasp and dropped to the ground.

Will dove across the campfire, throwing the armload of wood at Paddy. The branches hit Paddy in the chest, knocking him back a step. Will tackled him around the waist, driving the skinny Irishman hard into the ground. Their hats flew off.

"Humph!" Paddy exhaled sharply from Will's weight on his chest.

Paddy's foul breath caused Will to push backward. He kicked out with his feet and struck something behind him.

"Ah!" Jenny yelped.

Her cry distracted him and he looked at her. He'd kicked her where she still lay on the ground.

"Watch out!" she screamed.

Paddy lashed at Will with his knife. Will rolled to the side. The knife caught the side of his arm—slashing across the wounded bicep. Wow, that hurt!

The wiry Irishman jumped to his feet. He crouched, swinging the big knife back and forth before him with one hand. With the other he reached for the revolver. A grin snarled across his mouth. "Now what, Braddock?"

Will rose to his knees and reached behind him. His hand closed on Lone Eagle's knife, against the small of his back.

Paddy cocked the Colt once, then a second time.

Will threw the knife.

"Agh!" Paddy doubled over—the blade quivered in his shoulder, above his heart.

Blam! The pistol fired. The bullet slammed into the ground in front of Will. Dirt flew.

Will surged to his feet and smashed a fist into Paddy's face. Will felt the nose crunch under the blow, blood spewing down Paddy's lips and chin.

Will kicked up and knocked the revolver from Paddy's hand. It sailed away into the brush.

Paddy slashed out with the Bowie knife.

Will dropped to a knee. The blade swished above his head. His hand landed on one of the branches he'd thrown earlier. He grasped it and jumped back to his feet. He swung out, feeling the wood connect with Paddy's left arm.

Paddy grunted and stumbled back. His left arm hung limp beside him, blood soaking his shirt below the imbedded knife.

Will brandished the limb, keeping it between himself and Paddy.

Out of the corner of his eye Will saw Jenny scramble into the brush, searching for the revolver.

Paddy waved his Bowie knife before him. He looked at his bleeding shoulder, stole a glance to the side where Jenny combed through the brush, then faced back toward Will. He exhaled sharply, turned and ran down the slope.

Will joined Jenny in the tangle of bushes searching for the gun.

"Here it is," she said.

Will double cocked the Navy Colt and pointed it to where Paddy mounted a horse beyond the ring of pine trees. Paddy looked back at Will. "I'll kill you someday, Braddock!"

"Not if I kill you first!" Will pulled the trigger. He heard a click, but no explosion. He looked at the revolver. When he'd kicked it out of Paddy's hand the percussion cap had been knocked off that cylinder. He cocked the gun again, rolling a chamber into firing position that did have a cap. He fired, but the Irishman had ridden out of range.

Jenny stood beside him. "You all right?"

"I'm fine."

He turned her cheek to the side to look at her neck. The blood had dried where Paddy had stuck her.

She placed a hand over his sleeve and pulled her hand away to show him the sticky redness. "We need to stop this bleeding. I seem to be always bandaging you."

They both looked down the slope where Paddy had disappeared.

"Do you think the knife wound will kill him?"

Will shrugged. "I can only hope."

Chapter 50

"Halloo the camp!"

Will jerked awake. Jenny stirred against his shoulder where she'd fallen asleep. Will had promised himself he would stay awake, but he'd dozed off. He rubbed the sleep from his eyes. A thick fog engulfed their campsite. The fire was a pile of glowing embers.

"Halloo the camp!"

Will recognized the voice. "Bullfrog? That you?"

"Yep. I'm coming in."

Will heard the steps of two horses and the creak of leather, but could see nothing through the heavy white cloud cover. The horses stopped and Will heard feet thump the ground when Bullfrog dismounted. Like an apparition, the old mountain man emerged from the mist.

"How'd you find us? I kept the fire small—didn't think it could be seen."

"Didn't see it. Smelled it. Smoke smell was held low to the ground by the fog."

Bullfrog leaned his rifle against a tree, stooped by the fire, laid some twigs on it, and blew. The fire flared up. Bullfrog turned in his crouch and looked at Jenny. "This the little lady you were so determined to rescue?"

"This is Jenny McNabb, Bullfrog."

"Ma'am." Bullfrog touched the edge of his old hat.

"Hello, Mr. Munro," Jenny said. "Will tells me you're Lone

Eagle's father."

"That I am, ma'am. And call me Bullfrog." He stood. "What's for breakfast?"

"Nothing," Will said.

"Figured as much. When's the last time you two ate?"

"Yesterday," Will said. "Some pemmican."

"I reckon we can do better than that. Help me dump that antelope off the packhorse and we'll carve us off some steaks."

Will eased away from Jenny and stood.

"Little lady," Bullfrog said, "while we do some butchering how about you get this fire to blazing?"

"Certainly," Jenny said. She stood and look down at her bare legs. She was dressed only in Will's shirt. "But first I've got to get decent. Will hand me that dress. I expect it's dry by now."

Will pulled the buckskin dress off the branch where they'd hung it the night before. "It's dryer," he said. "A little moist from the fog. Once the fire is up, the heat should take care of that."

They devoured the antelope steaks, which Bullfrog seared in a skillet, and washed them down with strong coffee. While they ate, Will told about their escape from the Cheyenne village and their run-in last night with Paddy O'Hannigan. He also described how Lone Eagle helped them escape and hadn't given away their hiding place in the beaver lodge.

"That's good," Bullfrog said. "His ma would be right proud of what he done."

"We couldn't have done it without his help," Will said.

Bullfrog belched. " 'Scuse me. Nothing like a good antelope steak." He stood and kicked dirt onto the fire. "Time to skedaddle. How were you planning on getting to Fort Sanders?"

"Walk," Will said.

"Hmm. This fog will burn off shortly, then you'll be sitting ducks for any Injuns what's tracking you. I reckon we best ride.

I don't relish being caught out here in the open if them Cheyenne come snooping 'round."

"This isn't your fight, Bullfrog," Will said. "You get along fine with the Cheyenne."

"Come along now. We'll leave that antelope carcass by the fire. Mebbe that'll slow them bucks down if they stop to eat some of it."

The fog had thinned enough that Will could see Bullfrog's horses standing nearby.

"You two climb up on Ida. Only got the packsaddle on her. Not the most comfortable, but I reckon it won't be too bad. She's gentle walking. Don't need no bridle. She's been following behind her ma, Minnie, here for years. I'll load my gear on Minnie with me."

Jenny rode in silence behind Will. She wrapped her arms around his waist and leaned her head against his back. When Will turned to look up the trail behind them, she looked too. No sign of followers.

Suddenly she raised her head and leaned her chin on Will's shoulder. "Is that Fort Sanders?" she asked. "Where I see that big American flag?"

"Sure is," Bullfrog answered. "Reckon we made it all right."

"And to think I used to hate that flag," Jenny said.

An hour later they passed through the opened gate into Fort Sanders.

"Papa!" Jenny shouted. She slid off the horse from behind Will and ran to her father.

"Jenny." Her father embraced her. "I was afraid I'd lost you."

"Will saved me, Papa." She turned to Will, who'd dismounted. She reached a hand out to him, and Will stepped up beside her.

Jenny's father extended his good right arm. "Thank you, Will."

Will returned the strength of the grip that held his. "You're welcome, sir."

"Bullfrog Charlie helped us get here, Papa." Jenny smiled at the mountain man who stood nearby with his horses. "Thank you again, Bullfrog."

"Glad to be of help."

Duncan raced across the parade ground and charged straight into his sister's outstretched arms. "Jenny! You look like an Indian."

Jenny laughed. She wore the buckskin dress and moccasins. She'd rebraided her hair on the ride. Her days of captivity had tanned her face a golden brown.

"Where's Elspeth?" Jenny looked around.

Her father shook his head. "She left yesterday. Went with that saloon keeper, Kavanagh. He promised her a job . . . if you can call it that."

"She's going to work in the Lucky Dollar Saloon?" Will asked.

Jenny's father nodded. "Kavanagh came scouting out the next location for Hell on Wheels. He told Elspeth he'd learned she was stranded here and told her she could earn a lot of money working for him."

Jenny frowned. "Yeah, doing what? Paddy O'Hannigan had something to do with this, I'll bet. I asked him to help me escape from the Cheyenne, but he told me he'd only do it if I agreed to go to work at the Lucky Dollar. Oh, Elspeth. You think you've found freedom . . . but you've just made yourself a slave."

"What Kavanagh offered sounded more exciting to her than working for the stagecoach line," her father said.

"Stagecoach line?" Jenny asked.

"Wells Fargo has hired me to manage the Big Laramie home station here," he said.

"Yeah," Duncan piped in. "I'll be a stock tender and help the stage drivers change horses when they come through. And I'm going to learn Morse code, so I can operate the telegraph."

"There's work for all of us, Jenny," her father said. "I'm hoping you'll take on the job of cooking meals for the passengers. Elspeth didn't want anything to do with it."

"Of course, Papa. I'll be the cook. And I can help with the teams, too."

"As the railroad moves west we'll keep moving with it," her father said. "Wells Fargo has a good business hauling passengers and mail between the end of track of one railroad and the other. But the overland stagecoach business will cease when the UP and the CP finally meet."

"That's all right," Jenny said. "We'll eventually get to California this way. Who needs a wagon." She laughed and hugged her father's waist.

Lieutenant Moretti strolled across the parade ground twisting on the ends of his mustache. "Will," he said. "I'm glad you're safe. And this must be Miss McNabb?"

"Yes, Luey," Will said. "Meet Jenny McNabb."

Moretti took Jenny's hand and bowed over it. "Pleased to meet you, miss." He nodded to her father and brother, and raised a hand in greeting to Bullfrog Charlie.

"I must talk to you, Will. Your uncle left instructions." Moretti pointed to the Officers' Club. "Let's go in there."

Once inside, Moretti told Will that his uncle had departed with General Dodge, in the company of General Rawlins, two days earlier. "Major Corcoran left an envelope for you. He directed me to give it to you . . . if you returned."

His uncle Sean's crisp handwriting addressed the envelope to *The Honorable Judge Clyde Sampson, Burlington, Iowa.* Will extracted the guardianship transfer papers. They bore his uncle's signature.

The envelope also contained a note:

Will,

You may take these papers to the judge, if you have had enough of this life. Or if you decide to stay with the team, come west as soon as you can.

Your Uncle, Sean Corcoran.

Will looked at Moretti and grinned. "No way am I going back to become a blacksmith."

Moretti laughed. The tips of his mustache quivered. "Your uncle's a bit put out with you disobeying, but he said he thought that'd be your decision. Sergeant Winter is leading a detail west tomorrow. You can ride with them."

Will stepped over to the club's fireplace and tossed the judge's papers onto the burning logs. The pages flared briefly, then curled down atop the logs, disintegrating into ashes.

Chapter 51

"Detail! Mount!" Sergeant Winter bellowed his order. Leather boots squeaked against saddles as a dozen cavalrymen mounted. Each trooper's carbine hung suspended from a snap ring attached to a strap slung over his left shoulder, keeping the weapon within easy reach of his right hand.

Opposite the cavalry formation, Will sat on a horse. Jenny stood beside him. She wore her buckskin dress and moccasins. Her braided hair was free of tangles and shone with a black brilliance. She laid a hand on Will's knee. "You be careful, Will. I've already lost a mother, and probably a sister. I don't want to lose you too."

"You do look like an Indian." Will laughed. "A beautiful Indian." He felt his face flush when he said that.

"Why thank you, Will Braddock. As soon as I earn some money, I'll buy a regular dress."

"Oh, I like the buckskin dress. You look fine. But the Wells Fargo passengers may think it strange to be served their meals by a Cheyenne."

Duncan ran up with a bouquet of wildflowers and handed them to his sister. "Happy birthday, Jenny. I didn't have any money to buy a present. So I picked these for you."

"Thank you, Duncan." Jenny lifted the bouquet to her nose. "They're lovely."

"Birthday?" Will asked. "Today's your birthday? August sixth? I didn't know. I would've gotten you a present if I'd known."

"You don't have any money either. I know that. But you already gave me a present. In fact, you gave me the best present ever when you freed me from slavery." She smiled at him.

"You're fourteen?" he asked.

"Same as you. You told me when we first met you were fourteen. But you never told me your birth date."

"May tenth."

"I'll remember that," she said.

Bullfrog Charlie guided Minnie up beside Will. Ida trailed behind.

"You going with them Bullfrog?" Jenny asked.

"Nah. Too early to go to the cabin. I reckon I'll head back up into the Laramie Range to bag an antelope. Need one to trade with the sutler for some whiskey to see me through till spring. Snow gets mighty deep along the North Platte in winter. Once you settle in, you don't wanna move 'lessen you have to."

"Column of twos to the right! Ho!" Sergeant Winter's detail wheeled out of its single line into a marching formation, two abreast. The sergeant saluted Lieutenant Moretti, who sat his horse near the gatehouse.

"Stay alert, Sergeant." Moretti returned the salute.

"Always, sir." The sergeant pulled his horse's reins over its neck and fell in behind his troopers. The column of twos passed at a walk through the open gate of Fort Sanders.

Will and Bullfrog guided their mounts in behind the sergeant. Jenny walked beside Will's horse. When they came abreast of Moretti, Will turned to him. "Luey, keep an eye out for that rascal Paddy O'Hannigan."

Moretti raised a hand. "If I get the chance, I'll arrest that horse thief."

Alistair McNabb and Duncan stood off to one side of the gate. They exchanged goodbyes with Will when he rode by.

Will, Bullfrog, and Jenny had just passed through the gate

when one of the cavalryman reined in his horse and raised his carbine.

"Put that weapon away!" Sergeant Winter ordered. "We don't need to start a war over one Indian."

Beyond the column Will saw what had caused the soldier to raise his carbine. On a ridge, two hundred yards away, a lone Indian sat on a pony. Beside the Indian stood a black horse—the white blaze on its forehead visible even at this distance.

"It's Lone Eagle," Will said. "With Buck."

"Why, so it is," Jenny said.

Lone Eagle waived his coup stick above his head.

Will puckered his lips and whistled. *"Tseeeee, Tse, Tse, Tse."*

Buck's ears pricked forward. Lone Eagle slapped the Morgan's rump and Buck raced down the slope toward Will. The detail halted as if on command to watch.

Buck skidded to a halt, nuzzled Will's leg, and whinnied. "Welcome back, Bucephalus." Will patted his forehead and leaned over to stroke his mane.

Will looked back to the ridge. He drew Lone Eagle's knife from his waistband and raised it above his head by its blade, then handed the knife to Bullfrog Charlie.

"Thank Lone Eagle for the use of his knife," Will said. "And thank him for freeing Jenny . . . and Buck."

Bullfrog took the knife. "I'll see he gets the message." He snapped the reins over Minnie's neck and headed up the ridge. Ida trotted behind. Bullfrog called back over his shoulder. "When you find yourself near the North Platte, look me up. Only cabin north of the Overland Trail."

Sergeant Winter urged his horse to the front of his column. "Forward! Ho!" He ordered the soldiers back into motion.

Will dismounted and transferred the blanket and saddle to Buck's back. He removed the simple Indian bridle from Buck and replaced it with the Army bridle, then looped the Indian bridle into the saddle horse's mouth.

"Duncan, how about taking this horse back to the stable?" Will asked.

"Sure thing, Will."

Will mounted Buck, removed his hat, and looked down. "I'm not sure when I'll see you again, Jenny. Maybe next spring."

"Until spring then." She reached up and squeezed his hand.

Will shielded his eyes from the sun with his hat and watched the cavalry column approach the Laramie River, some distance from the fort. A lone eagle soared above the river's bank.

Jenny followed his gaze. "It is good to be free," she said. "Free as that eagle."

"Yes, it is." He gazed into her eyes. They were pale blue today. "You still have your eagle talon?"

She lifted the talon from beneath the neck of her dress. "And you?" she asked.

Will pulled his talon from his shirt front. He bent forward and tapped his talon against hers. "Think of me each time you feel its scratch, Jennifer McNabb."

"Likewise, William Braddock. May they continue to bring us good luck."

Will slapped his hat against the Morgan's flank. Buck leaped down the trail. Will swung his hat high overhead. "Run, Buck, run!"

HISTORICAL NOTES

Throughout *Eagle Talons,* Will Braddock encounters the following historical characters:

Grenville M. Dodge, Union Pacific's chief engineer

General John A. Rawlins, chief of staff to General Ulysses S. Grant

Jack Casement, Union Pacific's construction contractor

Dan Casement, Union Pacific's construction contractor (Jack's brother and partner)

Jack Ellis, Dan Casement's black servant

Thomas "Doc" Durant, Union Pacific's vice president and general manager

"Colonel" Silas Seymour, Durant's consulting engineer

Jacob Blickensderfer, Department of Interior railroad inspector

Doctor Henry Parry, Army surgeon (officially assigned to Fort Sedgwick's garrison)

Colonel John Stevenson, Fort D. A. Russell's commanding officer

Colonel John Gibbon, Fort Sanders's commanding officer

All other characters are fictitious.

Will's adventures in *Eagle Talons* take place during 1867, the first significant year of construction on the transcontinental railroad. The sequence of events in the book occurred when and as written.

Union Pacific, Central Pacific, and Wells Fargo are authentic companies, and the *Cheyenne Gazette* was a local newspaper publishing at the time. The other businesses Will encounters are fictional. The towns, mountains, streams, and other geographical locales mentioned in the book are real. Hell on Wheels, the itinerant shack town, moved and reestablished itself more frequently than described. Cheyenne, Dakota Territory (later Wyoming), was founded as depicted, except that General Rawlins's speech on the Fourth of July was not officially recorded and is the author's creation. The beaver dam is fictitious, but research reveals it could have been where it is sited.

ABOUT THE AUTHOR

Robert Lee Murphy graduated from the University of Oklahoma with a business degree. Throughout his career he worked with national and international agencies and institutions on all seven continents, including Antarctica, where Murphy Peak bears his name. He sold his first article, illustrated with his own photographs, many years ago to *Backpacker Magazine.* He has published technical articles in various trade journals and magazines, such as *Military Engineer.* Most recently, *The Gettysburg Magazine* published his annotated Civil War cavalry article in its July 2011 issue. *Eagle Talons* is Murphy's first novel, and the first book in his trilogy, The Iron Horse Chronicles.

Murphy is a member of the Society of Children's Book Writers & Illustrators and of Western Writers of America. The author invites you to visit his website at http://robertleemurphy.net.